GODS IN THE MIST

VIRGIL RENZULLI

Also by Virgil Renzulli
Caliburn: Merlin's Tale
Hero, Legend, Myth (publication date: February 2016)

Special thanks to Marshall Terrill, Liz Mays, and Liz Massey.

GODS IN THE MIST

CHAPTER 1: **The Grail Chapel**

Gawain was finally about to enter the fortress of the warlord Horsa, not as a conquering warrior over a vanquished enemy but rather in the disguise of a beggar. Just ahead the massive wooden gates of the Saxon castle were open wide. Far behind him the British fleet lay on the beach, and hundreds of King Arthur's knights, foot soldiers and archers rested in their camp. If discovered, there was no one here to aid Gawain or to rescue him. If caught, the Saxons would execute him and put his corpse on display.

For months, men had been maimed and killed; battles had been won and lost; strategies had been tried and abandoned. At times, he thought victory was at hand, lately that it would never come. The British war council, a handful of the most important knights and their advisers, had decided too much time and blood had been invested in this siege to abandon it without one last major assault on the Saxon fortress. Lancelot and his army had been called from Britain to join in the final attack, and to weaken the enemy's resolve, Gawain was selected for this mission, one that both terrified and thrilled him.

There were differences of opinion over whether Gawain's chance of success was worth the danger he was risking, and the Wizard Merlin would not even venture an opinion, unable to foresee either a good or bad outcome for Gawain. Ultimately it was decided anything that might help bring a victory was worth the risk.

During his entire reign Arthur had been plagued by Saxon raids and invasions, and he finally decided to put the enemy on the defensive and to send an army here, across the sea to Germania, to attack one of the most important Saxon warlords, Horsa. After long, cold months, what remained of the British army was locked in a stalemate with the Saxons, who remained secure behind their castle walls.

When Gawain first saw the castle he was now approaching, it was from the bow of his ship, and at the time he had difficulty distinguishing the features of the castle's limestone walls and towers against the surrounding hills. During the long siege, he became familiar with the castle's exterior, but he never had the opportunity to study the structure up close as he could now that he was a few steps from entering the hilltop fortress. The sight of its walls, rising fifty feet and higher, and its parapet-topped towers, rising yet another twenty-five or thirty feet, was overpowering.

But this was not a day when the Saxon stronghold would need to be defended, not a day of battle, which was why he was able to mix in with non-combatants to enter the castle. Still, sentries in full armor were stationed on the towers, ready, if necessary, to have the gates locked and the Saxon forces called to their stations.

Gawain, unshaven, dressed in a ragged cloak, a wool cap pulled down over his ears, drew in his shoulders and hunched over. He could not appear either muscular or well fed. Walking with a slight limp, he fell in behind a handful of tradesmen who were passing through the castle gates.

The courtyard was full of people, a hundred or more in his immediate vicinity. There were women and children among them, but most of those near the city gates were men, and most of the men were warriors who had either a sword or a dagger hanging from their belt. A few were mounted or walking while leading a horse behind them. If found out, Gawain would not be able to singlehandedly fight his way back out of the castle; even the powerful Lancelot could not win such a battle. Neither would he be able to escape on foot ahead of pursuing Saxon horses. And the Wizard Merlin hadn't been able to offer him any magical protection to prevent him from being recognized.

There was no alternative for Gawain but to succeed on his own in carrying out this deception.

Horsa's castle rivaled Arthur's Camelot in size and splendor. It was laid out in similar fashion, with defensive towers in the four corners of its walls and a large residential tower situated at the far end of the courtyard. Wooden shacks, stalls and tables lined the periphery of the courtyard, where tradesmen and craftsmen displayed weapons and cloth, performed metal work and carpentry, sold vegetables and roasted meats. The Grail Chapel, his destination, was at the back of the castle hidden behind the main tower, or so he had been told by a British knight who claimed to know where it was. Gawain did not want to go there directly. Being so direct would arouse suspicion. Nor did he wish to be conspicuous in observing the architecture and defenses of the castle too carefully.

It was not sufficient to look like a beggar; he must also act the part. Gawain withdrew a bowl from under his cloak and approached the fiercest looking Saxon he saw. He extended the bowl with his right hand and bowed in exaggerated fashion. The man ignored him. He performed the same act with the next passing man and was brushed out of the way.

Accursed Saxons.

Another passerby put a handful of dried fruit into his bowl. He bowed in gratitude and transferred the fruit from the bowl to a small sack he carried.

His attention was drawn to the figure of woman walking in his direction. Her form looked familiar but out of place in this castle. She was tall for a woman and slender, her arms and fingers long and delicate, her breasts disproportionately large for one as thin as she. And she moved with a certain grace and confidence he recognized. He could not help but stare when he saw her face. The remarkable complexion, whiter than any he had ever seen, was silken and still had its youthful glow although there were thin age lines in the corner of her eyes and mouth. Her light golden hair was backlit by the sun. Her eyes were gray; her mouth petite and bowed in a pleasing way; her nose slightly long; her cheeks a trifle hollow. She was beautiful. Exquisite. She was the embodiment of all that was feminine, including the less admirable qualities of being often too clever and sometimes deceptive, and of having a changeable mind.

Morgan le Fay claimed to be an enchantress – Gawain was skeptical anyone, including Merlin, possessed true magical powers – but with her beauty and charm she could certainly enchant men. Morgan, who was Arthur's half sister and the mother of his ambitious and scheming son Mordred, was not a supporter of Arthur and was given to intrigues to undermine the king. However, Gawain would not have expected she would be plotting with an enemy who could be a danger to herself as well as to the king, but there could be no other reason for her presence here. As the implications of her being in a Saxon castle ran through his mind, she noticed him staring at her. He lowered his gaze and began to walk away, sensing her eyes were following him.

"Gawain." Her voice was just loud enough to command his attention. He turned to face her as she approached. She looked him up and down, smiled and spoke in a soft voice. "Your disguise is excellent."

He forced a sarcastic laugh. "I thought so until it failed to fool you."

"It was your interest in me that gave you away, not the disguise. I saw a large man trying to look smaller than he is. A spy no doubt, and one who recognizes me. Who else would have the courage and cunning to enter Horsa's stronghold alone but Gawain?" She leaned closer to him and whispered. "And remember, I have the sight."

"Of course, the sight. You and Merlin both have it, but he neglected to see I would find you here."

"And you are most likely wondering exactly how I did get here." She gave him a flirtatious smile. "Let's say that a woman has her ways."

Given Morgan's height, Gawain would have preferred to stand erect to be more than eye-to-eye with her. Instead, he remained in beggar character, hunch-shouldered and bent at the waist. "I wonder more about why you are here."

"My presence here is not your concern," she said sternly.

Before he could respond, Morgan's attention was drawn away from him. Several warriors were passing nearby. She reached into her purse. "We must maintain your disguise." She withdrew a coin and placed it into his hand. As she did so, her warm, soft hand squeezed his. Her touch was exciting, and the flirtatious manner in which she looked at him caused him to briefly consider that she might have a sexual interest in him despite his dirty and ragged appearance. Such was the impact Morgan could have on a man.

She released his hand, backed off a step and smiled. "Whatever it is that has brought you into the enemy's castle, Gawain, I assume it must be a challenge of some sort and a chance for some glory."

There was no point in telling her he had not volunteered for this task; she would only respond that he could have declined to accept it. "Perhaps women don't understand about honor – and dishonor." Gawain looked around to see if they were being observed. A passing Saxon cast a long look in his direction. "And perhaps you could fetch another coin so our conversation doesn't appear unnaturally long."

She opened her purse and rummaged around in it. "Sir Gawain, one of Arthur's greatest knights, in the midst of the challenge of his life, daring to tread unarmed – I assume you are unarmed – among hundreds of enemy warriors; yet he finds himself at the mercy of a woman."

His eyes locked on hers. He had imagined dozens of ways he might have been caught entering or trying to leave the castle. Not once had it occurred to him he might be exposed by someone he knew. "Yes, a word from you. . ."

She gave an insincere laugh. "Please! I'm not threatening you. I'm merely making an observation. I'm a loyal Briton despite you finding me here in a Saxon castle. You don't think otherwise, do you? At least, you should never make such an unfounded and damning accusation about me to anyone. Nonetheless, we both find ourselves in a compromising situation. I came here for reasons that are no one's concern but my own, and those reasons are completely innocent. But here I am trapped under siege by my own people." She gave him another flirtatious look. "So, I will make you a bargain because some things are better agreed to explicitly and because you are said to be a man who always keeps his word." Gawain bowed in acknowledgment of her comment. "I won't ask you what your mission here is, and I'll forget we had this conversation and that I ever saw you. In return. . ." She paused to make certain she could observe his eyes. "In return, you will tell no one you saw me here – not ever. That's a fair bargain, isn't it? But there is more to this bargain, Gawain." The mention of his name caused him to look anxiously around. "If I need to flee this castle suddenly, I'll place a lantern in the highest window of Horsa's tower. When you see it, you will signal back with a torch, waving it three times from left to right; you will meet me at the small gate in the east tower and take me to a British vessel and back to Britain. Agreed?"

He hesitated.

Morgan looked over his shoulder to something or someone behind him. "Here comes, Willayne, the Saxon knight. What is your answer to my proposed bargain?"

Gawain glanced back in the direction Morgan was looking. He didn't recognize Willayne without his armor but didn't doubt the man approaching was the best of all the Saxon knights. Gawain lowered his head in resignation. "Agreed."

She took a coin from her purse and handed it to him. "Go."

Gawain took the coin, bowed and walked several steps away but stopped when a deep, male voice called after him. "Wait, beggar." He turned to face Willayne.

The Saxon was of average height but had an exceptionally thick torso and well muscled arms. His hair and eyes were dark; his large nose was bent to one side, a war wound no doubt. A woman, likely his wife, was beside him. She was much shorter than Morgan, full bodied, and attractive in her way, though not nearly as alluring as the enchantress. He heard the whimper of an infant and noticed a servant behind the couple was holding their baby, who was about the same age of Gawain's youngest son. The child even resembled his Lovell.

Being confronted now by Willayne, Gawain wondered if he could trust Morgan not to give him away and whether he would survive this day to see his son again.

But Willayne appeared neither suspicious nor hostile. The Saxon warrior struck Gawain as being as straightforward and virtuous as Lancelot. Willayne did not engage in deception and therefore, was not well prepared to recognize it. "Have you eaten in recent days?" asked Willayne.

Gawain withdrew the dried fruit from his pouch and held it toward the Saxon.

Willayne dismissed the fruit with a shake of his head. "Hardly a meal. No beggar goes hungry in this castle. We pride ourselves on our generosity. And besides, God appreciates a good deed; so, we both benefit. These days we should do as much as we can to please God and gain his benefits." Willayne took Gawain by the arm and led him to a food seller's stand. Willayne's grasp was firm, and Gawain hoped Willayne would not feel the muscle in his own arm, which was beyond what any beggar would have.

They stopped before a table behind which stood a man with a bloodstained apron. To the man's left a spitted ox thigh warmed over a small fire. Willayne ordered a meal by motioning to the seller and saying not a word. The tradesman sliced two large pieces of meat, placed them on a plate he garnished with a few cooked vegetables and handed it to Gawain, who smiled and bowed repeatedly to Willayne. Although he was not hungry, he tore into the meat like a half-starved man.

Gawain watched as Willayne walked away and was more than a little jealous of the Saxon warrior for being at home with his wife and child. Gawain also caught himself simultaneously longing for his own wife and lusting for the untrustworthy but appealing Morgan le Fay.

Continuing to nibble at his roasted ox, Gawain toured the remainder of the castle, careful to avoid every Saxon warrior he could. Horsa's stronghold was all it was reputed to be, well designed and expertly built. And the Saxon men, women and children were a healthy and comely race. It would have been altogether a pleasant place – had it not been Saxon.

The sun had reached the top of the midday sky. Gawain thought the Grail Chapel might be vacant while the residents of the castle ate their afternoon meal. He went in search of the chapel and found it where it was said to be, in a far corner of the castle, two-thirds of the way up the hill upon which the castle sat. It was a small stone building, no more than twenty-five feet square, and it was reached by means of several dozen stone steps. At the base of the steps was a large, marble statue of a supernatural being, a woman warrior with wings, a spear in her right hand, the shaft resting on the ground, the point facing skywards. At the top of the steps, the entrance had a small portico supported by two stone columns. It contained the Christian cross.

It was the same cross now decorating Lancelot's shield, the same cross to which Arthur knelt. The old enchanter Merlin was disappointed Arthur had embraced the new religion and once complained to Gawain that he thought it was a matter of expediency on the part of the king to consolidate his kingdom. Gawain disagreed, believing Arthur had too much integrity to espouse something he did not wholeheartedly believe.

It was sadly ironic, thought Gawain, that this siege pitted Christian Saxons against Britons, many of them also Christian, men in both armies praying to the same god for victory.

Gawain had just begun to ascend the chapel stairs when Willayne appeared from inside. Now he would have to fool this Saxon battle leader a second time, and seeing Gawain here and earlier with Morgan might be the only clues Willayne needed to realize the man dressed as a beggar was a spy. But the Saxon warrior only smiled at him, and Gawain again bowed in gratitude for the meal Willayne had given him. It had been, in fact, a generous gesture although Gawain had to remind himself that if Willayne knew his true identity and was given the opportunity, he would plunge his dagger into Gawain's belly or slash his throat without any remorse.

Gawain ascended the remaining steps, crossed the small portico and entered the dark chapel illuminated by several small oil lamps and a rack of candles. At the front of the chapel on either side of a large wooden cross was a statue of a supernatural winged warrior, one male, the other female. The firelight throwing shadows across their faces and the shadow of their wings against the ceiling gave them an ominous appearance. On a small pedestal stationed before the cross was the Holy Grail, a silver chalice with several vertical rows of large rubies running down the cup to its stem. This was the vessel said to have held the blood of Christ as he died on the cross, and the Son of God's blood was the source of its purported supernatural power. Looking at the Grail now and in this setting, Gawain could almost believe it had magical powers.

The Saxons believed the Grail was brought to them by Joseph of Arimathea and its mere presence in a place had protective powers. As long as the Grail was within this castle, its walls would not be breached. It was Gawain's intention to steal the Grail. The Britons with Lancelot and his men hopefully arriving in time to be among them would launch a major assault on the castle once the impact of the Grail's loss sank into the hearts of the Saxons. The British expected to put an end to this long siege and return home.

However, there were still several people in the temple offering sacrifices to their god and honoring the Grail. He would have to wait.

Gawain prayed in his own halfhearted manner both to avoid arousing suspicion about his presence in the chapel and just in case prayer might help ensure the success of his dangerous mission.

A woman stood, bowed to the cross and left the chapel. Almost the instant she left, an elderly man entered, and a short time after, a portly man appeared at the entrance. It seemed the chapel might be in use throughout the afternoon, and Gawain went back out to the steps to sit and wait.

There was a steady flow of people passing in and out of the chapel for most of the afternoon, many of them warriors, a few casting suspicious glances in his direction. It was too risky to remain here. Gawain, looking and beginning to feel the part of a weary beggar, decided to go in search of the east gate Morgan had mentioned. It would be useful to know exactly where it was because it might well be an entry point for the British forces when they made their final assault on the castle. He walked across the courtyard, found the gate, and sat down on the bare ground near it to rest and wait. He leaned his back against the castle wall and without intending to, eventually fell asleep.

Gawain awoke when a fly touched his face. As he came to full consciousness, he started to panic when he realized he was inside the Saxon castle. For an instant he could not remember how he had come to be here. He relaxed as he recalled his mission and saw his disguise was intact.

This would be a story to tell – if he survived this adventure. Gawain, the crafty, was so brave as to fall asleep in the center of the enemy citadel, surrounded by hundreds of Saxon warriors, any one of whom would have happily chopped off his head and hung the trophy from the saddle of his horse.

His lower back was stiff and his left knee sore from how he had been resting on the ground. Gawain stood, stretching both his back and his leg, and walked to the chapel entrance. He paused at the door and peered inside. The chapel was empty. His eyes swept the room from left to right, then back again to be certain he had not missed anyone in the dim light. He took a look outside. No one was approaching the chapel. He went back inside and hurried to the Grail's pedestal.

What if the Grail did have some magical power? If he touched it, would he be struck by lightening? Or bring a curse down upon himself? Don't be a fool, he thought. But who could blame him under these circumstances for being a little foolish and more than a little worried?

He looked one last time from side to side and behind him to the chapel entrance. Gawain gently wrapped his hand around the stem of the Grail. He thought he would feel some sensation as he had when Morgan le Fay touched his hand, but he felt none. He respectfully placed the Grail into a sack he had brought to conceal it. He hung the sack by a belt hidden under his cloak and hurried out of the temple.

The moment he left the temple, he wondered if there was a priest or temple attendant who had somehow sensed the theft of the Grail and had given an alarm that was at this moment bringing the entire castle running after him. He descended the stone steps in enough haste to have raised suspicion had anyone been watching. He reached the lower level of the castle, slowed his pace and withdrew his begging bowl. As much as he wanted to flee as fast as he could, his survival depended on maintaining his deception, especially if, before he managed to leave the castle, it was discovered that the Grail was missing.

He reached the courtyard. There were dozens of people milling about, and as luck – bad luck – would have it, the Saxons were in the midst of changing the guard, and a handful of armed warriors were headed his way. Trying to avoid them would arouse more suspicion than accosting them; so, with an exaggerated limp, he walked toward the Saxon sentries. As soon as he committed to this course of action, he worried the bulge of the Grail under his cloak would be easily detected.

After their watch, the soldiers were in no mood to deal with a beggar holding a bowl extended in his hand. They walked past Gawain as though they did not see him. He bowed toward them to help conceal the Grail protruding under his garment.

Gawain continued toward the tower gates as quickly as he dared. And just in time. The Saxons were preparing to shut the massive wooden doors for the night. He exited the Saxon stronghold, careful to maintain his limp, and got no more than a few dozen feet when he heard the castle gates closing behind him. It was safe to pick up his pace. The farther he got from the castle, the faster he walked.

In the distance ahead of him, barely lit by the remaining sunlight, was a man on horseback and a rider-less horse. It was Merlin, looking in the dim light even older and thinner than he normally did. The wizard began to ride in his direction. Gawain took off his wool cap, threw it to the ground, and followed it with his begging bowl.

Merlin brought the horses to a stop in front of Gawain and handed him the reins of his mount. "It took you long enough," said the wizard. "I was getting bored out here. You were gone so long it would have been easy for me to think you were dead or captured, but my intuition told me to wait for you longer."

Gawain mounted his horse. "I'm glad you still have some intuition left. I was delayed because I fell asleep for a time."

"Asleep! I am often accused of embellishing my stories – although I seldom do – but surely you are embellishing yours."

"No, I did, indeed, fall sleep. I had to wait until the Grail Chapel was empty before entering it and took a nap." Gawain put a hand to the small of his back. "The ground was uncomfortable. Oh, and another thing, I met the Saxon knight Willayne."

Merlin studied Gawain's face for an indication he was not serious. "And I suppose he invited you for a tankard of mead."

"No, but he bought me a meal of roasted ox thigh." The wizard raised a thick white eyebrow at him, and Gawain smiled. "I'm making it all sound more daring than it was, but I swear by the Christian God and all the gods you honor, Merlin, everything I just told you is true." They turned their horses back toward the British camp. Gawain was about to mention he had seen Morgan le Fay and explain she must be pursuing some treachery involving the Saxons when he remembered his promise to keep silent.

"But with all you accomplished, Gawain – taking a nap and meeting Willayne – you didn't mention the Grail. I assume you were unable to get it."

Gawain reached under his cloak, withdrew the chalice from his sack and held it before Merlin.

The old wizard looked at it. At first he appeared impressed, then skeptical. "And you believe taking this Grail will change the course of the siege?"

"The council does, but I think it has no magical powers, if that's what you mean, unless it influences the state of men's minds."

Merlin took a closer look at the silver, ruby-studded chalice. "In war, Gawain, the two biggest causes of defeat are desperation on the one hand and overconfidence on the other. I fear this planned assault of ours is equal parts of the two."

CHAPTER 2: The Saxon Response

Willayne was hurrying down the tower's rear steps, but the apparent urgency of his movement did not dissuade Morgan le Fay, who was coming from the opposite direction, from standing in his way. She hung her arms around his neck and was about to kiss him. He frowned, leaned his head back and pulled her arms away. "Not now."

She dismissed his concern with a wave of her hand. "No one is watching, least of all your wife. For a knight who is fearless in battle, you worry too much when it comes to being with me. Or am I misunderstanding you? Maybe you are tired of me."

She reached out for him again, and he grabbed her wrists to hold her off. "Not now. There is an urgent matter I must deal with." She had never before seen him so concerned, not even when he was about to enter a battle.

"So urgent you cannot pay any attention to me?"

He clearly was annoyed with her. "Yes, that urgent. You were serious enough when you were bargaining with Horsa to join you and Vortigern in deposing your brother from the throne. You should understand my urgency now when Horsa has called a meeting of the war council."

She put her hands on her hips and gave him a harsh look. "First, Arthur is only my half brother, and second, don't make it sound as though Vortigern and I are equal in this. He is but a minor British warlord with ambitions beyond his reach. I do the thinking for both of us." Some of her golden hair fell over her right eye. She brushed it into place as she stepped back and looked at Willayne. "Now, what is so urgent?"

"The Grail is missing."

"Oh that! The odd Christian relic you Saxons worship. So what does it matter if it's missing?"

"The legend is that the walls of this castle will not be breached while the Grail is within them. And Saxons rely on it."

"I've heard of this legend. Don't you think it's somewhat nonsensical?" She regretted using the word "nonsensical" as soon as she said it.

"It's not nonsense!" It was the first time he had ever raised his voice to her. "You told me you can work magic, and you told me Merlin concocted a magic potion and that's how your mother was fooled into sleeping with the wrong man. I believe what you told me. And if you and Merlin can work magic, so can the Grail. You, of all people, should not doubt its power."

Morgan, who now understood the reason for Gawain's presence in the castle, decided to take a more serious attitude for fear of jeopardizing her relationship with Willayne. "And you think the British stole it?"

"Yes."

"How could they manage such a feat?"

Willayne shook his head. "I don't know."

She wanted to demonstrate the sincerity of her interest and concern by asking yet another question. "Is there any reason why they would have taken such a risk now? Surely stealing the Grail from this castle must have seemed nearly impossible to the Britons. Why even try it at this moment in time?"

It was the right question to ask, and it seemed to deepen Willayne's concern. "Every possible speculation has been made. On the one hand, some say the British are desperate, can no longer maintain their siege, and will try anything to gain an advantage. On the other hand, there are those who say Lancelot and his men are on the way from Britain or Arthur, himself, will soon join the battle. First, they believe, the British stole the Grail to weaken our resolve; next, the British will launch a major attack to finish us off. And still others are saying that because we have lost the protection of the Grail, we should not wait to see what happens next and should ask for an immediate truce or even surrender."

Those words struck Morgan with force. Her situation might well become more dangerous than it was already. Before she had been able to return home after her successful negotiation with Horsa, the British invaded and laid their siege, trapping her in this castle these past months. The worst thing that could happen to her was the British taking this castle, finding her inside its walls and declaring her a traitor. This war could continue no longer, she decided. It was time to have a victor and a vanquished opponent. And now that she had extracted a promise from Gawain, she had a plan whichever way the siege was decided.

She looked at Willayne, pretending to have had a revelation. "The Britons stole the Grail out of desperation, of course. This is the explanation that makes the most sense. Why take the risk if Lancelot or Arthur is on the way? But your worry, Willayne, is that those among you who want to yield to the British will win the day at the war council?"

"Exactly."

She tilted her head toward Willayne and let some of her hair slide over part of her right eye as she often did when she intended to seduce him. "Since you have suddenly become a man of caution, at least when it comes to me, may I offer some advice? If the British stole the relic out of desperation – and indeed, your god didn't just spirit it away – then, now is the time for you Saxons to launch an attack to drive the British back into the sea. They would not expect it and would be totally unprepared."

Willayne appeared to mull over her idea, but just as he was about to answer her, his attention seemed to wander. "The beggar."

The corners of Morgan's mouth turned downward. "Beggar?"

"The one with you."

"With me?" Morgan hesitated, as she heard footsteps rushing their way from up the stairs. She dearly hoped whoever was approaching would interrupt them. "I saw several beggars today," she said finally, "if that's what you mean?"

"The one I fed, the one with you. There was something unusual about him."

"He wasn't with me. And why do you say he was unusual? He was like any other beggar."

"Willayne." Alpin, one of Horsa's advisors, was heading toward the ground floor. "Hurry. The war council is about to begin."

"I must go," Willayne said to Morgan's relief. When Alpin was down the stairs, out of sight and out of earshot, Willayne whispered, "I don't trust Alpin. He is weak and a defeatist." Willayne kissed her cheek and hurried after Alpin.

When Willayne arrived in the council chamber, he found Horsa in his regular seat at the front of the assembly, looking down at his hands, his expression pained. Several knights and battle leaders were already there, including Willayne's brother Isanbert and his cousin Eadhelm. The chamber, thirty-five feet by thirty feet, barely accommodated seating for the large war council. As the others arrived, they filled the room sitting in three rows of chairs arranged in a semicircle before their leader. Willayne, as Horsa's knight champion, stood at the battle leader's right side.

Horsa, who had grown thin and haggard during the siege, looked especially frail. His expression was so solemn that no one spoke to him or to any other person in the room. Finally Horsa raised his eyes and looked at the assembly. "As you doubtlessly know, the Grail has been stolen or is, at least, missing."

Alpin, who had only a hedge of gray hair remaining just above his ears, stood part way out of his seat. "Was it not under guard?"

His question elicited comments shouted from different parts of the gathering:

"It should have been guarded day and night."

"Perhaps it was taken back by God."

"And why would God take it back? We have properly honored Him and cared for the Grail."

"Cared for it! If we had cared for it, it would not now be missing."

"Men." Horsa held up a hand to quiet them. "Such talk doesn't help us now. The question is: What do we do next?"

"The castle is lost."

"The castle is not lost!" Horsa strained to see who at the rear of the assembly made the comment. "The castle is not lost, not at all. The legend is that no castle wall shall be breached while the Grail is within. It doesn't say the walls will fall or will be breached in the absence of the Grail."

Alpin stood up and pointed a finger at Horsa. "But the loss of the Grail makes us weaker today than we were yesterday."

Horsa nodded solemnly. "That much is true."

"Perhaps, we're not weaker but stronger." The comment came from Isanbert. "If the British have defiled the Grail Temple, the Almighty may turn his wrath on them."

"Then, why did he allow the desecration of his own temple? No, the loss of the Grail is the worst possible omen," said Alpin. "It leaves us only one sensible alternative to losing this siege."

Willayne stepped forward to confront him. "I can guess what you think the solution is."

"Can you? And can you also remember the time months ago, when you said the Britons would not maintain their siege long and I said just the opposite?"

"You want to seek a truce, even a surrender," said Willayne in an accusatory tone. "You would throw yourself – throw all of us – on the mercy of the British."

"Not surrender but yes, seek a truce." Alpin looked about the room as though appealing to the others to join him in opposing Willayne. "It may be the only way any of us survive this siege. There have been other truces in recent times."

The anger was mounting in Willayne's face. "Those situations were in Britain, on British land, not ours, and those conflicts were resolved when we withdrew to our homeland. Shamefully withdrew, I would add. Now we are in our homeland. Where do we go now to appease the British?"

"We could promise to not invade Britain again."

"And you think the British would accept a promise given from obvious desperation? I wouldn't, and neither will they." Willayne began to pace before the assembly looking man after man in the eye as he spoke. "We will all die in battle or from old age, some sooner than others. But our reputations will live on long after. To be cowardly now, to beg for a truce, to accept defeat on this day or tomorrow or the day after is to be cowardly for eternity."

Eadhelm stood to address the group. "God works in ways men often don't understand. Perhaps, God allowed the British to take the Grail because we have depended far too much on the safety of our walls."

"Yes, I agree," said Willayne. "This is God telling us to go on the attack, bring the battle to the British in their camp, push them back into the sea, act like warriors instead of hiding behind these walls and hoping to negotiate a truce. The British stole the Grail out of weakness, not strength. If we fight our way past their wooden fortifications, they'll break ranks and take to their ships." Willayne clenched his fist. "Here's my proposal. Take the battle to the enemy and do so while they think the loss of the Grail leaves us weak." He looked about the room. "Who favors an attack?"

Several knights voiced support for Willayne's suggestion, and the more they discussed the alternatives, the better the suggestion to attack appeared. As Horsa concluded when the debate finally ended, they could launch an offensive, and if it failed, they could return to the safety of their walls. There was no reason to make seeking a truce or surrendering the castle their next move, and every reason to follow the will of God, if the meaning of the Grail's loss was that they had been too complacent and should take the offensive.

CHAPTER 3: **Gods and Grails**

The night was moonless, and hardly a star was visible. Although dawn could not be far off, there was still no hint of sunlight in the sky. Gawain, staring into the blackness, had been alerted by one of the night watch to noises he had heard on the field between the British camp and the Saxon castle. Gawain turned to Percival, who stood next to him at the British line of protective fences. "I hear something, too."

Percival frowned and turned his right ear toward the field. "I hear nothing."

"There! The sound of wooden wheels rolling."

"A cart at this time of night?"

"I could think of a dozen things that might be on a cart, if it is a cart, and none of them are likely to be good. We'd better prepare for anything."

Percival ran back to their camp to rouse the troops from their sleep while Gawain continued to listen for movement by the Saxons. He thought he heard a second set of wheels and a third. The Saxons were preparing to launch an assault – that much was clear – and the wheels were more than likely on moveable catapults. Gawain did not remember seeing many large rocks or boulders on the field between the two armies that could be used in the catapults, but this observation didn't preclude the Saxons from having a large store of them.

The British wooden fortifications were only eight-foot-high stockade fences, ranging from eight to twelve feet in length, each section staggered several feet ahead or behind those on either side of it. The spaces between the fences allowed the British easy movement to and from the Saxon castle while the staggered fences presented a barrier against Saxon knights charging unimpeded into their camp on horseback. The fences would not afford much protection against catapults and would not stand up long to a well-planned assault.

British warriors, after hastily donning their armor and grabbing their weapons, began to arrive at the fence line. Gawain knew it would not be long before the catapults unleashed their deadly loads, and he listened intently for the first sound of a discharge as the British warriors took cover behind their wooden walls.

There it was, a loud snap in the distance. Gawain cringed waiting for a projectile to land. It fortunately fell short, making an odd sound, more of a slap than a heavy thud. A second snap. He sensed something flying overhead. It landed well behind his position, and the sound was again like a slap. A third projectile landed just short of his position, this time with an audible splash. A fourth hit against the wall close enough to spray him with a liquid.

It was oil. The Saxons had filled animal skins with oil, and the skins were bursting open on impact.

Gawain began shouting. "It's oil. Pass the word. And be prepared to move quickly."

Skins full of oil splashed down all along the British defensive line. Only a small percentage actually hit their primary target, the wooden defensive walls, but that was of little consolation to Gawain, who knew fire was always an unpredictable and dangerous weapon. He moved to the edge of the wall he was hiding behind and peeked around the corner just in time to see the first volley of flaming arrows arch into the sky and drop down around the British army. Wherever a lighted arrow struck oil, it ignited a fire. Flames were climbing up the fences in several locations and flaming up from the ground behind the British line.

The tunic of one warrior caught fire and quickly spread along his back, shoulders and one arm. He staggered, moving his arms wildly trying to put out the flames. Two men came to his aid. The first took off his cloak and used it in an effort to smother the flames. Before the second man could act, a flaming arrow dropped out of the sky and struck him in the upper back.

More oil-filled skins were crashing down on the British, and where they hit existing fires, they burst into flame. The walls were aflame in more than a half dozen locations, and several more warriors were on fire.

At the center of their line, the British hastily formed a battle formation, spearmen kneeling behind their large shields and archers crouching behind the spearmen. British archers began to exchange volleys of arrows with their Saxon counterparts while the spearmen prepared for a Saxon charge.

But the charge did not come at the center of their defense as expected but rather on the far right flank, where two hundred knights led by Willayne, a red tunic over his armor, a red plume in his helmet, attacked the British fortifications. Willayne withdrew one of the two throwing spears sheathed in a leather sleeve on his saddle, steadied himself as best he could on the galloping horse and threw the spear at the British warriors who were hiding behind the stockades. It hit no one. He waited until his horse closed on the British line and threw the second spear; this one struck an enemy warrior in the right shoulder and took him down. Behind him other Saxon knights did the same, launching their spears to soften the British line.

The Saxons dismounted and again led by Willayne rushed the fences. It was less a fight between armies than a sparring between individual warriors engaged one-on-one and in small groups. The first Briton to challenge Willayne was no match for him. Willayne unleashed a series of sword blows driving the man back and throwing him off balance. An overhand blow knocked the man to the ground, and before he could recover, Willayne finished him off with a thrust to the belly.

Willayne moved deeper into the British ranks and overpowered several Britons forcing them backwards with their shields held above their heads and leaving them unable to strike a single blow. He heard a shout behind him and saw his brother Isanbert was now supporting him at the rear. The two continued to penetrate the British line.

An arrow flew in seemingly from nowhere. There was a loud cry. Willayne turned to see Isanbert, an arrow in his chest, stagger and fall to the ground. He rushed to Isanbert and helped his bleeding brother to his feet. Other Saxons came to protect the pair as they retreated. But they didn't get far before Isanbert's legs collapsed beneath him, and he dropped to the ground. Willayne tried to lift his brother up again, but when he looked down at Isanbert, he saw his brother's eyes roll up into his eye sockets and his head drop to his chest.

Gawain and Percival learned of the breech on the right flank and arrived in time to find Willayne and several other Saxons trying to carry a body from the field. They charged in, Gawain going straight for Willayne. The two warriors stood almost toe-to-toe and exchanged a rapid series of forceful blows leaving dents in each other's shield. They broke off, circled and reengaged. Gawain's blows were coming fast, putting Willayne on the defensive and forcing him backward. Willayne teetered, almost losing his balance. Gawain moved in and hit him with his shield in an effort to topple him backwards. But Willayne held his balance and brought the butt of his sword handle down on Gawain's helmet with as much force as he could muster.

Gawain staggered backwards in a daze. Several Britons ran in to protect him and lead him to safety. The rest of the British surrounding Willayne retreated.

Willayne lowered his sword and shield, watching them back away, and shouted after them. "The next time you British, you and your mighty Lancelot, who didn't have the courage to come here and join this fight, the next time you brag about your prowess in battle, remember it was Willayne who sent you scurrying for your lives."

Brash statements are often made in battle. Willayne had not planned to issue a challenge to the mighty Lancelot, who fortunately was in Britain, but issuing a challenge is exactly what he had done.

The fighting continued throughout the morning with individual warriors occasionally returning to the rear of their line to rest, rearm or tend to a wound. And although the battle had an ebb and flow, the Saxons clearly had the advantage until late morning when the British began to take ground from the Saxons. Willayne rallied his men and gradually by midday, they pushed the British back, forcing them to retreat behind their stockades.

The two armies were exhausted, and they paused in their fighting to remove the dead and injured from the field, and to rest and have a meal.

Gawain, his head still throbbing from the blow he received from Willayne, walked hurriedly toward Balin's tent, where their war council was hastily meeting during the pause in fighting. Gawain was taller than average, lean but broad-shouldered. His features were even, if unremarkable except for the piercing brown eyes, and his sandy hair was matched in color by the stubble on his chin and cheeks. On the way to the council meeting Gawain came across an odd sight, Percival, kneeling on the ground just outside his own tent, his head hung low.

Gawain stopped before the young knight. "Percival, don't tell me you are praying."

Percival, his brow furrowed, looked up at Gawain and spoke in a soft voice. "I am praying, yes. I'm asking for forgiveness."

"Forgiveness! For what?"

"For the theft of the Grail."

Gawain slapped his hand against his chest. "I stole the Grail, not you. Did you forget?"

Percival's expression was no less pained after Gawain's comment. "I didn't stop you, and I should have. I knew it would be a sacrilege, and I allowed it to happen."

Gawain stared down at Percival, his voice a mixture of surprise and annoyance. "Don't tell me you blame this morning's setback on the Grail, on a superstition, on God?"

"He allowed it to happen."

"Are you saying God is at fault for what happened this morning?"

"No, one never faults God."

Gawain gave a sarcastic grunt. "Well, I fault Him if He is the reason we were bashed and battered today."

Percival waved his hands in Gawain's direction as though trying to erase his words from the air. "Please, Gawain, don't speak that way. It will only worsen the situation."

"If you insist on praying, must you do it out here in the open where others can see you?"

"You two prattle like old ladies." Merlin, as he often did, somehow managed to appear in the middle of an important conversation and walked up behind Percival. "No, you prattle like little girls."

"It's not prattle," said Percival indignantly. "Everything that happens is God's will, or it would not happen. And you, Merlin, you honor and ask favors of your gods although I doubt you ever ask for forgiveness from them."

"No, I never ask for forgiveness. And my gods tell me when you have suffered a thrashing at the hands of an enemy, you pick up your sword and fight harder." Merlin put a hand under Percival's elbow and prodded him up to his feet. "It wasn't the Grail or the theft of it that caused our defeat. And even if it was, you're needed at the war council, Percival, not on your knees. Come on, the two of you, before some foolish decision is made." Merlin began to mumble to himself. "Knights praying on their knees! What is the world coming to?"

The three continued to Balin's tent, where they were joined by Balin's brother Balan, as well as Bedivere and Erec, all Knights of the Roundtable. They sat on stools around a small, smoky fire in a brass brazier. Percival was the first to speak, and his conversation with Gawain had not changed his view. "The theft of the Grail was a mistake," he said in a soft but determined voice. "We should return it immediately."

Balin gave Percival a disapproving look. "Returning the Gail would indicate weakness if not defeat. It would encourage the Saxons to continue what they began this morning and drive us into the sea."

Gawain was annoyed by Percival's suggestion. "Not to mention that I had to spend a full day in the Saxon castle to acquire it."

"Acquire it! Steal it, you mean."

"If the Grail actually has any power, which I sincerely doubt," said Merlin, "may I remind you all it was in our possession during the battle and therefore, should have protected us. Or do none of you see that point?"

Bedivere was unmoved by the wizard's remarks. "God was against us this day."

"Your god," said Merlin.

"My god, then. He was against us and for the Saxons. It was clear to anyone who has eyes to see."

Gawain moved to the edge of his stool and looked from one side of the small gathering to the other. "Have you seen the Grail? It's made of pure silver and studded with rubies. Percival, you say the Grail acquired its power when it received Christ's blood as he died on the cross?" Percival nodded. "Tell me what destitute Jew or poor Roman soldier would have been at a crucifixion with a silver chalice decorated with priceless rubies?"

The group was silent for a few moments until Percival ventured an answer. "The cup may have been bronze or even wood originally but once it received the blood. . ."

Merlin interrupted. "Spare me! Bronze to silver? Please!"

Percival appeared shaken by the force of Merlin's comment but did not back down. "Why doubt it? You yourself, Merlin, have said you turned brass into gold."

"Brass into gold?' Merlin's eyes moved from side to side as though searching for something. "Yes, of course. The lad has a point. Bronze to silver. Why not?"

Now it was Bedivere's turn to become emphatic. "Whatever role the theft of the Grail played or did not play in our defeat, one thing is certain. God favored the Saxons over us today."

"Because they are more Christian than we are?" asked Gawain.

"Or perhaps we have become too Christian." Merlin appeared very satisfied with this appraisal. "We have been too quick to abandon the old gods and the old ways that served us well in the past."

Gawain stood up and gestured lavishly with both hands as he spoke. "Listen to yourselves. We shouldn't have stolen the Grail. We should return the Grail. We lost because God was offended by a sacrilege. We lost because God favors the Saxons. We lost because we are not Christian enough. We lost because we are too Christian. We could debate all this until the Saxons are outside this tent, and we might still reach no agreement. I am the only one here who has held the Grail, and I tell you I felt no power in it, no magic, nothing at all.

"The truth is that we lost because we were overconfident. We didn't expect an attack and were unprepared, and we didn't easily recover. What we should be discussing now is not grails and gods but rather what we should do in the next few moments before the Saxons resume their attack."

"What option to do we have besides staying behind our defenses?" said Balin. "Besides Lancelot and his men should arrive here soon. We need only hold out today and maybe tomorrow. "

"I don't think we can count on Lancelot arriving in time – if he's coming at all," said Merlin. "It always seems what we most expect is always the one thing that never happens."

"Merlin is right about expectations," said Gawain. "And what the Saxons don't expect is a counterattack. I suggest we try to outflank them as they did to us this morning."

The Saxon army was again taking to the field. The British left just enough men at the center of their defensive line to hold off an enemy charge while Balin took a group of warriors to circle the left Saxon flank, and Gawain and his men did the same on the right. Breathing heavily and their armor clanking, Gawain and his men ran along the shore, and he worried they had to travel too far a distance to outflank the enemy in time.

The Saxons began to march toward the charred British fortifications. What remained behind of the British force came forward to meet them. Focused on the enemy force before them, the Saxons did not notice the British warriors approaching them from the right.

The Saxons knelt and lifted their shields high. Archers stood behind them, loaded arrows, drew their bowstrings and aimed their weapons high. A volley of Saxon arrows dropped down on the British, the vast majority of arrows harmlessly bouncing off shields or penetrating them only a few inches. The British returned fire with similar results.

Shouting and waving their swords, Gawain and his men reached the Saxon flank and tore into it, immediately inflicting heavy damage on the enemy. The Saxon left flank turned as quickly as it could to meet them, and a pitched battle ensued.

Balin and his men now attacked from the other flank, again catching the Saxons exposed and again inflicting significant casualties.

The Saxons, caught in the pincer, regrouped after the initial shock of being outflanked. They turned their battle formation to face the British on three sides and began to hold their own. What had been a British advantage quickly turned into a stalemate.

Eventually Gawain's men on the right flank began to be pushed back, and he saw the reason why. Willayne was leading a thrust in their direction. Gawain started to fight his way toward Willayne intending to engage him in one-on-one combat. In his haste to reach the Saxon champion, he paid insufficient attention to the situation about him and found himself surrounded by three Saxons. He fended off the man on his left with his shield and parried the remaining two with his sword.

Horns began to sound from the Saxon castle. At first, the horns were ignored by the Saxon warriors, but as they continued to blow, the Saxons began to fall back. As the Saxons retreated, Gawain again caught sight of Willayne, who continued to fight and was urging the men around him to stay in the battle. But Willayne could not know what was happening elsewhere on the battlefield and would have been a fool to ignore the call to retreat.

Willayne was no fool, and he, too, began to fall back.

The British were too tired from fighting and too relieved to see the Saxons retreating to press any advantage they might now have. And they had to consider that the Saxon withdrawal might be an attempt to draw them into a trap of some sort.

Percival came up beside Gawain and watched as the Saxons returned to their castle.

"God granted us a miracle," said Percival.

Gawain turned toward Percival. He was tempted to give a sarcastic response, but he was too happy to see the enemy break off the battle to want to start an argument. "A miracle? It certainly seems so. I don't understand the timing or cause of their retreat. In fact, I thought the Saxons were about to gain the upper hand."

Willayne, his face and neck flushed red, mounted his horse and raced back to the castle. As he approached the Saxon stronghold, he noticed Horsa atop the castle wall near the front gate. Willayne rode into the courtyard, slid off his horse without bothering to tether it and rushed up the stone stairs to the top of the wall, to where Horsa waited for him.

"Why sound the retreat?" Willayne's breathing was labored, and his words came out unevenly. "We were winning. We could have finally defeated them."

Horsa said not a word. Instead he turned and pointed out to sea. Willayne's eyes followed Horsa's motion out to the horizon where he could see at least a dozen white sails. The lead vessel bore a blue cross on its sail, the insignia of Lancelot.

CHAPTER 4: **Death of a Warrior**

Gawain and a handful of other British knights were on the shore watching as Lancelot's fleet beached. Merlin observed the arrival as well. Lancelot was a big man, tall with a large chest and broad shoulders, and hands that were big even for his size. He had wavy, shoulder-length brown hair and a protruding jaw that added to his appearance of being both strong and determined. Dressed in a long white robe with a blue cross on its front, Lancelot was the first of his men to climb down from his vessel to the beach. He withdrew his sword, knelt on one knee, rested the blade point in the sand and bowed his head.

Gawain leaned toward Merlin. "What's he doing? Giving thanks for managing to cross the sea, as though sailing was a dangerous undertaking, while we fought a desperate battle this morning and saw some of our men burn to death."

Merlin glanced at Gawain from the corner of his eye. "I'm surprised you concern yourself about such things. I wish the two of you got along better."

"We get along well enough," said Gawain sarcastically, "when his arrogance doesn't vex me."

"We need his arrogance at the moment." Merlin took another look at Lancelot and scowled. "Of course, you have a point, at least in the way he dresses. He looks more like a Christian monk than a knight. I suppose when you *speak* for the Christian god, you must look the part as well as act it. It's his speaking for his god more than his pride in his battle skills that vexes me."

Lancelot stood, approached Merlin and Gawain, and was immediately surrounded by warriors who wanted to welcome him. He acknowledged their comments but with little enthusiasm. He looked over the heads of those who had come to greet him toward the burned-out British fortifications. "I see I arrived just in time." Looking at Merlin, he said, "Arthur needs this siege to end immediately." And turning to Gawain: "While you have been bogged down here fighting one Saxon warlord, another Saxon battle leader, Hengst, has been raiding our coast."

"We were planning to storm the Saxon castle as soon as you arrived," said Percival.

Gawain focused on the words "bogged down" and did not take Lancelot's criticism well, especially after the many warriors who had died or been wounded in the battle that morning. "Had you arrived *just in time*, you would have been here before the battle." He looked back over his shoulder at the smoldering wooden walls. "We have been here fighting for many months. The Saxons launched a powerful offensive this morning, and we beat them back while you were taking a sea voyage."

The tone of Gawain's comment caused Lancelot to bite his lips and open his eyes wide. "And yet your defenses, instead of the Saxon castle, are in ashes. Perhaps those who have been fighting here have had insufficient faith or perhaps insufficient courage to win this battle. Something here is lacking."

Gawain took a step toward Lancelot in anger. Percival held him back by his sleeve, and Merlin stepped between Gawain and Lancelot. "We don't need our best two knights fighting each other," said the wizard. "Both of you back off a step – with both your feet and your tongues."

But Gawain was not yet finished. "Be careful whose courage you question, Lancelot."

"Control yourself," said Merlin sternly.

"You are wrong to question our courage, Lancelot," said Percival. "Gawain has shown great bravery. He has faced the best of the Saxon knights, a warrior so brave he even issued a challenge to you."

Percival's comment drew Lancelot's attention away from Gawain. "Which knight issued the challenge?"

Percival ignored the question. "Gawain also snuck into the Saxon castle and stole the Grail."

Lancelot was awed by this information. "The Holy Grail," he whispered. He turned toward Gawain. "The Grail is here? You have it?" Gawain nodded and gave Lancelot a self-satisfied smile. "I must see it."

Merlin held out a hand toward each man. "I suggest everyone take a long breath, compose himself, and then, we can visit the Grail. Do you still have it, Gawain?"

"Yes, follow me." Lancelot, Percival and Merlin accompanied Gawain to his tent. Gawain held open the tent flap to let the other three enter. Lancelot's head turned in all directions. "Where is it? I don't see it."

Gawain went to his cot, bent over and withdrew a cloth from underneath.

"Damnation, Gawain," said Lancelot, as he watched Gawain unwrap the ruby-studded, silver chalice. "This isn't how you treat God's Holy Grail. It should be in a shrine, not wrapped in a towel under a cot." Lancelot held out his hand for the Grail. Gawain gave it to him. When he touched the Grail, Lancelot's body grew rigid and his eyes closed. And he remained motionless for so long Gawain thought he had gone into a trance.

"Hand it back." Lancelot seemed not to hear Gawain's words but opened his eyes with a start when Gawain pulled the chalice away from him. "I feel nothing." Gawain, who was holding the Grail by its stem, now wrapped both hands around the cup. "Still nothing."

"It's not surprising the Grail's power is hidden from you." Lancelot held out a hand. "Let me keep it."

Gawain would have allowed anyone else to take the Grail but not the sanctimonious Lancelot. "God found me worthy enough to take the Grail from the middle of the Saxon stronghold. So, I assume he considers me worthy enough to hold onto it – at least for a while." Now that Gawain had tried speaking for God he rather enjoyed it and would make that observation to Merlin after Lancelot left. "If you wish to erect some kind of appropriate shrine or altar here in my tent, you are welcome to do so."

It was a rare defeat for Lancelot, who stared angrily at Gawain. But Lancelot won a victory later in the day when at a meeting of the war council, he outlined his plan to attack Horsa's castle. During their months-long siege, the Britons had avoided going against the castle walls because of the certain cost in casualties. Lancelot insisted there was now no alternative to a direct and risky assault, and many of the others had already come to the same conclusion. They would storm the castle walls – but with a twist that just might catch the Saxons off guard.

Willayne stood atop the castle walls staring down at Britons who were building a siege tower in the open a short distance from the Saxon stronghold.

Horsa, a puzzled look on his face, stood next to him. "I'm confused, Willayne. On the one hand, I understand the sense of building a siege tower close to the castle walls where they intend to use it. On the other, being this close puts it at great risk of us attacking and destroying it. I wonder what they have in mind." Horsa waited for Willayne to comment, but he did not. "I also wonder why, if they are building their tower so close to the castle, the Britons don't have more warriors protecting it." Horsa pointed to one Briton who stood facing the castle, hands on hips. "But mostly I don't understand why Lancelot – I assume that is who the knight in white is – stands and stares this way."

Willayne spoke slowly and in a somber tone. "Yes, it is Lancelot who stares this way. He is waiting for me."

Horsa turned toward Willayne. "For you?"

Willayne nodded. "The best knight in the world knows I challenged him."

"Challenged him! When?"

"He stands and dares me to face him and dares us to attack his siege tower."

"But when could you have challenged him? He has only just arrived." Horsa stared at Willayne, waiting for an answer.

Willayne hung his head and spoke softly. "Not directly. I didn't challenge him to his face. It was something I shouted during battle. He wasn't there, but he must have been told. He does nothing but stand there, but I know the challenge is for me."

"You will, of course, refuse his challenge, Willayne. You cannot allow yourself to be baited by him."

Willayne looked up at Horsa; there was worry, not confidence, in his face. "Have I not proven myself a capable warrior, Horsa? Do you give me no hope against this man?"

Horsa rested a hand on Willayne's shoulder. "You are a great warrior, our best, but if this is Lancelot, he is said to be unbeatable. What purpose would it serve for you to be killed by him?"

Morgan le Fay appeared on the wall. She stood far enough away to not be intruding on their conversation, but close enough to hear it.

"It's matter of honor, Horsa. We will all die. . ."

"Yes, yes, I know. In battle or in bed, but reputations live forever. But reputation is not sufficient reason for going to the next world sooner than you have to."

"There are things worse than death and living without honor is first among them. And, Horsa, you forget an aspect of battle. Call it the fortunes of war. . ." Willayne paused to look skyward. ". . . or the whim of God, but a man can be killed cowering at the rear of the battle formation as well as leading the charge. I could defeat Lancelot today and tomorrow fall dead to an arrow shot by the weakest Briton. Should I fear a weak archer as well as Lancelot? A warrior cannot enter a battle worried he will die." Horsa was about to speak, but Willayne continued. "One last thing, if I take his challenge, we will destroy their siege tower."

"They will just build another."

"We will destroy the next one too." With that, Willayne turned and walked away.

Morgan let him pass by without saying anything. She approached Horsa. "I'll speak to him," she said.

"Please, Morgan, make him see the folly of his plan. If we lose Willayne, it will be a blow equal to that of losing the Grail."

Morgan walked away at a fast pace and caught up to Willayne just as he was about to descend the stone stairs leading from the wall down to the courtyard. "Wait, Willayne." He turned to face her, and she stood so close to him their bodies were almost touching. "I overheard your conversation, and I agree with you, but for a reason other than your need to defend your honor." Her comment appeared to pique his interest. "As you explained to me, the walls of this castle were secure as long as the Grail was within them. But the Grail is gone. You know I have the *sight*. I can't always see the future, and truthfully, it is seldom that I do, but this I see with great clarity. This castle will not stand; the Saxons will not emerge from this siege victorious while Lancelot lives. He must be defeated." She pointed over her shoulder in the general direction of where the Britons were constructing their siege tower. "If you don't fight him out there, then you will face him in here, in this castle when the stakes are much higher."

"I know," he said. "I have no choice but to face him. But I do have the choice of when and where. I choose out there and at dusk today."

The sun was dropping below the horizon. The carpenters building the British siege tower, which already rose twenty-feet high, had returned to their camp, and in the twilight the dozen Britons guarding the tower sat around three campfires. Inside the Saxon castle, more than a score of knights commanded by Willayne waited on horseback by the castle gates.

Horsa suggested his men burn the siege tower as they had the British defensive walls, but oil was in short supply and animal skins even scarcer. They decided to use ropes and grappling hooks instead in an effort to pull down the tower. No one could be certain how difficult a task that might be.

At Willayne's signal the castle gates were opened, and the Saxon knights charged into the night. The first wave of Saxons rode toward British guards, who rose to their feet, spears in hand, shields held high, to meet the attack. The second Saxon wave, Willayne in front, whipped grappling hooks in circles over their heads and flung them at the tower. Willayne's hook caught. He wrapped the rope through a notch on his saddle and urged his horse forward. The tower would not budge. The Saxons whose first throw failed to hook onto the tower turned their horses around for another pass. Another half dozen hooks caught the tower, and as the horses pulled, it began to tilt forward.

Lancelot appeared from inside the tower just as it was beginning to fall. The tower crashed to the ground and broke into pieces. Saxon riders loosened the ropes fastened to their saddles, let them fall to the ground and wheeled their horses around to return to the safety of their castle. The Saxon contingent fighting the British guards began to disengage and withdraw.

Willayne caught sight of Lancelot and rode toward him. He raised his sword, leaned over the side of his mount and swung at Lancelot's head. Lancelot rolled under Willayne's blade and back up to his knees, sword in hand, in time to chop through the right rear leg of Willayne's horse. The horse fell, throwing its rider and rolling over the top of him.

On the walls of the castle Saxon archers stood ready to cover the retreat of their knights. If any of the Saxon riders knew Willayne had been left behind, none of them turned to go to his aid.

Willayne survived being rolled over by his horse, but his left arm was broken, his vision blurry and his head throbbed. He stood up, his useless left arm dangling at his side, and scanned the field until he found Lancelot standing a short distance away. Lancelot did not take the offensive but waited for the Saxon to make the first move. Willayne feigned an overhand attack but backed off. The two circled one another. Willayne again feigned an overhand attack, then whipped his sword around in a half circle, delivering a blow that Lancelot easily caught on his shield. Now Lancelot took the offensive, unleashing a series of blows the shield-less Willayne had to deflect with his sword.

A group of British warriors, Gawain among them, was approaching and halted their advance a short distance from where the two dark figures were fighting in the campfire light. At first Gawain could not make out who the warriors were, although he guessed one was Lancelot, the taller of the two, and the other Willayne. As they fought across the campfire, Gawain caught a glimpse of Lancelot's white tunic and Willayne's red, but they quickly became gray shadows again.

One of the figures raised his sword overhead, but before he could bring it down, the second figure thrust his sword low at his opponent and the first shadow doubled over and fell to his knees.

Gawain spurred his horse forward and found Lancelot standing over the fallen Willayne and watching the life drain out of him. There was an eerie silence among the Britons present, as well as among the Saxons who lined the castle wall.

Gawain dismounted and knelt by Willayne just as the last flicker of life left him. Speaking to Lancelot but keeping his eyes on the fallen Saxon, Gawain said, "He knew you were waiting for him. He understood why you stood staring at the castle and knew you would kill him. And he came to destroy the tower anyway. Such courage should be honored." Gawain stood and faced Lancelot. "Unless you have an objection, I will return his body to his people."

Lancelot shook his head indicating he had no objection. Balin and Percival dismounted to help Gawain lift Willayne's body onto the back of Gawain's horse. Gawain rode to the castle and was met by a handful of men who took Willayne's body down from the horse and carried it into the castle. Not a word was spoken by anyone.

Gawain rode slowly back toward the British camp. For some unknown reason he turned back for a final look at the Saxon castle. There in the highest window of the tower was a single light. It was Morgan le Fay's signal.

CHAPTER 5: **Night Journey**

Sleep would not come to Gawain. He thought about some of the Britons who died in the recent combat, but mostly he thought about Willayne. There was something about the death of the Saxon that upset him to his core. Gawain had been less disturbed by the loss of some of his own men, and he wondered why the death of an enemy would strike him so hard. Perhaps it was because of the kindness the Saxon had shown him at Horsa's castle in making certain a beggar did not go hungry. Maybe it was because Gawain had seen Willayne's family – his wife and young child. More likely it was because Willayne had gone to fight Lancelot knowing he would die, while Gawain, if called upon in similar circumstances, would be far less willing to make such a sacrifice. Even when he entered the Saxon castle dressed as a beggar, Gawain was fairly confident he would survive. Certainly it wasn't a suicidal effort. But Willayne must have known Lancelot was waiting for him, daring him to one-on-one combat, when Lancelot stood staring up at the wall of Horsa's castle. And still Willayne came.

Gawain could not get the troubling images out of his mind and was beginning to find his tent confining. After lying on his cot for a time, he took a stool outside the tent to sit in the night air, hoping it would clear his head. The sky was full of stars, and he occupied himself by seeing how many he could name. There were not many. When he lowered his eyes from the heavens, he was startled to see a figure approaching from a short distance away. Because of the man's small, thin frame and hooded cape, Gawain at first thought it was Merlin come to visit in the middle of the night. But as the figure came closer, he knew it was not the wizard even though the front of the man's hood was drawn down in such a way as to prevent Gawain from seeing his face.

The figure held out a boney hand and beckoned Gawain to follow. Gawain had no intention of following whoever or whatever this was but found himself standing up and involuntarily walking after the hooded figure.

Gawain was led to the edge of their camp, past tent after tent, not a single person awake or even visible or making a sound. They went to where there should have been the sea, but instead there was a mountain where none had been before. And in the mountain there was a cave. The hooded figure stood by the cave entrance and directed him to enter. Again he did not intend to follow the creature's instruction; yet again he found himself doing exactly what he was bid to do.

Inside the cave, there was nothing ahead but blackness. Gawain turned back to look at the entrance. It had disappeared. There was no way to go except forward. He moved cautiously through the darkness not knowing what was ahead until he saw some light in the distance. Farther inside the cave the walls were lined with torches on either side. Gawain walked forward hoping there would be an exit a short distance ahead. The cave narrowed. This, he was certain, meant he was coming to its end and there was a way out. But that was not the case. The first cave only led to another torch-lined cave. He moved quickly into this second one, looking for an exit and wanting to escape as soon as he could. The cave narrowed, and he hoped it meant he was approaching an opening of some sort. But this path only led him into yet another cave.

The third cave also came to a tapered end. This time there was something on the other side. Taking a torch from the cave wall, Gawain examined his surroundings. The first thing he noticed was a tree. It was leafless and dead. Next he saw a boulder and more trees, all leafless and dead. Such was the Underworld, and he should have expected nothing better.

Finally he saw something other than boulders and lifeless trees, and he approached it cautiously. It was a small boy. The boy stood perfectly still, and his eyes were unseeing. The boy looked familiar, but Gawain could not identify him until he noticed the bruises on his face and arms. When he was a youth, Gawain saw a boy accidentally trampled to death by a horse. This was that boy, the first person he had ever seen die.

Gawain did not know if he could or should speak to the boy, and since the boy did not seem to notice him, he moved on. The next figure he encountered was an adult male who stood among dozens of other figures. He held the torch up to the figure's face. "Uncle?"

"Greetings, Gawain. Have you joined us so soon?" The voice was eerily hollow, and Gawain was not certain his uncle's lips had moved.

"I don't know why I'm here or even how I got here." He waited for his uncle to say more, but he did not speak again, which was fine with Gawain. He found the dead man's hollow voice disturbing enough that he moved on from his uncle without trying to foster further conversation. He walked among the other figures examining most of them. They, too, were relatives and friends who had died years before. They all had unseeing eyes, and not wishing to hear the eerie voices of the dead again, Gawain did not speak to any of them and was relieved that none called out to him.

He continued to walk in the darkness and entered another area of only boulders and lifeless trees. After he walked through it, he reached another grouping of several dozen figures. He examined their faces in the torchlight but did not recognize the first or the second. But he knew the third; it was a man he killed in war. He examined a few more figures and soon realized these were all men he had killed during one battle or another.

He was overcome by guilt and grief. He could not face them and turned to leave when a hollow voice called his name.

"Gawain, I have a message for you."

He knew this must be the reason he was brought here, to receive this message, and he slowly walked toward the location of the hollow voice. His torch lit the spirit of the Saxon knight Willayne, dressed in the armor and red tunic in which he had died, the tunic stained with blood at his belly where it had been pierced by Lancelot's sword.

Gawain approached cautiously. "Willayne, do you know who I am? I am Gawain, a knight of Arthur's Roundtable but also the beggar you fed in Horsa's castle."

Willayne's eyes never moved and never blinked remaining locked open and staring straight ahead. "Yes, I know who you are, Gawain. We know many things in the Underworld, but the knowledge comes far too late."

"And how do you fare, Willayne? Do you suffer here?"

Willayne never looked at him, did not have eyes that seemed capable of sight and hardly moved his mouth as he spoke. "Not in the way you imagine, but I am in perpetual misery. I would rather be a living cleaner of stables or the lowest servant rather than what I am now." Despite the nature of his words, there was no emotion in Willayne's voice. "Do not make the same mistake, Gawain."

"Of being prideful?"

"Yes, pride was my mistake and a fatal one. You confronted Lancelot as a matter of pride. I did also. I could have avoided doing battle with him, but I was concerned about my reputation, about my legend, that which would endure after my death. I made the wrong choice in challenging him although I knew I would lose. This is my message for you Gawain: Choose as much life as you can."

He did not know what kind of answer would satisfy a man no longer alive. "I understand and know your message is why I was led here."

"Do you understand, Gawain? You sneaked into the castle to steal the Grail. You could have easily been caught and killed. Would you risk everything again now to prove your worth with Lancelot or against a Saxon knight?"

"I would choose not to – if I had a choice." The uncertainty was clear in Gawain's voice. "We are warriors. Battle is our world. I would try not to take unnecessary risks, but risks always find us."

"You have a wife and children, Gawain." Every time Willayne said his name, Gawain felt a chill. "I left my wife and young son behind. I was more wedded to duty and to glory than to my wife. But there is no duty here, no honor or glory, no reason for courage. There is nothing here. Your wife and children, they are your most important duty. Return to them as soon as you can. This is my message for you."

"I want nothing more than to return to my family." Gawain hesitated. The words came hard to him. "I saw others here, men I have killed, and I truly regret killing them now. I don't suppose there is any way I could make amends except not to kill more men." Gawain waited for Willayne to give a response, and when none came, he turned to leave.

"Wait, Gawain. I have a request as well."

He turned back toward the unmoving figure. "Ask anything. Willayne. I remember your generosity to me."

The Saxon's dead eyes remained locked in a sightless stare. "This request is for more than just a plate of meat."

"Ask anyway."

"Lancelot has a plan to take the castle."

Gawain nodded although he was not certain Willayne could see him. "Yes, we intend to attack before dawn."

"And you will be among the first Britons into the city because you will meet Morgan le Fay at the east tower gate."

"You know about Morgan? Yes, that is also correct."

Willayne turned his head slightly to more directly face Gawain although his eyes still appeared to be unseeing. "Then, this is my favor. The British will storm the castle burning with a blood lust. They will take my son, although he is an infant, and crush his head against a wall or throw him from the castle gates for fear he will grow into a great warrior who seeks vengeance for the sack of our castle. Protect my son, Gawain. This is my request."

Gawain was not sure he could fulfill the request, but he also thought it unwise and ignoble to deny a request from the dead. "You have my word, Willayne; I will do my best."

Willayne retuned his head to its original position, and without knowing why, Gawain thought Willayne had withdrawn from his body. Whatever the reason, Willayne did not speak again. Gawain decided it was time to flee the land of the dead and took his leave of Willayne with a slight bow. He retraced his steps back through the series of torch-lined caves, worried the caves would be endless or he would not be able to find his way back or the cave entrance was still closed and had disappeared forever. But the caves did end, and he did find the entrance. The hooded figure was awaiting for him just outside and silently led him back to his tent.

Gawain was shaking from the experience and breathing hard. He sat down in his chair to recover and looked up at his guide. The hooded figure waved a hand over him, and everything turned to black.

CHAPTER 6: **Final Assault**

Merlin, as sometimes happened the night before an important battle, was too anxious to sleep, and he walked through the British camp checking that all was in order. Everyone else, except the night watch, was sleeping, or should have been asleep, but he noticed a light in Gawain's tent. He approached it and stopped to watch a shadow reflected on the inside of the tent wall, a figure lifting a tankard to his mouth. He went around to the entrance, called to Gawain and entered.

Inside he found Gawain on a stool hunched over a fire, a tankard in his right hand. The tent smelled strongly of mead. Merlin moved closer to Gawain, who looked up at him, his eyes watery. "You've been drinking too much," said Merlin. The comment was part question, part statement.

Gawain took another swallow of mead. "I've been drinking, yes. Too much, for certain."

Merlin stood before Gawain and scowled at him. "Have you lost your senses? You'll be in battle before the sun rises and hardly appear in condition to fight."

"Exactly so. There will be a battle. I will fight. And that is exactly why I've been drinking." Gawain started to lift his tankard, but Merlin caught his arm and took the mead away from him.

"You need food and lots of water." The wizard dumped the remaining mead onto the ground and searched the tent until he found some bread, fruit and a jug of water.

Gawain glanced over at him and smiled. "The great Merlin making me a meal! Imagine. You may be a good cook, Merlin, but you would not make a good wife or even a good woman."

"You are talking nonsense," said the wizard, the anger mounting in his voice.

"Now, Morgan le Fay would make a good woman but most likely not a good wife."

"Morgan le Fay. Why do you mention her?"

"No reason. I should stop talking."

"Morgan le Fay! Babbling, that's what it is. You should stop talking nonsense. You must come to your senses, or you will be in woeful condition for the coming battle."

"The coming battle is exactly why I've been drinking. It's hard to deceive a wizard. They're too perceptive. You are a wizard, aren't you? I'm never sure. But you can confide in me. You'd be surprised at the confidences I keep."

Merlin ignored the comment and handed Gawain a jug of water. "Drink if for no other reason than to interrupt your inane babbling." Gawain drank, spilling water down his face and neck. The wizard pulled up a stool and sat next to Gawain with a plate of food in his lap.

Gawain wiped the water from his chin and turned serious. "Tonight I went to the Underworld, Merlin."

The wizard extended a piece of bread in Gawain's direction. "You dreamed you went to the Underworld."

He refused the bread. "No, no, you're wrong. It was real. At least, I think it was real. Can't dreams be real?"

"Not this one, not if you think you were in the Underworld. No one returns from the Underworld."

"Oh, but I did, and I think I was actually there. I saw people, dead people, people I didn't even remember knowing. So, how could I dream of them if I didn't even remember them or even know some of them were dead? How did I know they were in the Underworld if it wasn't real?"

Merlin's tone became more sympathetic. "Your point seems logical, but sometimes we know things in dreams we don't know when we are awake."

"People in the Underworld, if that's what they still are, people there learn much after they're dead but learn it too late. Far too late, I was told. And that's exactly my point. I learned something in the dream I didn't know before the dream. So, I must have been in the Underworld." He took another swallow of water. Merlin tried again to hand him the bread, but he pushed it away. "When I was in the Underworld, I saw Willayne, the Saxon knight."

"I'm well aware of who Willayne is – or was."

"Exactly. Who he *was*, not who he *is*. He is no more. And you know what he told me? He said to grab as much life as I can. And avoid the Underworld as long as I can. And not take unnecessary risks." Gawain put a hand to his chest. "And I said we are warriors and cannot avoid risk."

Merlin lifted his head back as though he had just come to a realization. "And now you are fearful about the coming battle?"

Gawain did not answer at first; he merely stared down at the fire. "Every warrior experiences some fear before every battle, before the actual fighting begins. Some fear is natural. But not this, not being so frightened you feel sick in your belly and feel too weak to walk. And Willayne said something else. He made me promise him something, to protect his infant son."

Merlin extended the bread to Gawain a third time; this time he took it and bit off a piece. "It will more than likely be a very bloody battle – not that any battle is bloodless," said the wizard. "There is cause for concern for Willayne's son – not that I'm agreeing you were actually in the Underworld. Our men have had months of being in this hostile land, and it has taken a toll on them the Saxons will be expected to pay. And Lancelot's warriors seem to be exceptionally self-righteous and hard men; they have little humor and seemingly no compassion – not any compassion I've seen. I'm not sure what will happen." Merlin shook Gawain's shoulder to be certain he was paying attention. "But when the sun reaches the top of the midday sky tomorrow, the battle will be over. Do you understand?"

Gawain looked at the old wizard with his watery eyes and shook his head. "I'm afraid, Merlin, afraid of dying, of returning to the Underworld and standing there in the dark, motionless and sightless for eternity. I would admit this to no one except you because you say you know things about worlds beyond this one if there are any."

Merlin leaned toward Gawain and spoke more emphatically. "The battle will be over before the sun reaches the top of the midday sky. Can you hold yourself together that long?" Gawain hung his head and did not answer. "Can you? Can you just keep yourself together until then?"

"What choice do I have?"

At the wizard's urging Gawain tried to nap and did sleep for a time with Merlin watching over him. When Gawain awoke, he was more alert and rational but his head ached. He drank more water, ate more bread and his head began to clear. When he decided he felt as good as he was going to feel on this day, he dressed in his armor, donned his helmet, strapped on his sword and grabbed his shield.

Merlin caught him by the arm, as he was about to leave the tent. "Remember you need only to make it to midday." Gawain nodded and exited the tent.

The British warriors were quietly assembling in the dark, grouping themselves around long, crudely made ladders. Using the ladders had been Lancelot's plan all along. The siege tower was a decoy. Lancelot wanted the Saxons to destroy it in the hope the enemy would relax their guard while they thought the Britons were con-structing a new one. His deception being achieved, as far as they could determine, Lancelot planned a rare night assault using the lad-ders and was prepared to accept heavy losses if it meant the attack would be successful.

The chances of the plan's success increased greatly when Gawain told Lancelot he thought he would be able to get a contingent of men inside the castle through a gate in its east tower.

While the rest of the British army remained in place ready to ad-vance at a signal, Gawain and forty other men, including Percival, crept toward the castle. Gawain's legs were unsteady, from mead, yes, but also from fear. And he did not feel much strength in his arms. This weakness he also attributed to both mead and a mounting sense of panic.

Gawain now regretted trying to drink away his fear.

How quickly things change. It was only days ago – two or three, he could not remember how many – when he entered this castle alone and unarmed and had the audacity to walk casually among the Saxons and steal their most valued possession. Now, accompanied by an entire army, he feared approaching it.

There were a half dozen fires burning on the walls of the Saxon stronghold, two on either side of the main gates and one by each of the four towers. There were probably sentries by each fire, but none were visible in the dark. Gawain raised his eyes and saw Morgan's light still burning in the highest window of the main tower. He gave her the signal, three times waving a torch from side to side. The light in the tower was moved up and down.

With Gawain in the lead, the Britons crossed the dark plain between the two armies, and when they neared the castle, they moved more slowly and cautiously toward it in single file. They reached the wall and crept along it, staying close to its stone face to prevent being spotted from above. They made their way to the east tower. Gawain turned back and waited for his men to catch up. When they were all in position, he tapped on the thick wooden tower door. There was no response. He tapped again. On the inside, he heard a large metal bolt being pulled back from the center of the door. A second was pulled back from its top and a third from its bottom. The door was drawn back and open. In the doorway stood what appeared to be a servant boy carrying a large sack.

"What took you so long? I expected you shortly after nightfall."

The voice was Morgan's, and with a closer look he was surprised he could have mistaken her for a male even for an instant. Gawain ignored her question to inspect the tower interior. The thick wooden exterior door she opened was only the first line of defense. There was a second, equally thick interior door leading to the castle court-yard; it had been closed but was unlocked. And between the two doors a thick metal gate had been raised into the stone ceiling. The way for the British troops was open.

"I want to leave this place." The impatience was clear in Morgan's tone.

Gawain took her gently by the arm and led her outside, where he was met by Percival. "Escort this boy to my tent, Percival, and see that he is safe from both Saxons and Britons."

Percival protested. "I would rather remain here with you and fight."

"This is a very important task, and I trust you more than anyone else. There will be plenty of time for fighting later."

Reluctantly Percival took the *boy* by the arm and led him away.

Gawain went to the inner castle door, opened it and cautiously peeked out. The courtyard appeared empty, but it was too dark to be certain. He motioned for the other soldiers to follow as he stepped into the castle's interior. They lined up behind him in single file, and again they crept along the wall to keep from being seen from above. Ahead, fires burned atop the main gates. The castle entrance seemed a far distance off, too far off to be reached safely. His footsteps and those of his men seemed louder than they had outside the castle, and their armor seemed to be clanging almost as loud as bells, every sound causing Gawain to cringe. He felt a mounting sickness in his stomach, and his legs were on the verge of giving way.

They were nearing the halfway point to the main gates and had not been spotted. Maybe they would make it.

"Who's there?" someone shouted from above.

They were caught.

The Britons pressed their bodies flat against the wall, and the voice atop the wall called out again. "Who's there?"

The sounds of a great commotion erupted. At first Gawain couldn't identify what was going on; then, he realized Lancelot and the others were attacking the castle from outside. He could hear wooden ladders being thrown against the walls, and the Saxon sentries calling out the alarm.

Gawain and his men broke from their cover and ran for the main gates. Above them on the walls he could hear battle cries and the sounds of swords and shields colliding. A horn sounded from atop a tower. A body crashed down from the wall to the courtyard, whether Briton or Saxon, he could not tell.

Gawain and his men reached the gates and began to fight the outnumbered Saxon guard. The courtyard was chaotic as Saxons rushed in from every direction to join the battle. Gawain's men overwhelmed the guard trying to protect the castle's main gates and managed to pull open one of the two large wooden doors. Britons began to pour in.

Gawain had succeeded in what he had come to do – help Morgan escape and open the main gates. Now that there was fighting all about him, he grew oddly numb, a lingering effect from his journey to the Underworld. He was there at the battle but not part of it. He walked about like a specter, unnoticed and unchallenged, observing and not engaging. None of it seemed real; none of it seemed reasonable in the least – men hacking at each other, chopping off limbs, slashing throats, stabbing backs, slicing open bellies.

He paused when he saw two Britons pulling frail-looking Horsa from the castle tower. Horsa resisted at first, but an armored elbow to the head convinced him to be more cooperative. Horsa pleaded for his life. "My brother Hengst will ransom me, a sizable ransom," he said. A third Briton joined them, and at his command, Horsa, was forced to his knees. The Saxon leader continued to beg for mercy as the Briton behind him raised his sword and lopped off Horsa's head with a single blow.

This sight brought Gawain back to reality, and he remembered his promise to Willayne. He hurried to the tower and began searching the bedrooms from the second floor up. All the rooms were empty of living people, and most had bodies lying in pools of blood on the floor. His hope was running out. Nowhere had he come across Willayne's wife and child. There was one last, unlikely place to check, and he climbed to the highest point in the tower. There he found only Morgan's lantern, its flame nearly burned out.

There was no sign of the infant. He had failed Willayne.

CHAPTER 7: **Change of Heart, Change of Mind**

The fighting had ended and the remaining Saxons were being taken prisoner when Gawain left the castle and began the long walk back to his tent. He expected to find no comfort there, but he could not remain here, the site of so much carnage. Someone was approaching from behind. He looked from the corner of his eye to see the wizard catching up with him. Merlin fell in next to him and said not a word.

Behind them they could hear the sounds of warriors shouting, their words indistinct.

It was Gawain who finally broke the silence. "Everything has been undone. Everything I have accomplished and everything I have believed in for a lifetime has been destroyed in a single night and day – or perhaps *changed* is a better word than *destroyed*." He went silent again, and Merlin seemed to know he should allow Gawain to proceed at his own pace. "I was always so sure, so certain, so un-questioning. All those battles we fought *needed* to be fought. All the men we killed *deserved* to be killed. But now. . ."

Merlin appeared uncharacteristically subdued. "I understand."

"And I failed Willayne."

"You did what you could." The wizard spoke softly and slowly as though his mind were someplace else. "All these years, I have had to satisfy myself with knowing that I did what I could rather than enjoying the successes I sought. Of course, I've had a few modest victories and a major one with Arthur. But beginning with Uther Pendragon, then with Arthur and even here now, I have tried to influence the affairs of men and to encourage them to see things in a different way, and I have failed miserably. I have even assisted them with their battles because the enemy was usually worse than us. And I tell myself I have done the best I can. Worse still, I sometimes believe as time passes I am able to do less and less."

Merlin became more present and spoke with more intensity. "What I have learned, Gawain, is that the world is difficult to change. Beliefs carry from one man to another. There is right and wrong, up and down, and no in-between; there is what we have done before and what our fathers did before us and never anything new. If you have changed everything you believe in, it is not a tragedy but rather the mark of a mind willing to explore."

Gawain would not be consoled. "Oh but there is tragedy, Merlin. I was eager to fight those battles and more than willing to dispatch to the Underworld as many of our enemies as I could." He raised his eyes toward the sky. "The gods, if there are any, forgive me if I sent anyone to the Underworld before his time."

"You cannot fault yourself too much for being a man of your time and place. But you've changed. That's good." Merlin studied Gawain's face. "And this change, did it begin when Willayne fought Lancelot?"

He stopped walking to look at Merlin. "In some ways, yes. How did you know? Your sight?"

"No, dark as it was, I merely observed your expression when they were fighting, and of course, you returned the Saxon's body to his people. But it was mostly your expression."

"I didn't even realize you where there, but you are correct," said Gawain, as they continued walking. "I liked Willayne. He treated a ragged beggar well. And Lancelot increasingly annoys me. I found myself hoping the *wrong man* would win their fight. And as for the battle just fought, I always saw bloodshed as a part of the normal course of events." He shook his head vigorously. "But not today, not during the senseless carnage I witnessed today as though I was not actually a part of it. Strange how you see things when you detach yourself from them."

Merlin gave a sarcastic grunt. "You don't have to tell me. Remember, I'm the most detached person you know."

There was a flickering light against the clouds in the morning sky. Gawain turned back to see flames in several of the castle's tower windows. "A beautiful castle, it rivaled Camelot. I even had sympathy for its master, Horsa, who begged for his life. The warriors who had hold of him could have earned themselves a substantial ransom, but they preferred to see his head rolling on the ground."

Merlin took him by the arm. "Gawain, listen to me. I am old and perhaps a little addled, but I still know a thing or two. You condemn yourself – and I don't say your concerns and opinions are wrong – but it's not as simple as you make it out to be, not so easy to have avoided everything that happened here this day. There was, after all, a legitimate reason to attack Horsa, to take the fighting to the Saxons, who have often enough invaded our shores and attacked our people, usually helpless villagers."

In his mind Gawain could see the warriors he had killed standing like a forest of dead trees in the Underworld. "Yes, Merlin, there was a reason to be here, but not an absolute necessity. And there was no absolute necessity for me to kill the men I killed in battle and no absolute necessity in how I hastened the destruction of the Saxons by taking men through an unlocked gate in their wall."

"Perhaps not, but once in battle – and you know this better than I – it's killed or be killed, isn't it?"

"Yes, but it's also true that once the killing starts, killing itself becomes a goal." He could hear Willayne's hollow voice calling to him, asking him to save his son, and he wondered how the infant boy died.

Merlin relented. "All good points. I merely state a mitigating argument that has some value. I understand how you feel, Gawain, but remember every man is also bound by circumstances no matter what he believes – unless you want to live in the woods like me, outside society. I doubt you do. Few people want to."

They walked silently for a while. Gawain looked back at the fires in the castle, opened his mouth to speak but did not. They went a distance farther, and he finally got the words out. "Worse than the thought of killing is the thought of dying. To spend an eternity standing in the Underworld unable to move, an eternity staring yet unable to see, I cannot imagine it. I would lose my mind. Tell me, Merlin, is the journey from life to death, a journey from sanity to insanity?"

"No, I don't believe so." The question seemed to trouble Merlin. "And I don't think you actually visited the Underworld, despite how real it seemed to you, because I don't believe it actually exists."

Gawain was surprised by his remark. "I'm not sure your lack of belief is good news for me. The Christian hell might be worse than the Underworld, and maybe nothingness, to be totally removed from existence with no trace you had ever lived, might be even worse. At least, I would have company in the Underworld."

Merlin again grabbed Gawain by the arm and turned him so they were face to face. "There are no words I could say now, Gawain, that would give you any real comfort, but every man and every beast, every blade of grass in every field and every leaf on every tree that ever lived also died. You are just trying to come to terms with your own mortality. It is more difficult for you because you see and question more than most."

Gawain gave the wizard a bitter smile. "There is actually a humorous aspect to all this." Merlin appeared puzzled. "With all I just said, I also feel guilty I didn't fight today, and I worry I have become a coward and am not the warrior I was a day ago."

CHAPTER 8: **Next To A Warm Body**

Morgan le Fay, who had dispensed with her boyish disguise, waited in Gawain's tent. She had combed out her long golden hair, put on a dress – which she considered a temporary measure – and dabbed just a little perfume on her neck. She pulled a lock of hair down over the edge of her right eye. She believed a fallen lock made her appear vulnerable and gave men – the male in this case being Gawain – more courage to be assertive. Now that she was in the British camp, she could easily make up a story to explain her presence among her own people even though she was in the land of the Saxons. While not as renowned as Merlin, she did have a reputation as an enchantress, and the more simple-minded Britons would believe almost anything she said about using her magical skills as long as Gawain kept to their bargain.

And it was Gawain who was her immediate concern. She had plans for him, and they would begin as soon as she brought him under her *spell*, as she liked to think of it.

There was tapping all across the tent roof, the pleasant sound of a light rain. Morgan went to the tent entrance and pulled back the door flap. The sky was overcast, and the morning was almost as dark as dusk. She caught sight of two figures approaching in the distance. The first she recognized as Merlin, and the second, after he came a few dozen feet closer, as Gawain. Morgan cursed under her breath. If the wizard came in here with Gawain, it would ruin things – perhaps not ruin, but certainly delay them. She watched as the two men stopped walking, faced each other and continued their conversation. The rain increased in intensity, and both men covered their heads. Morgan smiled when she saw Gawain take his leave of the wizard and walk toward his tent.

On an impulse she abandoned her original plan to be subtle. She hurriedly slipped out of her dress and climbed into Gawain's cot, pulling the blanket up to her neck. Gawain entered. Not noticing her, he filled a tankard with mead, sat by the fire and began to drink.

She leaned her head up from the pillow. "Have you forgotten about me?"

Gawain, in mid-sip, was startled, spilling some mead down his chin and quickly wiping it with his sleeve. "Morgan! Yes, in fact, I did forget. Actually I didn't think you would be here. Actually, I didn't give any thought to where you might be. I have much on my mind."

She propped herself up on her elbow. "It's time to unburden yourself. The battle is over, I assume?"

He took another swallow of mead. "It is for me, if not for everyone else."

"And we won, or you would not be here now?"

"Yes, we did win. Certainly Horsa and his head have gone their separate ways, and the tower of his castle is in flames." Gawain's eyes ran up and down the cot as though finally realizing she had made herself at home in his bed.

She looked down at herself. "Forgive me for taking the liberty, but I was tired." She feigned a yawn. "I was awake all night waiting for you to take me from the castle."

His eyes lingered on her bare shoulders. "You are naked?"

She dropped the blanket to her waist revealing her breasts, which were only partially covered by her long hair. "I always sleep naked. They say it is good for the body. But I'm sorry if my nakedness disturbs you."

He turned away, seemingly more interested in his mead. "I have far more important things than your nakedness or anyone else's nakedness to be disturbed about. Please don't be offended."

She realized he was not going to join her in bed, at least, not yet. She sat up on the edge of the cot, wrapped the blanket around herself and walked to where he sat. She came up beside him and ran her fingers through his hair. "You can relax now, Gawain. The battle has ended, and you helped win it by helping me. We have become allies. Now you can relax, and we can enjoy our victory." He did not answer, but neither did he resist her touch. She kissed him on the cheek. "Do you find me attractive?" She placed her hand under his chin and turned his face toward hers. "Do you?"

There was sadness in his face. "Very attractive," he said, but the comment was made without passion or enthusiasm.

She pulled down one side of the blanket and placed his hand on her bare breast. He began to fondle her, but before she could pretend to be getting aroused, he withdrew his hand.

"I have a wife," he said nonchalantly and turned his attention back to his mead.

She studied his expression. "But she is not the reason for your lack of interest, is she?"

"It's not so much lack of interest as this is just not a good time, not so soon after a battle. Anger and fear well up in a man during battle, and it's difficult to back away from them soon after. Don't take offense."

"I understand. . .and I can wait." Morgan pulled the blanket back over her shoulder, returned to the cot and sat on its edge, watching as he finished one tankard of mead and poured himself another. After he downed three more tankards, she got up again and sat opposite him. His eyes were watery and droopy. "Are you drunk?"

"A little."

She stroked his hair from front to back. "And are you tired?"

"Very. I, too, was awake most of the night."

"Then, sleep." She stood up and coaxed him to his feet. He walked unsteadily to the cot. "Your clothes are still wet from the rain." He still exhibited no passion but was too drunk to resist as she helped him off with his tunic and his leggings. With her assistance, he got into the bed, and she laid the blanket over him.

The rain was coming down with more force, pounding the tent roof, the wind causing its sides to billow. It was a good sound, she thought, because the rain made her feel safely cut off from the rest of the camp. They would not be interrupted. She waited until Gawain was sleeping and crawled under the covers with him. Nestling her body next to his, she whispered, "It's nice to have a warm body next to you on a chilly, rainy morning, isn't it?"

He grunted a noise she took to mean yes. She rubbed her hand across his body and began to massage him. It was not long before she got the desired response. He turned and rolled over on top her. He grabbed her right leg and lifted it up and back. And then he stopped. He dropped back to his side of the cot and turned his back to her.

Something was wrong with this man. Morgan needed someone close to Arthur; Gawain was as close as anyone except for Arthur's brother Kaye and, of course, Lancelot. And she needed a powerful knight; Gawain was a powerful knight or at least he had been one of the best. She never expected controlling him would be easy, but behind the tiredness and the mead and even his wife, she sensed a resistance in Gawain, perhaps a weakness, that might make him useless to her. Certainly if she couldn't even seduce him, she wouldn't be able to bend him to her purposes.

With Horsa dead, his army defeated, his castle – or what was left of it – under British control, she needed to find another ally, a willing or unwitting ally. Gawain was tired and drunk and battle weary. He might be a different man tomorrow, but it was possible she might have to forget Gawain and find another of Arthur's knights.

CHAPTER 9: **Crossing a Deadly Sea**

Gawain awoke startled to find a woman in bed with him. He was even more surprised to see it was Morgan le Fay, breathing lightly, who lay next to him. He searched his memory and recalled her being in his tent when he returned from the battle at Horsa's castle but had no recollection of their getting into his cot together. Lying as he was against the tent wall, he had to carefully climb over her to get up without waking her. He found his clothes on the floor and glanced back at her. She was still asleep. He quickly dressed, combed his hair with his fingers and found some water to rinse out his mouth.

He did not know whether it was day or night, although now that he noticed, there was dim light illuminating the roof of the tent. He also didn't know if it was the same day they fought the final battle with the Saxons or the day after. He tried to recall what had transpired with Morgan and remembered speaking with her and that she stroked his hair, even that she exposed her body to him, but he could not piece together how they went to bed together.

It would come back to him later.

The tent was cold; the fire at its center was nearly out. He went to get some wood from a corner of the tent and noticed the Grail was missing from the altar Lancelot had erected for it. "That's right," he said softly to himself. He wanted to hide the Grail while he was away from his tent and removed it from the altar himself, wrapped it in a cloth and stored it back under his cot. There was no reason to think the Grail was not where he left it, but he decided to check anyway. He knelt by the cot, careful not to wake Morgan, and looked underneath. He did not see it. He felt around the floor under the cot. Nothing. He laid flat on the ground and looked under the cot from top to bottom. The cloth was there; the Grail was not.

Lancelot! He was the only person who knew where Gawain had originally hidden the Grail except for Merlin, and he could not imagine the old wizard cared enough about the Grail to steal it. Lancelot must have taken it or sent someone to steal it because he considered Gawain unworthy to possess it. Yesterday such a trick would have disturbed him. Today it didn't matter.

He stood back up as Morgan began to stir. She opened her eyes. "Good morning, Gawain – if it is morning."

"I think it may be afternoon, but I'm not sure, and I don't know what day it is." He lowered his eyes rather than look at her directly. "I want to apologize. . ."

She interrupted him as she propped herself up on her elbow. "You have nothing to apologize for. Actually, you do, but not for the reason you think."

"I don't understand."

"Your virtue is in tact. But . . ." She pulled back the covers exposing her naked body except for her lower legs and feet. "It isn't too late to have something worth apologizing for."

He stared down at her delicate, white body and thought how he lusted for her when he encountered her in the Saxon castle. There was no sex in the Underworld – if there was an Underworld despite Merlin's doubts about its existence. He should take advantage of every opportunity to enjoy the flesh now. And he might not have another chance soon and likely not ever again with a woman as beautiful and seductive as Morgan.

Now it came back to him, how he started to take her in the cot and lost all interest when the vision of the sightless, motionless Willayne in the Underworld crossed his mind. As much as he might want to have her now, he could not know what trick his mind might play on him, what visions he might have and how badly he might embarrass himself. He decided to distract Morgan.

"The Grail is missing." He pointed to the empty altar.

"The Grail again!" She bothered to pull the blanket up only as far as her waist. "Willayne and the other Saxons were overly concerned about it. I'm surprised you are as well. It has no magic I have seen."

"I'm not concerned, just curious about who would take it and why."

"Do you believe it has power, Gawain?"

"It has some power if people believe it does. If it influences their minds, it also influences what they do."

She sat up, wrapped the blanket around her and got out of bed. "Yes, belief is power."

There was noise mounting outside just beyond the tent. Gawain went to the entrance and pulled back the tent flap. Dozens of men were gathering despite the light rain. They were forming a circle around Lancelot, who stood at its center expressionless and motionless. When the men were fully assembled and quiet, Lancelot led them in a prayer of thanksgiving for their victory.

Morgan, still wrapped in the blanket, came up behind Gawain and leaned against his back to look over his shoulder. "It's ironic, isn't it?" he said, his eyes remaining on the prayer service. "They are praying to the Christian god in thanks for their victory over the Christian Saxons."

"Ironic? I think it's humorous," she said without a trace of sympathy.

He glanced back at her. He saw nothing humorous about all the Saxon dead. She had finally shown a little of the other side of her nature, the cold, untrustworthy, ruthless Morgan she was reputed to be. Judging from how quickly she offered herself to him, she had probably slept with Horsa or Willayne or both, but she did not grieve in the least for either. In fact, she had opened the east tower door hastening their destruction. And it occurred to him only now that there must be some motivation for her interest in him although he could not think what it might be and was in no mood to guess. Gawain was glad he had not yielded to her attempts at seduction.

But she was tempting, and he thought it best to get away from her and this unfortunate place as quickly as he could. "Morgan, I will be leaving here very soon."

Her attention was locked on Lancelot. He cut an imposing figure, especially in his white robe and with his long hair blowing in the breeze. "What? Leaving?"

"Yes, soon. Leaving for Britain. I need to see home again."

She appeared indifferent to his words. "I am not yet ready." She motioned toward the dozens of vessels beached on the shore. "There are many ships here. I will find a way back. Don't concern yourself about me."

Gawain studied her face as she continued to focus on Lancelot. Perhaps whatever she wanted from him she would now seek from Lancelot. "No, I won't worry about you."

Gawain left the tent and went in search of his favorite servant, the young and energetic Bem, and found the short and slightly built boy on the periphery of Lancelot's prayer gathering. The boy came to attention the moment he saw Gawain approaching. "We are leaving, Bem. Tell the men to break camp and prepare the ship. Get some others, dismantle and pack my tent, but before you do. . ." Gawain motioned the boy closer and whispered in his ear. "Search the entire tent, search every corner, every container, and under every object and see if the Grail is hidden somewhere in it. But you search, only you, Bem. There is a woman there now; wait until she leaves before you begin."

"The Grail, Sir." The boy appeared surprised and a little frightened. "If I find it, dare I touch it?"

"Yes, you can touch it or come get me if you prefer. I'm trusting you with this search, and it's very important. Do you understand?"

"Yes, Sir." The boy left him.

Gawain went to say goodbye to Merlin, who was also watching Lancelot from a distance. The wizard looked up at the heavens. It had stopped raining, but the sky was heavy with clouds. "This storm has not yet ended," said Merlin, "and maybe it has not really begun. If you are leaving, Gawain, leave soon before it resumes."

"I intend to leave immediately." Gawain lowered his eyes, embarrassed about what he was about to say next. "Thank you for listening last night to my concerns about death and the Underworld. Not many would understand."

The wizard rested a hand on his shoulder. "Those are topics worth discussing."

"Perhaps we can speak again when I see you in Britain."

"Whenever you are ready. Just come find me."

Gawain left him and said goodbye to several other of his friends before returning to where his tent had been standing. It had already been disassembled, and several of his men were carrying it and its contents to their ship. Morgan was nowhere to be seen and had surely managed to find another knight to take her back to Britain.

Bem approached him. "No Grail, Sir. Looked everywhere, but it wasn't to be found."

"You look relieved, Bem."

"I am, Sir. The Grail gives me the shivers."

Gawain smiled, the first time he had done so in some time. "It's nothing to be frightened of. It's just a chalice, although a very valuable one."

All was ready for his departure, and Gawain took a final look back at the encampment where he had spent the last few months. He was about to board his ship when he saw Lancelot rushing toward him.

"Gawain, glad I caught you." Lancelot appeared different – more relaxed, less arrogant, almost likeable. Perhaps it was the aftermath of the battle. "I wanted to see you before you left. Now that the battle has been won and the Grail has proven its power, would you like me to relieve you of it? Save you the responsibility of caring for it? I don't think the safety of the Grail is something you want to concern yourself with."

This was clever on Lancelot's part, pretending he didn't know the Grail was missing. Gawain considered accusing him of stealing it, but the Grail and its whereabouts were no longer of much importance to him, and Lancelot was being unusually gracious. He decided to play along with Lancelot instead. "I would like to keep it a while longer, Lancelot. Besides, my men have already packed up everything. You understand. I've done well so far, wouldn't you agree? Keeping it would give me comfort during the voyage home."

"I certainly understand. It makes sense that the Grail could protect a ship at sea as well as a castle." Lancelot seemed pleased with Gawain's request. "Then, safe journey."

Gawain was the last man to climb aboard his vessel. The crew rowed out to sea, and Gawain put Lancelot's attempt at deception out of his mind. He sat in the stern of his vessel near Coswyn, the helmsman, watching as the oarsmen pulled them farther away from the shore and as Bem secured the last of the items he had carried on board. Gawain wondered if leaving the Saxon homeland might clear his mind of troubling thoughts and periodically looked behind to see if the shoreline was still in sight. It was.

When they were finally in the open sea, there was sufficient wind for the crew to pull in their oars and hoist the sail. Gawain was eager to get home, to see his wife and how much his young son had grown. He hoped it would be a fast and easy journey. But he was still not completely over the aftermath of his overindulgence with mead, and the continued rocking of the boat began to disturb both his head and stomach. As they sailed, he braced himself against the movement of the ship, the lack of sleep occasionally causing his eyes to close and his head to bob. Eventually he drifted off to sleep and was awakened with a jolt much later when the ship climbed a large wave and dropped down the opposite side. Gawain cleared moisture from his eyes and looked ahead to the horizon. The air was heavy with mist; the sky was overcast, and there was a bank of black clouds ahead of them reaching down to the waterline directly in their path. He turned to the helmsman. "Do you think we should turn back?"

"Would be wise, very wise." Coswyn pointed to the black clouds. "I'm not lookin' forward to learnin' what lay out there."

Several bolts of lightening flashed inside the cloudbank. Moments later, peals of thunder cracked overhead. The wind began to pick up.

Gawain stood up, bracing himself with a hand against the side of the ship. "Bring the sail about, and man your oars. We are turning around and heading back to shore."

The men hurried to their duties with the precision of a crew that had worked together for years. The ship began to turn. The wind was blowing with force now, and the seas began to rise making their maneuver more difficult than Gawain anticipated. A wave tossed the ship sideways as the bow came around, and lightening cracked directly above them.

It started to rain. The rain quickly turned into a downpour soaking the men and accumulating water in the bottom of their vessel. The wind gained in force and occasionally gusted, whipping the rain against them. There was precious little visibility in any direction. With the wind behind them, they made headway, and Gawain hoped the shoreline would soon come into view. But the storm was completely overtaking them. The sea rose with six- and eight-foot waves tossing the ship about and threatening to capsize them. A wave splashed across the vessel, adding to the accumulation of rainwater soaking their feet, and the crew began to bale out the vessel with any container they could grab hold of.

Gawain had faced danger in battle many times before but almost always with some control over the situation. Armed with sword and shield, he could defend himself or take the offensive. And retreating was usually an option albeit one he rarely used. But now he was completely helpless. His ship and everyone and everything on it were tossed about like a leaf caught in a rampaging stream. Gawain wanted to pray for help. But to whom?

Gawain focused on surviving one wave at a time, the ship climbing to a crest and crashing down the other side. This approach helped for a time, but as the waves got higher and the inevitable splashdown more violent, he feared the ship would be torn apart.

The ship's bow was turned by the wind, and the vessel ascended a wave at a dangerous angle. A giant wall of water crashed over the bow, and when it drained away, Gawain saw it had washed away several men, his tent and much of their supplies. "Try to come around," he shouted to Coswyn. "We need to find those men."

Coswyn cupped a hand by his mouth and shouted back. "I dunno that I can come about."

Gawain moved next to the helmsman, grabbed onto the tiller and together they began to swing the ship around. The sky was dark, the sea black. It was almost impossible to see anything. Someone at the bow of the vessel was shouting and pointing. The man thought he saw one of the crewmen who were swept overboard. Gawain struggled against the unsteady footing to reach the bow of the ship to see for himself. He looked in the direction the man was pointing but saw nothing.

Gawain was hit hard from behind by a wave. Without immediately realizing he had been knocked overboard, he found himself in the black sea, completely underwater and struggling to keep from sinking deeper. The water was cold, the sea endless in every direction. He struggled to the surface, coughed out water and took a deep breath. The moment he rested his flailing arms, he sank below the water again. Once more he fought his way to the surface. This time he shouted for help. But the crew had not been able to save the men who were first washed overboard, and he knew there was no chance he would be rescued. He took a breath and moved his arms furiously to keep from being pulled under by the weight of his wet clothes. He looked for his ship but could see nothing beyond the waves surrounding him.

Again he went under, this time sinking farther than he had before. He gave up all hope of survival and thought he should just yield to this inevitable death. He stopped fighting the water and sank farther down. In an instant he found himself home in his own castle. His wife was being informed he had been lost at sea. He saw the scene clearly but was observing it from a distance. Her face was a mixture of shock and desolation; she was devastated.

He could not allow this vision to become reality without a fight.

He was aware of being back in the water again running out of breath and struggling toward the surface. His head struck something. It took an instant before he realized it had to be the bottom of his ship. He reached up and felt the ship bottom moving away from him. He pushed his way to the surface, shouting for help and swallowing water. He tried desperately and unsuccessfully to catch hold of the vessel.

He was grabbed by the hair, then by the collar and pulled along with the ship. Another set of hands took hold of the shoulder of his tunic, then his arm, and he was pulled partially out of the water. More hands clutched at him, and he was lifted over the side and into the vessel's interior.

Gawain was stretched out on his back in several inches of water, gasping for breath, his body quaking from the frigid water, his mind numb. The ship continued to be tossed about, and he clutched the leg of a bench to keep from being thrown overboard again, too exhausted and too frightened to be of much use to his crew.

Two men held the tiller and struggled to keep it nosed into the coming waves. The others held onto whatever they could. There was nothing Gawain could do to help, and had there been, his body and mind were not in a condition to do much. He continued to hold onto the bench.

After a seemingly interminable length of time, the storm weakened enough that each wave no longer seemed life threatening. He was beginning to think they might survive.

By late afternoon the storm abated, and the sky lightened. They could take their normal seats, and Gawain was able to make a quick assessment of their losses. Four men were gone, including his favorite Bem, along with most of their food and all of their water. He didn't know where they were with no sun or stars visible to tell him, but his instinct told him they had been pushed north or perhaps northeast, which meant they were farther away from both home and the camp they had just left.

This might have been the worst day of Gawain's life. Certainly leaving the safety of the shore in this storm was the worst decision he had ever made, and he wished Merlin had some real magic that could take him back in time and allow him to alter the course of the day's events. Gawain was especially upset about the loss of Bem, whose body was still in the black sea that had almost become Gawain's own tomb.

There was excitement at the bow of the ship. Something was in the sea, maybe a man, maybe he was still alive. Gawain rushed to the bow hoping by some miracle they had found Bem.

As the ship pulled near, Gawain could see the man had long dark hair and he was clinging to a piece of wood. It was not Bem and did not appear to be any of their crew. The man looked up at the approaching vessel and waved to them.

One of Gawain's crew began cursing. "Damnation! I think it's a Norsemin."

As they came closer, the longhaired, dark-bearded man did, in fact, appear to be Norse. A crewman raised his oar overhead.

"Hold," shouted Gawain. "What are you doing?"

"Gonna kill him, o'course."

"No! No one else dies in the sea today if I can help it." Gawain reached down to pull the man in. No one helped him, but the Norseman had enough strength to pull himself onboard with only Gawain's assistance. The Norseman was huge. He looked at Gawain and bowed in thanks for the rescue.

"You're not gonna let 'im stay aboard? He'll kill us in our sleep."

"Even a Norseman must have some sense of gratitude." Gawain motioned for the man to sit down, and the Norseman took a seat on one of the benches. Gawain could hear Coswyn whisper at the rear of the boat, predicting the Norseman would slit at least one throat before they touched land.

The wind picked up again, and the roll of the sea grew more violent.

CHAPTER 10: **The Second Lesson**

Lancelot's eyes never left Morgan le Fay, who sat in his tent across the table from him. He lifted a goose leg to his mouth, bit off a large chunk, and continued to speak as he chewed. "I'm glad you came to me, Morgan. There is much I can teach you. I would hate to think anyone as beautiful as you would remain a Pagan and be consigned to the fires of hell for all eternity. Such a fate would be a pity."

She tilted her head toward him and raised an eyebrow. "I wasn't certain you had even noticed I'm female." He looked her up and down but said nothing. "And what does your religion say about love?"

The question seemed to surprise him enough to cause him to stop eating. "Love, except for the love of God, is far less important than correct behavior."

"But he forgives bad behavior, does he not?"

He ignored her comment as he took another bite of meat. "You still haven't told me how you got to Germania and when. But know I am Christian and do not believe in the magic of enchanters and enchantresses, only the supernatural power God, Himself, possesses."

"Then, I shall simply say a woman has her ways. After all, how did I end up in your tent?"

"You invited yourself," he said nonchalantly.

She expected him to praise her beauty and charm – most men did – and was surprised and a little embarrassed by the bluntness of his remark. The way he ate his meal was not the only indication that Lancelot's social skills might be wanting. "You should never speak to a lady in such a manner." Her tone was harsh. "You make me feel uncomfortable even being here."

Now he was the embarrassed one. "Oh no, you are more than welcome. I would have invited you, but you spoke first."

"Surely, Lancelot, you know enough about women not to say such things. But if you must know how I came to be here, I was Gawain's guest. He is a great warrior." Lancelot made a noise, which she assumed was a grunt of derision. "What does that animal sound mean? That you believe you are a superior warrior?"

"Not believe. I know I am superior to Gawain and every other knight, including the Saxon champion."

"It must be a comfort to be so certain of things. Gawain is also a very skilled lover – so I'm told." Lancelot did not answer but turned bright red. She lifted her head back and laughed. "By all the gods, yours and mine, you are bashful when it comes to women."

"I'm not as bashful as you may think."

Few things delighted Morgan more than this. She had made a battle-hardened knight wilt like a delicate flower exposed to a frost and hadn't needed to use any of her potions. And Lancelot was no ordinary knight. He was said to be the best in the world.

Morgan rose and went to his side of the table. "I'm sorry if I embarrassed you."

"You didn't. I'm just not accustomed to a woman speaking so bluntly."

She stroked his hair and kissed the side of his neck. "Don't be upset, my dear Lancelot. You will teach me about your religion, and in return, there are things I can teach you." She bent over and gently bit him on the neck. He put his arm around her, slid it down her back and caressed her buttocks. He pinched her hard. She screamed, slapped him on the shoulder and broke out of his embrace.

"That is your first lesson," she said, backing away, "not to be rough. I prefer the gentle, spiritual Lancelot I saw when you were leading the men in prayer to the powerful and ruthless warrior. You are not in battle now."

He appeared genuinely contrite. "I'm sorry. I didn't mean to hurt you. It was harder than I meant."

She recognized the growing look of lust in his eyes. "Well, you did hurt me whether you meant to or not."

"I think you're teasing me. But I'm not a man to be teased." Looking self-assured, he got up, stood toe-to-toe with her, kissed her on the lips and placed his large hand under the top of her low-cut dress and onto her breast. He squeezed her once gently. "That didn't hurt, did it?"

"I am much more than a tease, but only when I am ready." He found a dagger point pressed against his belly. "You're standing too close. Back off a step or two." He backed away from the dagger, staring down at it in disbelief. "I'm not a helpless little girl."

"I didn't think you were." He quickly overcame his surprise and seemed to be enjoying her boldness. "You're not helpless. Not in the least. Any man who thought so would find himself in trouble."

"There is much I can teach you, but I won't teach you anything except on my own terms. You apparently think you can just take whatever you want."

"Usually I can." He smiled. "And it's inevitable that we will bed together. That's already been decided by both of us. Why waste time?"

"We can waste a few moments." She pointed to his chair with the blade of her dagger. "Now, go sit down." She did not know which passion was stronger in him, his lust for her or his desire to take command of the situation, but she could tell from the smile he was trying to suppress that he was enjoying the game. She looked about the tent. "Had you not been so aggressive, I might have agreed to spend the night here since I have nowhere else to stay. But you haven't asked me. And I won't invite myself."

"You are welcome to stay here. You know full well you are. Besides, as you say, you have nowhere else to go, and I have lessons to learn. I assure you that whatever small issue you might have had with my behavior – and I apologize for it – you will find me more gentle and accommodating than any man in this camp." He looked her up and down. "And I think I can be quite pleasing."

She put a hand on her hip. "You are not as pure as they say."

"Hardly." He shrugged his shoulders. "No one could be."

She looked about the tent again. "There is but a single cot. One cot is not acceptable."

"You can take the cot. I'll throw a few blankets on the floor and sleep there." He smiled slyly. "And I will be nearby should you decide to give me my first lesson."

"If there is a lesson, it would be the second. The first was not to play rough. Remember lesson one, or you will never get to lesson two." What would the men at the prayer service think of their spiritual leader had they witnessed his behavior toward her? "I'll agree to stay the night as long as we understand each other."

He again suppressed a smile. "We understand each other far better than you think."

"Then why don't you finish your meal?"

He looked down at his food and ate with little enthusiasm, his eyes locked on her. She went to the far side of the tent and sat on the edge of the cot watching him watching her. After a time, she stood, turned her back to him and dropped her gown to the floor. She hesitated long enough to give him a good look at her bare legs and bottom. She climbed under the covers and lay on the cot with her eyes closed.

Morgan heard the sound of his clothes being pulled off and dropped to the floor. His footsteps approached, and the blanket was pulled away from her. Lancelot stood over her naked and was about to climb on top of her. She produced the dagger again and held him suspended half bent over her.

"I asked you before, Lancelot. Do you think you can just take what you want?"

"In this case, yes."

She laughed. "That is lesson two. Sometimes it is wise to stoke the flames of passion." She dropped the dagger to the floor and pulled him down on her.

CHAPTER 11: **Lost**

The Norseman sat in the bow of the boat watching with suspicion the dozen Britons who were gathered at the center of the vessel. He must have sensed they occasionally discussed throwing him overboard, and they would have killed him except for Gawain's insistence that the man not be harmed unless necessary and thrown overboard only as a last resort.

The rain had stopped, and the wind had subsided. But the sky remained overcast, and the seas continued to roil, rocking their vessel from side to side. The main topic of the crew's discussion was not the Norseman, although an occasional glance was shot in his direction, but rather an assessment of how far they had been blown off course, where they might be now and how long it would take to get home – when they were finally able to determine which way home was.

"With no water and little food," said Gawain, "we can risk a sail of no more than a day or two's duration, and if the storm resumes with any intensity and we are again blown off course, even a short sail will become deadly."

"What do ya propose?" asked Coswyn. "We can't stay here in the middle of the sea."

"Of course not. Before we decide anything, we need some sense of where we are or we may end up farther away from where we want to be."

Coswyn looked up at the clouds. "We need a sky that's clear to know where we are, and the heavens aren't cooperatin'."

"I plan to ask the Norseman. If we were blown northeast, as I suspect, he would know these waters far better than us."

Several of the men made faces to indicate their displeasure at this idea. "Knows the waters, yes," said Coswyn. "Him tellin' you the truth, I'm not so sure."

"It's his life too. I doubt he would take us off the edge of the world, and there's no harm in asking."

"There's harm, indeed, if he leads us ta a Norse village, and they were to chop us in little pieces with their battleaxes."

Ignoring Coswyn's concerns, Gawain went to the bow and sat next to the Norseman. Gawain did not speak his language, and the Norseman did not speak theirs. All Gawain knew was the Norseman was named Alrood. At least, he thought Alrood was his name. He found the Norse language impossible to follow. Gawain pulled his dagger causing Alrood to flinch. Gawain held up his other hand to reassure the Norseman he meant him no harm. Gawain used the point of the dagger to scratch out the crude figure of a boat on the wooden bench between them. He pointed to their ship. Alrood nodded his understanding. Gawain drew a castle with a coastline to represent Britain and pointed to his chest. Again the Norseman nodded. Finally Gawain drew a curved line to represent the coasts of Gaul and Germania.

Alrood looked down at the carving and extended his hand for the dagger.

"Don't!" shouted two of the men simultaneously.

Gawain looked at the crew, several of whom appeared ready to grab their swords and attack the Norseman. He handed over the dagger to Alrood.

Alrood stared at the crew for a few moments and turned his attention to adding to Gawain's drawing. He scratched out what looked like part of an island above Germania and indicated it was his home. Norseland, Gawain assumed. Next he added another drawing of a ship, south of Norseland and north of Germania, and pointed to himself. Finally he traced a line from the drawing of the British vessel to that of his own.

Gawain shouted back to his crew. "If I understand his meaning and I think I do, we are far north of where we were. Our vessel was blown toward his, which was between Germania near Norseland when it must have sunk."

"How can ya be sure?" asked Coswyn.

"I can't, but we certainly are closer to Norseland and Germania than we are to home, and we need to make landfall soon. When the sky clears, I think we should sail east a distance, look for land, preferably in Germania rather than Norseland, go ashore and resupply." Gawain turned back toward Alrood and extended his hand for his dagger. The Norseman held it toward him point first. With a twist of his wrist, he flipped the blade into his palm and with a laugh handed the dagger back to Gawain handle first.

They allowed the vessel to drift through the afternoon and into the night. When the night watch saw the North Star and a few others through a break in the clouds, he roused everyone from their sleep. They quickly approximated their position. The Norseman's reckoning about their position was fairly correct. They all were thirsty and hungry enough to take immediately to their oars, the Norseman included, and they began to row due east.

First light confirmed they were heading in their intended direction, and shortly after dawn, they could make out the thin line of a landmass in the distance. The men cheered, and Gawain felt his decision to trust the Norseman had been vindicated.

As they approached the coast, Alrood strained for a better look. He talked excitedly, but no one understood what he was saying. He pointed to the northeast, and Gawain instructed the helmsman to change course. It was not long before they saw a small cove, surrounded by large boulders on either side. They made for the beach with Alrood continuing to chatter. As they neared the cove the Norseman stood up, pointed to the water and began to shout. He pointed from his eyes to the sea, and finally the Britons understood he was warning them to look for underwater rocks.

Too late. There was a scraping sound along the hull. The right side of the ship lifted up and fell down again. A two-foot long section of the ship's bottom was torn open, and water poured in. The Britons rowed harder and were assisted by a wave that picked up the rear of the vessel and carried it to shore. The bow of the ship hit the beach and lodged in the sand. The crew jumped overboard and pulled the boat onto the land.

Gawain and several of his men examined the damage. Without their carpentry tools, which were washed overboard earlier, and no substance to seal a patch, it would be difficult, if not impossible, to adequately repair the ship. Of course, they had to try.

Gawain divided his men into four groups: one to search for fresh water and a second to make containers to carry the water, a third to hunt for food, and a fourth to work on repairing the ship.

It was then he noticed Alrood was gone. Coswyn came up beside Gawain. "Has the Norsemin ran away?"

"It appears so."

"He'll probably be back with lots of his brothers, and they'll murder us in our sleep."

"Why would he return? We have nothing of value except a ship that may never again be seaworthy."

On the first day they found a stream for fresh water but had little success in finding food, only managing to gather some edible roots and to catch a rabbit and several small birds for their meal. The second day's great success was happening across four goats, three of which they caught. The goats would give them much of the meat they needed for their voyage home, and their skins could be made into containers to carry water. Meanwhile, the men repairing their ship made progress. Using their daggers and their lone remaining battleax, they did a reasonably good job of replacing the damaged section of hull with a piece of wood cut from a tree trunk, and they used tunic cloth to wedge the new wood tightly into position. They sealed the patch with tree resin, but Gawain, thinking it might not hold, instructed them to test the seal by taking the ship out a short distance from shore.

Several men took the ship out, and it was not long before the seal leaked, not badly, but enough to convince Gawain it would not last the voyage back home. "We will need a better substance to seal the patch," he said.

"Only needs another coat a resin," said Coswyn. "The patch leaks, but not badly. All it needs is another coat a resin, maybe two. And the leak was small. We can always bale out what little leaks in."

"And what if the whole patch comes out when we are half way between here and home?"

"I'll take my chances." Several others voiced their agreement. "It's better than stayin' here and waitin' to run out of goats or be murdered by Saxons or Norsemin."

Gawain looked from one end of the group to the other. They seemed all to agree with Coswyn, and indeed, they did have a point. "Patch it, then. But there's no harm in testing it again. Just be certain to test it thoroughly."

More resin was applied to the patch, and seven men boarded the vessel to test its seaworthiness. Gawain and the remaining five other crewmen who stayed on the shore watched them row out a good distance. One of the older crewmen, Mawgan, stood next to Gawain. "They're goin' out a bit far, aren't they?"

"Not so far. They need to stay in the water long enough to test the repair. It's a lot farther to get home."

The men aboard ship hauled in their oars and let the boat drift.

Gawain left the beach to go in search of food. He returned empty-handed a while later and was surprised to see the ship had drifted out close to the horizon. The patch obviously was holding.

In the distance he could see the sail being raised. The ship came about and made for shore. Gawain thought the vessel had a slight list. As it approached closer, he saw it did have a list. There was hardly any wind, and the sail appeared to be of no help. He could make out oars splashing into the sea. The ship listed more.

Mawgan came up beside him. "What's happenin'?

Gawain's eyes never left the ship. "They are taking on water and rapidly."

"They aren't sinkin', are they?"

The ship leaned to a dangerous angle. It leaned farther and rolled onto its side as the mast and sail splashed into the sea. Several men jumped overboard. The bow began to slide under the water. Gawain and Mawgan watched silently as the rest of the ship and all the men who had been on it disappeared under the surface.

Now they were trapped here for certain.

CHAPTER 12: **Return to Camelot**

Arthur happened to glance out his bedchamber window and noticed riders approaching Camelot. The king had retained his muscular frame and youthful good looks although he had gained a few pounds in the years since he was crowned, and there were more than a few strands of white mixed in with his black hair and many more in the short beard he had recently grown. During the last two days his knights had been returning from their victory over the Saxon battle lord Horsa, and he hoped his favorite knight was among these riders. Arthur smiled. There was no mistaking the lead horseman, who was large and dressed in white. It was Lancelot. There was a woman riding next to him, but from this distance she was not recognizable.

The king turned around and found himself face to face with Merlin. "You gave me a start! Why are you always popping out of nowhere? And this time in my bed chamber!"

Merlin was not bothered by the comment. "I wish I could just pop out of nowhere. It would be a very useful skill indeed."

Arthur took a deep breath and softened his expression and tone. "I assume, old friend, that you have come on a matter of some importance or you would not have come unannounced. And I also assume you are here to deliver some caution, correct?"

"If you already know what I am about to say, there is no need for me to say it."

"But you will say it anyway."

"Yes, I will." Merlin leaned toward Arthur and whispered. "Do not believe all your battles have been won and certainly not that the worst of them have been fought."

Arthur appeared relieved, almost pleased, by the comment; it was a typical Merlin warning. "Rest assured I make no such assumption. However, we just defeated a Saxon battle leader in Germania. Can't I savor the moment?"

"Of course, you can. I never said you couldn't but. . ."

"But – another caution?"

"Yes, a caution to be cautious." Merlin paused for a moment. "I suppose that sounded strange. Nonetheless, what have I always told you about caution and doubt?"
"They have always held you in good stead. I've learned your lessons better than you give me credit for. But please, Merlin, no lessons now."

The old wizard's expression betrayed a sudden decrease in confidence. "I know, Arthur, you believe I concoct conspiracies to increase my worth to you as an advisor."

Arthur laughed. "Isn't that exactly what you do?"

"Well, yes, but only when there isn't a real conspiracy to be concerned about. In any case, none of the history between us has anything to do with what I am telling you now. Just be cautious. This is all I ask of you. Be cautious."

"I will be cautious. I promise. But I will also celebrate our victory – with caution. And now I will go to greet Lancelot."

Arthur left Merlin, hurried down to the courtyard and stood smiling as the approaching party rode through the castle gate. He called to Lancelot, who spurred his horse into a trot and rode directly to the king. Lancelot, dressed as usual in a white robe with a cross over the breast, jumped down from his horse, and he and Arthur embraced.

Arthur then saw who the woman with Lancelot was; it was his half-sister Morgan. It took him a moment to overcome his surprise to see her. He then greeted her, helped her down from her horse, and gave her a hug. Morgan, who could be intense and ill-tempered, appeared relaxed and happy, which prompted Arthur to extend an invitation. "I hope you will stay at Camelot for more than a brief time, Morgan."

She glanced up at Lancelot. "I certainly will stay at least a few days."

Guinevere was coming to join them. The queen had long blonde hair, fair skin, and cheekbones and a chin that were too pronounced. She had a slender shape and moved with elegance. She was not a great beauty, not like Morgan – few women were – but men found the queen attractive.

After more greetings were exchanged, Guinevere instructed a servant to show Lancelot and Morgan to rooms in the tower while Arthur announced he would hold a banquet that evening in their honor and in honor of all the returning knights.

As the servant led the two visitors away, Guinevere turned to Arthur. "I cannot think of two people who are more unalike than Morgan and Lancelot."

"Pairings can be strange. Think of Uriens and Maeve."

"And you consider them a good pairing?"

"No, but they have been together a long time. In any case, I don't know that there has been a *pairing* of those two."

Guinevere took a last look at Lancelot and Morgan, who were almost out of sight. "Pardon me for saying this, but given your sister's history. . ."

"Half-sister."

"Given your half-sister's history with men and Lancelot's physical appeal to women, I would think they have *coupled* at every opportunity."

"I wouldn't be so certain. Lancelot is odd in some ways. He believes his physical strength is rooted in his strength of character. He would be the ultimate challenge for Morgan, and I will bet you this, if Morgan spends too much time with Lancelot, she will become more like him than he like her." Guinevere appeared unconvinced. "Morgan is not quite the villainess people have always made her out to be. Her reputation has more to do with the bad feelings between her and Merlin than anything else. Besides, people can change."

"I'll admit I may be misjudging her," said Guinevere. "But I'll take your bet. Men are still men, and there are certain things they can't resist – even Lancelot and his strength of character can't resist."

The servant led Morgan to her bedchamber, and they paused just inside the door with Lancelot standing in the hall behind the servant. Morgan mouthed the word "Mordred" to the servant, and he gave the slightest nod to indicate he understood. The servant put her bags down and beckoned Lancelot to follow him to his own bedchamber.

Morgan unpacked her bags on the bed and spread out her clothes. She started to change out of her riding clothes and had barely finished pulling off her boots when there was a tap on the door and the door was pushed open. "I thought you understood my meaning," she said before she saw who the visitor was. It was Lancelot, and he looked puzzled by her comment. "It's you," said Morgan. "I thought it was the servant again."

He entered and stood before her. "You sound disappointed it was me at the door and not the servant."

"I'm happy you are developing a sense of humor. You were far too serious when we met – that is, when we got to *know* each other." He sat next to her on the bed and kissed her neck. She moved away. "After the banquet."

"Before." He kissed her neck again. "I'm ready."

"I'm not." She stood up, walked several paces away and turned to face him. "And that is another lesson for you: a woman isn't always ready just because her man is. After the banquet."

"Why do I have to wait?" His tone was more pleading than angry. "And why do you get to decide?"

"Because I'm not a person you can bully or overpower, and my strength of character, dear Lancelot, is why you find me so interesting."

He laughed at her remark. "I would still find you interesting if we bedded now. Probably more interesting."

She took several steps toward him, moving her hips in an exaggerated fashion, bent over and kissed him on the neck. "It will be worth the wait. I promise. Now let me get ready for the banquet. I want to look beautiful for you."

The banquet was one of the largest and most lavish Camelot had seen in years despite the short time Guinevere had to organize it. Every knight who lived in or near the castle and those newly returned from the Saxon siege attended with their ladies – if they had ladies. Two couples attracted the most attention. The king and queen, of course, were one. Arthur, wearing a purple and white robe and his silver crown, and Guinevere, dressed in a pale blue gown with a matching bow tied at the back of her long blonde hair, made the rounds of the great hall welcoming their guests. Of equal or greater interest to those assembled were Lancelot in his characteristic white tunic and Morgan in a high-necked white gown. It was the first time they had been seen together in public, and both seemed to enjoy the attention.

Sufficient time was allotted for people to mingle, and when at last the guests were invited to sit down to dinner, Lancelot and Morgan were placed with Arthur and Guinevere at the center of the head table. They were joined by Arthur's father, Ector, and brother, Kaye, as well as Balin and Bedivere, their wives, and Percival.

As the servants began to serve the meal, the conversation naturally turned to the recent victory over the Saxons. Lancelot bragged about his defeat of Willayne and his night assault on the walls of Horsa's castle. Percival let him finish, then started to tell how Gawain snuck into the Saxon stronghold disguised as a beggar and stole the Holy Grail, which, he said, might have caused the Saxons to give up any hope of victory.

Arthur, a concerned expression on his face, looked from one end of the table to the other. "Speaking of Gawain, I don't recall seeing him. Has he returned?"

"I think not," said Percival. "I have yet to see Gawain here, and he left Germania first."

"I don't recall seeing Gawain either," said Bedivere. "The rest of us waited until a storm ended. He may have sailed directly into it."

Percival appeared worried. "Could he be lost at sea or shipwrecked?"

"He may have been diverted by the storm," said Arthur. "Perhaps, the storm forced him to sail back to Germania, and he'll arrive in another day or two."

"What about the Grail?" said Lancelot. "Gawain carried it on his ship. The loss of the Grail hastened the fall of Horsa's castle. I thought it would protect Gawain. But he stole it, and maybe acquiring it in an unethical manner changes its protective powers. And he didn't treat it with proper respect, not when he showed it to me in his tent. He was keeping in a cloth under his bed. I told him that was no way to treat the Grail."

 Arthur tried to calm the group. "Let's not get overly concerned. We don't know that Gawain and the Grail are missing. Gawain may have gone straight to his own castle. He may be eating a feast there now while we sit here and worry about him unnecessarily. I'll send a rider to his castle in the morning to check. If he is not there, he and his ship will most likely arrive in another day or two."

"And if he doesn't arrive in another day or two or three?" asked Percival. "What then?"

Arthur shrugged his shoulders. "Well then I suppose we must organize a search."

"Of the open sea?" asked Ector. "How can we accomplish that?"

"We must make the effort – if it becomes necessary. Maybe he has lost his sail or his tiller or mast broke. His ship may not be far off shore for all we know. But let's give him more time before we panic."

Despite Arthur's reassuring comments, as the dinner progressed the conversation at the head table consisted mainly of speculation about what disaster might have befallen Gawain's vessel, if it was possible that he was safe somewhere, the consequences of losing the Grail, and whether the Grail could be recovered even if Gawain could not be found.

Morgan took the opportunity of this discussion to excuse herself for a few moments. She went to the far end of the great hall and pausing to be certain Lancelot was not following, climbed the steps to her chamber. Mordred was waiting for her there sitting on the bed. Not yet twenty, the youth far more resembled his mother than his father. He had her fair coloring, light hair, and slender build.

She closed the door behind her. "We must be quick. Lancelot may be knocking on my door any moment."

"Lancelot!" Mordred stood up. "What has he to do with anything?"

"Don't concern yourself with him right now. Has your man any news for us?"

Mordred frowned. "The servant? Only what you would expect. Arthur and his inner circle are happy and confident after their victory – all but Merlin."

Morgan's expression soured at the mention of the wizard's name. "He has always been a problem but not for much longer."

"And most people are crediting Lancelot for the victory."

"Good."

Mordred was puzzled. "What's all this about Lancelot?"

"You need to concern yourself about Vortigern at the moment, and you need to go to him immediately."

"Vortigern! What about Horsa? Doesn't his death ruin the plan?"

Morgan took a step closer to her son. "Horsa isn't the only Saxon warlord. He has a brother who is more powerful than he was."

"Surely you don't mean to turn to Hengst now," he said dismissively. "He and a small army have been raiding in the north. From what I've heard it's hardly a major force."

"I'm sure he kept the bulk of his forces in Germania. And even a small Saxon army can always grow bigger. After the defeat they suffered, the Saxons should be eager for vengeance." She forced a laugh. "How do you think Hengst will react when he finds out his brother Horsa was taken alive and uninjured and could have been ransomed but was decapitated by common foot soldiers?"

Mordred mulled over this information. "If Hengst knew how his brother died, it could make a difference."

"Of course, it could, and it will." She lowered her voice and spoke with more intensity. "You need to get to Vortigern, and then, the two of you must go to Hengst and convince him to join with us as his brother planned to do. And to make the idea even more enticing, Vortigern should offer to pay a portion of Hengst's expenses to bring a large army to Britain."

"Perhaps, you should come with us. Hengst would find you more convincing than Vortigern."

"Yes, I might be more convincing if only because Vortigern is a dolt. But I have too much to do here, and the things I must finish here will take time. The loss of Horsa and his army changes things for the moment – until we know we can count on Hengst. I need time to weaken Arthur's alliances, to isolate him as much as possible. Isolating him is a good thing to do regardless of how the negotiation goes with Hengst."

Mordred appeared doubtful. "You mean weaken the Roundtable?"

"Don't look so skeptical. It's not impossible. Let us say that certain things, which I do not have the time or the desire to explain now, have already been set in motion." She pointed to the door. "But you must go now, go before you are seen."

She ushered him toward the door. He turned back with a broad smile on his face. "Is that why you mentioned Lancelot? Is he what has been set in motion?"

"You just be on your way and leave me to my work." She hurried him into the hall and closed the door behind him.

CHAPTER 13 Death in All Directions

Gawain stood watching as two more fifteen-foot logs were strapped into place. The raft now had ten across. The plan was for several men to work adding a few more logs while others simultaneously fashioned a tiller, paddles and a mast. They still had no idea of what they might use for a sail unless they were able to hunt down a dozen or more goats.

Devaid, the oldest member of his crew and one of only five remaining survivors from Gawain's ship, was leading the construction. He took a break from his work and stood next to Gawain, wiping sweat from his forehead and neck. "The work 'id go much faster if we'd a second ax."

Gawain still had a vivid image of his vessel listing to one side and sinking beneath the surface without a single man surviving. "We're lucky our one ax and the goatskins of water were not on the ship when it went down."

"Yur certain ya'll not come with us?"

Gawain looked at the frail looking raft and then out over the water. He couldn't think of the sea without remembering his near drowning in the storm and his earlier visit to the Underworld, and in his mind the depths of the black sea and the Underworld were fused together and waiting to take him. "Devaid, I'm not certain I would willingly venture out onto the sea even in a large, well-crafted ship unless there was no alternative."

"But what are yur alternatives?"

Gawain sighed. "None of them are good. If I were to walk up or down the coast or inland, I would likely encounter Saxon warriors eager for British blood or Norsemen eager for anyone's blood."

Devaid motioned to the beach. "But ya can't stay here."

"I can stay here for a time as long as I can find food. Food is also a problem for you. You don't have enough for your voyage. Providing it will be my contribution to your journey. I'll hunt for your food even if I have to go far inland."

"Be careful if ya do."

"Don't worry. I'm always careful."

Gawain strapped on his sword and dagger, took a goatskin of water and a blanket, and started to hike inland with the intention of going farther in search of food than any of them had gone so far. As the leader of these men, he felt responsible for their current plight. He always ate last during their one and occasionally two daily meals and usually had far too little to eat. He planned to give everything he was able to gather or hunt on this trip to the men for their voyage. Their raft might sink or they might get lost at sea – sinking was his expectation – but he wanted to ensure they did not die of starvation.

He ventured far into new territory but was only able to find some roots as well as a few plants he was not certain were edible. At twilight he began to look for a place to spend the night. He settled on the grass before a small cluster of trees. The trees would protect his back from attack by man or beast, and although the night would be cold, he thought it too risky to build a fire and call attention to his location. He propped his back against a tree trunk, his sword by his side, listening to the periodic hoot of an owl as he tried to sleep.

The second day of his hunt was more successful: several rabbits and a squirrel. The third day luck was with him. He came across a large deer grazing by a pond. He crept closer to it, his dagger in hand. He got within striking distance, and the deer suddenly raised its head and turned an ear in his direction. Gawain stood up and threw his dagger. It spun through the air and struck the animal in the haunch penetrating it several inches.

The deer, the dagger hanging from its thigh, ran, and Gawain went after it. The animal quickly disappeared into the brush, but he was able to follow the trail of blood. Finally he caught up to the deer collapsed on the ground but still alive. He finished it off with his sword.

Why was it necessary to kill to live? Why didn't Lancelot's god make a world in which people and animals could eat without killing? Gawain didn't know the answer, but killing was certainly nature's way. Merlin might say Gawain and the deer were of one spirit. It was a thought that prompted him to do something he had never done before in his life: in the manner of a primitive Celt he gave thanks to the animal for surrendering its life so he and his men might live. "Might live a few days longer," he said aloud.

The deer was too large to carry. He had to skin and butcher it. He wrapped as much meat as he could carry into the skin and started back to their camp.

It was a two-day hike for him to reach the others, and when he arrived, he saw the raft was complete except for a mast and sail. The men decided to rely on makeshift paddles and the hope of catching a current. In the afternoon they smoked the deer meat and fashioned a water container from its skin. The next morning the men, as they were setting out to sea, tried unsuccessfully to convince Gawain to go with them. Gawain, waving goodbye from the shore, wished them luck. Worried the raft would sink like their ship, he watched them as the raft was paddled into the distance and disappeared at the horizon.

Gawain sat down on the beach and sank into self-pity. He was a Knight of the Roundtable, or at least, he was once. He could not say exactly what he was now except he was alone and not even sure where he was, away from his home and family with little chance of returning to them, obsessed with his own mortality, his thinking muddled from not having eaten much in several days. He knew he needed to eat and he should go back on the hunt, but he was too tired and weak to move. He dropped down on the beach, staring up at the sky, and soon fell asleep under the morning sun.

He was awakened by the gnawing in his stomach. He sat up realizing his body was shutting down. He was dying from lack of food. This was ludicrous, he thought. His obsession with death was killing him. He thought of the deer and his need to kill it. He thought of Merlin and his mysticism and Lancelot and his newfound religion. Maybe one day he would understand why the world was the way it was, why people lived and died, why people, at least some of them, lived in constant fear of death and others did not, but he would not reach that understanding now, not today.

What made no sense was to allow himself to starve to death on this beach.

Gawain got to his feet, limbered his weak arms and legs, and walked slowly in search of food. After he found something to eat and his strength and stamina returned, he would have to decide what to do next. Certainly taking to the sea was out of the question especially in the kind fragile raft the last of his crew had built. The only real option was to walk south although he was not yet ready to undertake such a journey. When he finally did walk south, maybe he would find some Britons who could take him home. More likely he would find only Saxons seeking to avenge Horsa's defeat.

Gawain had to laugh to himself. He once entered a Saxon castle disguised as a ragged beggar. Now his former disguise was his new reality, a derelict eager for food any way he could obtain it. On a journey south he was certain to encounter a Saxon village, town or castle, and he hoped his present appearance would fool them as well as his beggar's disguise had. He would be tempting fate to try that twice, but he might not have any option better than walking up to some Saxon and asking for food.

CHAPTER 14: **Mordred's Bargain**

Mordred rode through the gates of Vortigern's castle and directly to the tower, where he was met by a servant who took hold of his horse's bridle. "I will stable and feed your mount, sir."

"That isn't necessary." Mordred dismounted. "I won't be staying long. Is your master in?"

"Yes, sir. He is in the great hall having supper. I'll tell him you are here."

"I can tell him myself."

Mordred went into the tower and found Vortigern eating alone at a small table by the fireplace. Vortigern was a middle-aged man with a large belly and fleshy neck. He had a wide mouth, wide-set eyes and wisps of gray hair across his baldhead. He stood the moment he saw his visitor. "Mordred, just in time to have supper."

Mordred looked down at Vortigern's meal as though he smelled a foul odor. "I won't be staying long. I bring news from my mother."

Vortigern motioned Mordred to the chair opposite his own. "Sit down at least."

Mordred sat and folded his arms across his chest. "You no doubt heard about the victory over Horsa."

"Yes, of course."

"And you know Horsa was killed?"

"Yes, I have heard."

Mordred placed both hands on the table and leaned toward his host. "And have you also heard he was captured alive and uninjured but was decapitated by British warriors as he pleaded for his life and offered them a ransom?"

Vortigern paused in mid-chew. "No, I hadn't heard he was taken alive and executed. Does Hengst know this as well? I assume we will approach Hengst next with the same bargain we offered Horsa, and surely, he will join with us if for no other reason than to avenge his brother."

"My mother's thought exactly." Mordred reached over and pulled a piece of meat from Vortigern's plate. "It seems Hengst was busy raiding here while his brother was under siege." He took a small bite of the meat and put the remainder on the table. "Hengst should be suffering from a sense of guilt, and we can exploit it. We must also inform him that Morgan is working to weaken Arthur's alliances." Vortigern, who appeared lost in thought, did not respond. "Did you hear me?" asked Mordred impatiently.

"Yes, I heard you, and how will she accomplish this weakening of the Roundtable?"

"Morgan's methods are not your concern."

"As I am your ally, they are my concern, but I will let this pass for the moment because of another matter I wish to discuss with you." Vortigern pushed away his plate of food. "Mordred, there is a proposal I wish to offer to you and to you alone." Mordred tilted an ear toward him. "It concerns your mother. "

"What about my mother?"

"Don't look so suspicious. It's nothing bad." Vortigern lowered his voice to a whisper. "Your mother is a very beautiful woman, a prize."

"Come to the point."

"If we are successful in our joint enterprise and I become king in Arthur's place, I would want Morgan le Fay as my queen." Mordred laughed, causing Vortigern to take offense. "I am serious. I am a prosperous man and would treat her well."

"You are not the only man in Britain to notice my mother is very attractive," he said sarcastically. "Half the knights in Britain would chase after Morgan if they thought they had a chance of capturing her. Indeed, many of them have tried, and none has succeeded. It is my mother, not they, who does the choosing."

"You don't understand. Morgan means more to me than she does to them."

"Spoken like man who has no idea of what other men feel about Morgan."

"I'm serious, Mordred. I am not certain the effort to become king and this whole plot is worth the risk without Morgan being part of what I would gain."

Mordred took this comment seriously. "Are you saying our alliance depends on this?"

Vortigern lowered his eyes. "Not exactly."

"Be clear. Does it or doesn't it?"

"Let's just say it would add an important incentive."

"Let's say it would, but why tell me? I have no control over my mother."

"But you can help."

"Me! How?"

"I don't know how. You understand her as well as anyone. Can't you figure something out? You would benefit as well. I'm a man of some wealth."

"You will need your wealth to help pay the expenses for getting Hengst's army to Britain if we are able to make a bargain with him. Paying part of those expenses is one of the things Morgan sent me to tell you."

"I doubt I will need all my wealth for that purpose." His tone became almost pleading. "Help make Morgan my queen and a sizable portion of my treasure is yours. But I am no fool, Mordred. The payment will not be made until she is my queen. Realize also, Mordred, that you would also benefit by such a union by becoming crown prince and being in line for the throne."

"A tempting offer, Vortigern, but you ask the impossible. Surely you realize as much. No woman is of a stronger will than my mother. I don't know what you expect me to do." Mordred stood up to leave.

"You won't even consider the offer?"

He turned back toward Vortigern. "No, but I do have an alternative proposal that might interest you."

"I'm listening."

Mordred sat back down at the table. "What if I succeed in getting Morgan into your bed? A night with her is an accomplishment in itself and well worth a reward. Most lords in Britain would give a sizable portion of their wealth for a single night with her. Once there, in your bed, it would be your affair from that point on to convince Morgan to be your queen."

Vortigern was more than a little interested. "You can arrange this?"

"I can. You would pay me one-quarter of the reward now for my effort. Another quarter when you bed Morgan, and the remainder if you succeed in making her queen."

Vortigern looked at Mordred with suspicion. "Why should I pay anything now?"

"Because you want Morgan more than I want the bounty. Besides, why should I trust you to pay me later?"

"Because we are allies in the effort to dethrone Arthur."

"I repeat, dear Vortigern, why should I trust you to pay me later? And consider this. It's not in my nature to leave a reward on the table. Rest assured, I will deliver her."

Vortigern looked down at his hands for several moments, then back up at Mordred. "I need some assurance your efforts will have results. Tell me your plan so I will have some confidence in what you intend to do."

"I'm disappointed you have so little faith in me. Suffice it to say that I know of a potion. . ."

Vortigern grew excited. "I have heard of such a potion. Do you have it?"

"No, but I can get it."

CHAPTER 15 **The Search**

Five British ships were putting out to sea. Lancelot, standing in the stern of the last vessel, waved goodbye to Morgan, who stood on the shore with Guinevere. The two women returned his wave. The ships raised their sails and headed northeast in the direction of Germania. Gawain was not at his castle, and his vessel was six days overdue. Lancelot's concern about the Grail and what its loss might mean for the future of Britain prompted the search they were now beginning. He managed to convince Arthur and the other knights that the Grail had supernatural properties that would help them find it even in the vastness of the sea. When the vessels were a distance from shore, they began to spread out. The plan was to comb as wide as swath of the sea as five ships could manage while no ship moved too far away to hear a horn blown from the vessel closest to it.

The shoreline slowly receded behind them. The wind picked up, and the sails billowed. Lancelot's ship began to move at a brisk pace, the wooden slats of its hull creaking as it rose and fell with the waves. One by one the ships running parallel to them began to disappear in the distance.

Lancelot moved to the bow of his vessel and called his crew to attention. "It is unlikely we will find anything this close to shore. For now only one man need keep watch on each side of the ship. One man on each side. When we are farther out to sea, I expect all of you to keep a sharp eye. And not just for a ship, but also for men or bodies in the water, wreckage, anything, including things that appear to be mere flotsam. Anything at all. And look for the Grail. Do all of you know what it looks like?" Most of the men indicated they did, but Lancelot told them anyway. "It is a silver chalice with rubies." He moved his hand up and down. "Rows of red rubies running along its cup."

One of the men amidships shouted back at him. "I thought it was made of wood. How can it float if it's metal?"

"The Grail is no ordinary cup. It may well float. Indeed, I believe it may be impossible to sink, but we might only come across a clue, a sign of some kind, as to where it is. So, all of you must look for anything in the water, anything out of the ordinary, and if you see something, be sure to call me. It's more than just a matter of searching. I believe the Grail might find us."

Percival, who was sitting near to where Lancelot stood, appeared to be the only member of the crew not puzzled by this remark. He had as much faith as Lancelot, who earlier told him he wanted the two of them to pursue the search together in the same vessel. "At the risk of seeming immodest," Lancelot had said, "you and I are the most pious and devout of all the knights. Our being together on the same ship increases the likelihood we will find the Grail or it will find us."

Lancelot sat down next to Percival, who whispered to him. "Do you believe there is any hope of finding Gawain and his crew? I mean if they are not with the Grail."

"It's unlikely we would find them in the open sea, not unless they had sufficient food and water to sustain them these last days and the reason for their delay is a problem with their ship that did not cause it to sink. More likely they had to put into shore somewhere perhaps in Gaul or Germania or even an island. It is equally likely they sank in the storm or were attacked at sea."

"If so, did the Grail go down with them?"

"The Grail." Lancelot repeated the words with reverence. "No, it has supernatural powers invested in it by God. Metal or not, we might find it floating gently on the surface of the sea or see it elevated above the water with a bright light circling it. An arc of light."

"I hope that is how we find it," said Percival enthusiastically, "suspended in the air as you describe. But I also hope we find Gawain and the others safe."

"If it is God's will," said Lancelot, as he made the sign of the cross from his forehead and chest to both shoulders, "we will find them all."

At midmorning Lancelot and Percival joined the crewmen scanning the sea. They saw nothing in any direction not even a piece of driftwood. By late morning Lancelot had to admonish some of the men who were not paying attention to the search.

"I understand how they feel," said Percival to Lancelot. "I was excited when we started, but there is a lot of sea, and we find only more and more water."

"Have faith. When God wants us to find something, we will find it, whether it is wreckage or the Grail itself."

In early afternoon Lancelot saw something sparkling on the water. "Bring the ship about." He pointed to his right. "Come about." As the ship changed direction, he lost sight of the shinning object. He scanned the water, caught sight of it again and fixed its position in his mind. "Steady, hold your course."

Percival stood next to him. "What is it that you see?"

Lancelot pointed directly ahead of them but again lost sight of the object. "I saw the reflection of the sun on something that must be metal. But the sun must strike the object at a certain angle for the sparkle to be seen." He turned to the crew. "Man the oars. We need more speed."

Oars were dropped into the water. The men began rowing. And the vessel picked up speed.

"We are nearing the place," said Lancelot. But he could see nothing ahead of them and nothing to either side. The boat continued beyond the place Lancelot indicated. "We must have gone by it," he shouted. "Come about again." The ship turned and went over the same section of sea; again they found nothing. Lancelot next had the ship sail in a large circle. Still nothing. "I was sure I saw something that could have been the Grail," he said, but offered no explanation about what it might have been. He did say, however, that whatever mishap had befallen Gawain most likely happened closer to Germania than Britain and it was far too early to think the search might be unsuccessful.

They sailed back to their original search lane and continued east. Several more times Lancelot saw similar bright objects in the water, sometimes two, three or more at a time, but he said nothing. They were only the reflections of the sun off the peaks of waves.

At midafternoon, Percival sat erect in his seat. Lancelot was about to speak, but Percival held a finger to his lips. "Listen," he said. "I hear a horn."

Lancelot listened and heard it as well. "They've found something," he said to Percival and shouted to the helmsman, "Come about due south. Listen for the horn. Listen and follow it."

The expressions on the men's faces indicated they were eager to learn what the other ship had found, none more eager than Lancelot, who moved to the bow of the vessel, rested one foot on the stem and leaned forward.

A ship was approaching them. Percival also came forward to see Bedivere's vessel pulling into view and closing on them.

"What have you found?" shouted Lancelot, but the ship was too far away. He waited until the ship came closer to try again. "Have you found something?"

Bedivere was in the bow of his ship shouting something they could not hear. He pointed behind him. Both Lancelot and Percival looked to the southern horizon and saw the distant storm clouds.

Bedivere was finally within earshot of them. "It's a southern storm. When storms come from the south and not the west, they are bad ones, very bad. We must warn the others and get back to shore."

Lancelot was reluctant to abandon the search, but Percival convinced him it was the prudent thing to do. First, they had to warn the remaining three ships, and it took some time, even with the use of horns, to reach them. As the five ships turned back to shore, the storm clouds became larger and darker in the distance. The southern portion of the sky turned from blue to gray, and the wind began to blow with force.

They ran ahead of the storm and soon reached the shore. There was still no rain, and only a few clouds were in the sky, but the wind was blowing even harder, bending trees, and lifting leaves, dust and debris into the air. Ships were being dragged onto the land and tied down. Nearer the castle, mothers were ushering their children indoors, horses were being led into their stables, chickens, geese and goats into their pens.

Lancelot left his men to secure his vessel and went straight to Camelot. The wind at his back pushed him along and blew dust into his eyes. In the courtyard leaves and dirt were swirling in the air. He entered the tower, pushed the door shut against the wind, and brushed himself off. The castle residents who were not busy securing doors and closing window shutters were gathered in the great hall talking about the coming storm.

Morgan was among them. When she saw Lancelot entering, she rushed to him and pulled him aside. "What do you make of this storm?" she asked.

"What do you mean, what do I make of it?"

She leaned closer so she could not be overheard. "Gawain stole the Grail in the service of Arthur." She motioned back to the great hall. "Most believe Gawain was lost at sea in a storm because of his sacrilege. Now another storm descends on Camelot."

"I can well accept that Gawain met his fate, if he is at the bottom of the sea, for his violation of the Grail Chapel and his irreverent handling of the Grail itself. But those of us here don't also bear his guilt."

"Oh no? Not even Arthur? It was to win Arthur's battle that Gawain committed the desecration. And if Gawain's ship went down, it took with it men who had no part on the Grail theft." She leaned even closer rising up on her toes to whisper into his ear. "At this very moment Arthur is with Merlin, the old fraud. Arthur hasn't abandoned the old ways and the old beliefs, at least not completely. Isn't that also an offense for a king who claims to be Christian?"

Lancelot was silent for a time mulling over her words. "It's too soon to make a judgment about the storm, although I can't dismiss what you say, not entirely. After the storm passes and we can resume the search, I intend to find the Grail and return it to a suitable chapel or church. And all will be as it was."

"And if you don't find it?" He did not answer. "Listen to the storm, Lancelot. If it isn't the wrath of God, it is certainly the wrath of nature."

CHAPTER 16: The Edge of the World

Gawain walked the shoreline looking for any additional fish, clams and mussels that might have washed up on the beach. He already had a pouch full. The sky was clear and the sun bright, but the sea was turbulent, and all manner of debris and sea life was washing ashore. He had been eating better lately, and his vigor was returning. Still, he was left in this hostile land with no means and little hope of being able to return home.

He reached the end of the beach and turned back for his camp, which was not much, just a fire pit and a small shelter made of tree branches and covered with twigs and leaves. Inside was a makeshift bed made of twigs and leaves covered with a blanket.

He dropped his load by the pit and stoked the fire. This evening he would treat himself to a large supper, not that he particularly liked seafood. He was eating now solely for nourishment, and one of the fish he picked up was a good twelve inches long and would make a substantial meal accompanied by some of the shellfish he had gathered. He cleaned the fish, spitted it and roasted it over the fire.

During his stay here he had begun to eat like a savage, gobbling down his food, indifferent to the juice running down his chin or the mess he made of his hands. Although he had been eating well, he was still not sleeping through until morning, often awaking shortly after falling asleep or in the middle of the night, fearful of the imagined horrors of the Underworld and the real threats posed by men and beasts that might be near this beach. It was barely twilight, but when Gawain was finished eating, he felt he might be able to sleep. He did not want to miss the opportunity to get some rest whether it was night or day, and he felt more comfortable when there was enough light in the sky for him to see an approaching danger. He threw more wood on the fire, stretched himself out next to the fire pit, closed his eyes and fell asleep.

Gawain slept comfortably for a time but grew cold. He opened an eye and looked at the fire. Although it could have used more wood, it was still burning fairly strong, and he was too tired to get up to tend to it. He rolled over to expose his back to the warmth of the fire and happened to notice two odd shadows a short distance away. As he focused his eyes, he saw the shadows were legs. First there were two legs, then four of them. Gawain sat up with his hand feeling cautiously and blindly for his sword or dagger, neither of which was in reach. Into the firelight stepped two large men, and they were followed by three more, all dressed in animal skins and wearing helmets with metal pieces covering their jaws and noses. Norsemen.

Unarmed and outnumbered, Gawain decided to remain still in the hope they would not see him as a threat and would let him live. One of the Norsemen, their leader perhaps, stepped forward and removed his helmet. The man laughed.

"Alrood!" Gawain took the laugh as a good sign and stood to greet the man he had rescued from the sea. Alrood laughed again and slapped him on the arm in the manner one warrior might greet or congratulate another. "I'm happy to see you," Gawain said, as Alrood began to speak to him in his own language.

Another Norseman stepped forward from the darkness. "He says he thought you might still be marooned here. He says you saved his life twice, once from the sea and once from the other Britons. He says it is his happiness and his duty to save you now."

Gawain spoke to the young man who knew his language but continued to look at Alrood. "Tell him I certainly am in need of rescue and am happy to see him, and whether done by a Briton or Norseman, one good act always invites another."

The man spoke in Norse to Alrood, who nodded his understanding and agreement.

The translator turned back to Gawain. "I am Raevil my Norse name. I was born a Celt but raised a Norseman."

From what he could see in the shadows, Gawain thought the young man's features were indeed Celtic rather than Norse. "And I am Gawain. You were taken in a raid?"

"Yes, long ago. I remember my first language, some of it anyway, but seldom is there a need for me to speak it."

Keeping an eye on the three Norsemen who remained back in the dark, Gawain, through Raevil, offered Alrood what little food he had. Alrood declined, indicating they had brought their own.

More Norsemen, at least a score of them, appeared from the black night, and none of them, including Alrood, paid any attention to Gawain as they set up their camp and searched for more wood to build several additional fires. Nonetheless, it was unsettling for Gawain to be among a group of men every Briton considered barbaric and murderous.

The Norsemen made their meal, and as they sat by their fires, Raevil occasionally asked Gawain a question about life back in Britain. Gawain would answer and reciprocate by asking him about life among the Norsemen. They had accepted Raevil as a full member of their tribe, and Gawain wondered if there was any chance Alrood would take him back to Britain or if he intended to make him a Norse raider as he had Raevil.

Angry words were exchanged at one of the other fires. Gawain strained to see what was happening, but he could make out little in the firelight. The shouting continued. There was no doubt two of the Norsemen were arguing. "What's that about?" asked Gawain.

"Nothing, Gawain," said Raevil, who, in fact, appeared concerned. "Often there are arguments during meals, mostly when the men have gone a long time with no fighting."

The shouting ended. One of the men stood up and walked in their direction. As he approached, Gawain saw in the dim firelight the man was wild looking even for a Norseman. His hair was long and straggly, his beard ran far up his cheeks, and where his left eye should been there was only a white eye socket. He walked directly to where Gawain and Raevil were sitting, pointed a finger at Gawain, shouted at him, and walked away.

Raevil watched him disappear into the darkness. "He says you'd better stay away from him, Gawain, and I think it would be a very good idea."

Later the group bedded down for the night. Gawain, his dagger in his hand, doubted he would sleep much. He was camped with a group of Norsemen, a more savage enemy than the Saxons, and already one of them, the one-eyed Norseman, had threatened him. He would have to put aside thoughts of getting home for the moment to concentrate on staying alive, and his survival depended on maintaining the good will of Alrood and fitting in as best he could with these wild men. And, of course, remaining always on alert.

Gawain slept very little that night, and at sun-up the next morning, he thought it was best not to rise until his protector was awake; so, he pretended to be asleep until Alrood was finally up and about. Gawain was invited by Raevil to join him for breakfast, and they sat away from One Eye, who seemed to be paying no attention to the British guest this morning. Nonetheless Gawain's attention never left him. As Gawain was finishing his meal, Alrood brought him some animal skins to wear over his clothes and said something in Norse.

Raevil translated: "These you will need. We are going somewhere very cold." Raevil added his own explanation: "We are sailing north, Gawain. North and west, very far west."

Gawain put on the skins, and when the Norsemen were ready to leave, he carried his few belongings to their vessel. He still was not comfortable about going to sea, but on this voyage there was more danger above the water than beneath it. Alrood assigned him a seat next to Raevil and away from One Eye. At Alrood's command, the Norse longboat with a dragon head carved into its stem put out to sea and raised its sail.

They made good progress through the morning until the wind died down. The Norsemen took to their oars, and Gawain joined them. The more useful he was to them, the better the chances he would continue to live.

They rowed until midday when they again caught the wind, and they continued to sail into the night with only a helmsman and a night watch on duty. This pattern continued day after day. Gawain had grown more at ease with the sea, and so far he had no further trouble with One Eye – although it would be a long voyage. On their fifth night at sea Gawain studied the stars. By his reckoning they were farther north than he had ever been and heading west-northwest.

If they went far enough on this course, they would near the edge of the world and risk sailing over it and into oblivion.

CHAPTER 17: **The Storm**

Thunder ripped across the sky directly overhead. Guinevere, who sat next to Arthur on their bed, squeezed her husband's hand. He wrapped his arms around her. "It's only a sound," he said.

"It's the most terrible sound I've ever heard. It's as though the heavens themselves were being torn apart and Camelot was under siege."

Another but less menacing crack of thunder sounded, and she cringed. He released her and stood up. "I need to see what damage the rain and wind are causing." He walked toward the bedroom window.

"Arthur, must you open the window?"

"I'll open the shutter only a crack." He pushed the right shutter open several inches. It was immediately blown out of his hands, and the shutter smashed against the outside of the window frame. The force of the impact caused it to bounce back on its hinges. Arthur was able to grab it with one hand, but it took two to pull it shut again.

Guinevere came up behind him. "It's too dangerous to even be near a window."

"But I have to know what's happening outside. A storm this bad could do serious damage." He walked toward the door of their bedchamber and turned back toward her. "I'll return shortly."

Guinevere appeared panicked. "Where are you going? Not outside."

"Just for a quick look, a quick peek from the tower door. The sound of the thunder frightened you. But the storm is just water and wind."

"Then, why must you check it? And you said it could do serious damage."

Despite her objections, Arthur took a cloak and wrapped it around himself. "If there is any danger at all, I'll turn right around. I promise." He kissed her cheek and went downstairs. He paused at the bottom of the tower steps to lift the hood over his head and pull the cloak more tightly closed.

From the great hall, Kaye called to him. "You're not going out in this storm, are you?"

"Only for a few moments. I'll get wet and wind-blown but nothing more."

Arthur went to the tower's large wooden front door and opened it. Wind and rain whipped in. He had not even gone outside yet, and the entire front of his body was wet. He bent his head down against the wind, pulled the door shut behind him and went out into the courtyard.

The rain came down in great volume and with great force. Black clouds hung low over the castle. There were several inches of water covering the courtyard in rippling waves driven by the wind. Arthur was completely drenched. He walked carefully farther into the courtyard, his feet splashing in the water, his legs soaked above the ankles. He saw some broken and splintered wood and the bodies of several chickens scattered across the flooded ground. The wooden peddler stalls and animal pens had been blown away. A mangled goat lay at the base of a stone wall, where it must have been driven by a gust of wind. The other goats and livestock were nowhere in sight. The flags on the castle wall were drenched and hanging limp. One flag, along with its pole, was missing. Wind hammered the towers. Debris was being blown across the courtyard. A wet piece of discarded cloth slammed against his shoulder with enough force to sting, and nearby the wind was bouncing a bucket across puddles of water.

Arthur had seen enough. He turned back to the tower entrance and made slow progress against the wind toward the tower door. The wind was gusting, and he positioned himself against a protrusion in the tower wall to brace himself until it subsided.

There was a cracking and groaning overhead. Arthur looked up to see the wooden tower roof lifting up from its base. The roof rose up several feet on one side and blew off, coming down in the courtyard with a loud crash, pieces of wood breaking off and flying in all directions.

Arthur looked at the roof wreckage for a few moments, waiting to see if anything else would blow down. He resumed fighting his way back to the tower entrance. He opened the door, and it was blown out of his hands and against an interior wall. With the wind whipping rain against his back, he entered the tower, grabbed hold of the door and helped by Kaye, managed to shut it again.

Guinevere ran down the tower stairs. "Thank God, you're safe. I saw the roof crash and thought it might have hit you."

"I'm okay, just soaked. With the roof blown off, I need to see what damage we've suffered."

Arthur, followed by Guinevere and Kaye, ascended the tower stairs. Rainwater was already running down the steps leading to the fourth story. They continued up to the top floor and found Merlin there, oblivious to the rain, staring up at the sky through the missing roof. While Guinevere and Kaye remained back on the stairs where it was relatively dry, Arthur pulled up his wet hood and stepped into the downpour next to the wizard.

"I don't know what you can do about it, Arthur." Merlin's eyes remained on the rain blowing in from where the roof had been. "I suppose if you had some sails handy, you could lash them over the opening. Of course, if the roof blew away, the sails would likely blow away too."

"You forget about the men who would have to climb up there to lash the sails."

"No, I haven't. They would be blown away."

Arthur wiped rain out of his eyes. "Merlin, what is the meaning of all this?"

The wizard, water dripping from his head and beard, looked at Arthur. "The meaning of what? The storm?"

"Yes, is this a punishment?"

"A punishment? For something in the past?" He shook his head. "I don't know about such things, about the past determining the present. I only know about the present influencing the future."

"Portends?"

"Yes, portends and omens."

"If this is an omen, what does it mean?"
Merlin forced a laugh. "It doesn't take a wizard to tell you what this storm will lead to. It's nothing good, nothing good at all." Merlin leaned toward Arthur. "I can tell you what it brings without the use of any special sight." He pointed overhead. "If the castle roof blew away, so too have the cottages of villagers." He pointed to the water on the floor and to where it was running down the stairs. "If it flooded in here, it is flooding elsewhere. Crops will be washed away as will livestock. Maybe, people too. There will be much rebuilding, replanting and restocking that will need to be done."

"I understand that. But does the storm portend anything beyond the kind of damage storms are known to cause?"

Merlin weighed the question. "I can't say. Such visions must come to you. You can't simply pluck them out of the air. And nothing comes to me now, but you can be certain there will be many unhappy people."

Morgan and Lancelot were among those who arrived to see the damage. Morgan saw Guinevere, who stood near the open roof being pelted by rain, and gently pulled her back. "You're wet, my dear. Step back here where it's dry. You don't want to become sick."

Lancelot called to Arthur. "There is water dripping elsewhere in the castle, even in the great hall."

"I feel completely helpless. I can't do anything here and probably can't anywhere else." Arthur turned back to Merlin. "All I can do is see how bad things are in other parts of the tower."

Arthur started down the stairs, the others following except for Morgan and Lancelot. She waited until they were alone. "This storm, Lancelot, it's as though Camelot itself was being destroyed."

Lancelot was visibly concerned. "I think you were right, Morgan, in what you said before. There could be a supernatural aspect to this storm. I believe it could be a punishment from God."

"How could it be any clearer? Gawain and the Grail missing in a storm at sea. Another storm attacking Camelot. Yes, 'attacking,' that is the word."

"And I am disappointed Arthur seems not to take a step without consulting with Merlin, the same as in the old days."

She lowered her voice to a whisper. "We'd be safer with someone else in command."

Her remark confused Lancelot. "What do you mean?"

"He won't be king forever."

"As long as he is"

"He'll have your loyalty, I know. I just hope he will have earned it. In any case, you need to leave here, Lancelot, as soon as this storm relents. There is no reason for you to pay for Arthur's sins, is there? If a castle roof is going to fall on him, you couldn't prevent it, could you? But you can avoid being crushed by the same roof. For the sake of Britain, the king and his champion should not be victims of the same storm."

He looked at the missing roof, at the rain pouring in, at the water streaming down the tower steps. "You'll come with me?"

She smiled and caressed his cheek. "Of course I will."

CHAPTER 18: **Ritual in the Forest**

Silwyn, Mordred's servant, sat by their campfire while his master slept. He slowly extended a hand toward Mordred's shoulder but quickly drew it back. Silwyn looked into the night forest and turned his head to the side with a hand cupped to his ear. The odd noise sounded again in the distance, this time louder, causing Silwyn to panic. He grabbed Mordred's shoulder with more force than he intended. Mordred woke with a start, sat up and reached for his sword.

The servant raised his hands. "It's me, Silwyn. Only Silwyn."

Mordred dropped the sword and gave his squire an angry look. "Touch me again, and your head will no longer be situated on your neck."

Silwyn pointed back to the forest. "There was a sound out there, actually many sounds."

Mordred started to lie down again. "Field mice."

"No, not field mice. Sounded like people. But only *like* people. Maybe it's forest demons or witches."

Mordred took a closer look at Silwyn's face. His squire was truly frightened. The sounds came again. Mordred listened to them carefully. "I will investigate these sounds, Silwyn, just to put you at ease." He pulled off his blanket, stood up and grabbed his sword. "But I hope for your sake there is something out there worth investigating, waking me up the way you did in the middle of the night." He motioned with the blade of his sword. "Go on. Lead the way."

Mordred allowed Silwyn to lead him deeper into the forest, where the tangle of tree branches and bushes made passage difficult. Mordred's feet got caught in vines; branches and leaves brushed across his legs and upper body; and he cursed under his breath when the thorn of a vine pierced the side of his calf. They continued farther into the brush. Silwyn paused to listen for the sounds but heard nothing. He resumed walking and pushed out of his way a young tree branch that snapped back and hit Mordred with force across the chest.

Mordred grabbed the branch and broke it in half. "Damn you, Silwyn, you fool." Mordred pulled his squire back by the shoulder of his tunic and took the lead.

Silwyn fell behind his master and started to look from side to side although it was nearly impossible to see anything in the night forest. The sound came again. "Did you hear that?"

Mordred stopped walking. "Yes, but I can't place what it is."

"Doesn't sound human to me. Maybe we should turn back. Maybe it was a bad idea to go lookin' for trouble."

"No, Silwyn. I want to see what's out there – especially if it isn't human as you suggested." He continued to advance toward the sound. Silwyn kept falling behind, and Mordred needed to keep motioning for him to keep up.

Ahead there was a light in the forest, a shimmering glow. The sounds were clearer now. "That's chanting," said Mordred. "There's nothing supernatural about it."

Silwyn was so nervous his voice cracked as he spoke. "Don't witches and warlocks chant?"

Mordred ignored the question. He continued moving toward the sound, only more cautiously now. The light from the fire grew brighter, the chanting louder. Mordred held up a hand to stop Silwyn from coming closer. He held a finger to his lips, motioned Silwyn forward and pointed to something beyond the bushes immediately before them.

There was a large bonfire in a forest clearing and standing around it were two dozen people, several dressed in hooded cloaks. Silwyn, the fire reflecting in his wide-open eyes, stood next to Mordred. "They're Druids," whispered Mordred. "And this bunch has returned to their ancient ways."

Silwyn did not respond and appeared incapable of speech, his eyes locked on the figures standing around the fire and chanting in some ancient language.

In unison the Druids began to sway from side to side; their chanting grew louder and their swaying faster. Into the center of the group stepped a woman. She chanted more feverishly than any of the others, and the swaying of her body was faster and more extreme. The louder the group chanted the faster she moved until her body began to convulse. Two women rushed to her side, each taking her by an arm to hold her up. All the others stopped chanting as the woman spoke in a trance-like state.

Silwyn tapped Mordred's arm. "Let's leave this place."

Mordred roughly brushed his hand away. "Nonsense. I want to see this."

The woman who was the center of attention spoke for a time words neither Mordred nor Silwyn could hear; then she grew silent and still. Her two attendants led her away. A hooded man, leading a lamb by a rope, took their place at the center of the circle. He withdrew a knife from his belt, held it pointed to the sky and swept it in a circle pointing at all those around him. He lowered his head, grabbed the lamb by the back of its neck, and slit its throat.

Silwyn let out a yelp that was lost in the sound of the chanting Druids. Mordred scowled at him, took him by the arm and led him back the way they had come.

At first light Mordred and Silwyn, who was still recovering from his night encounter with Druids engaged in some weird and frightening ceremony, resumed their journey to the land of Sir Agravain, a knight who was anything but an admirer of King Arthur. The ground was still wet from the torrential rain, and where there was a trail, it was usually through mud and puddles of brown water. Their progress was slow, and Mordred insisted they push on without resting the horses to get to Agravain's manor house as soon as they could.

Agravain's estate was in a valley. The closer they got to it, the deeper the mud and the more numerous and larger the puddles of discolored water. They rode through a cluster of trees, and the manor house came into view on the other side. Mordred stopped his horse to take a look at it. Several of the shutters were missing, several more hanging by their hinges. The roof of the stable was partially collapsed, the fence of an outdoor animal pen knocked flat.

"Beautiful." Mordred spurred his horse forward.

"Beautiful?" Silwyn took another look at the devastation and followed his master to the estate.

As he rode closer, Mordred could see the stained remnants of the floodwater eight inches and higher around the base of the manor house. Piles of mud had been shoveled from inside the house into mounds by the front door.

Agravain came out to greet them. He was a thin man with graying hair. His boots and the lower portion of his leggings were covered with mud, and he was wiping mud from his hands with a cloth. Agravain waved to the visitors but never broke into a smile. He motioned to both his right and his left. "What you see gives you some small sense of the situation here, of the destruction I have suffered." Agravain pointed to the damaged stable. "The collapsed roof killed two horses, including my favorite."

"A terrible storm, indeed." Mordred's statement of sympathy was perfunctory.

Agravain stood by the side of Mordred's horse looking up at him. "Here is the fact that is most surprising and most troubling to me. I was hunting the morning of the storm – before it struck, of course. And there was no game of any kind to be seen anywhere, not a rabbit, not a bird, not even a snake or frog. Somehow they knew this great punishment was about to descend on us."

"Punishment is the word, Agravain, and the storm will have its aftermath. I must tell you what we, Silwyn and I, saw in the forest last night."

Agravain was annoyed by this comment. "Don't you first want to see the rest of the storm's destruction? Isn't that why you came?"

GODS IN THE MIST

"Yes, of course."

Agravain called for a servant to saddle a horse. The three men, Agravain and Mordred in the lead, Silwyn a distance behind, rode beyond the manor house to a large, flat field barren of everything but mud.

"The planting finished just a few days ago," said Agravain. "As you can see, everything was washed away by the storm. There's enough time to plant another crop if I can purchase or borrow – or maybe steal – enough seeds."

On the far side of the fields sat what remained of the estate's peasant village. The houses and huts were not as well constructed as the manor house, and the damage to them was greater, walls caved in, roofs blown off, a few huts washed away all together. Some of the peasants were working to repair the damage and tending to the livestock that survived the storm and did not run away. Others were sitting dejectedly on stools or pieces of debris. Near several of the damaged houses were new graves.

"We lost a few people," said Agravain. "Mostly the youngest and the oldest." He turned toward Mordred, his expression troubled. "Do you suppose they blame me for what happened?"

"Of course, they do." If Mordred had any empathy for Agravain or the peasants, it was not apparent from his tone. "Such is the nature of things, isn't it? They work the fields for you and obey your commands. In return, you protect them against brigands and invaders, and you and the priests serve as their intermediary with God, protecting them from pestilence, crop failure, droughts and floods. To their way of thinking, either something you did or did not do was the cause of this destruction, or you, at the very least, did not protect them from it."

Mordred let Agravain sit silently for a few moments considering his comments, then continued. "I told you we observed something in the forest last night." Agravain did not appear particularly interested. "It was a gathering of Druids. At least one hundred of them, perhaps two hundred." The remark caught Agravain's attention. "They were performing some ancient and evil ritual, dancing and chanting until they all went into convulsions and then into a trance. While my servant and I watched from hiding, they took a young woman to the center of their circle of evil and slit her throat. Then they cut open her belly and removed her entrails."

Agravain raised his eyebrows at this news. "They would do that to one of their own?"

"They are trying to appease their gods."

Mordred's explanation struck Agravain with force. "This is what they do to appease their gods! They are capable of anything, and I must prepare to defend myself and my family."

"I would do exactly that if I were in your place. You wouldn't want some Druid butcher to remove your entrails. But there is more news you should know. The damage wasn't restricted to your lands, as you surely can imagine. Camelot, itself, was battered as badly as your estate was. The very roof of the castle tower was blown off and almost came down on Arthur's head. So, you see, Agravain, the problem and the punishment extend far beyond anything here and reach as far as the crown itself."

"I think you know the situation with me, Mordred. I have never been a supporter of the boy-king, not that he is a boy any longer. But hasn't he been somewhat of a good king or at least an adequate one?"

"No better and no worse than most, I would say. But he is not exactly what he pretends to be."
"How so?"
"For one, he seduced his own sister."

Mordred delivered his comment in a tone of condemnation, but Agravain did not react strongly to it. "He was very young at the time, and magic was said to be involved."

"He proclaims himself a Christian, a man who has changed with the times, but he continues to consult and consort with the Druid Merlin. Remember it was the Druids who performed a deadly ritual a short distance from here only last night. And in Arthur's service, Gawain stole the Holy Grail. Did you know the Grail carried a curse?"

"I know little about the Grail or its powers."

"Anyone who takes the Grail or uses it for a selfish or evil purpose is punished. The Saxons paid the price for not protecting the Grail when their castle fell. Gawain paid the price for stealing the Grail when he failed to return from the sea. And now we all pay a price for what Gawain did on Arthur's behalf. You, yourself, Agravain said all the game disappeared in advance of the storm. That is not the natural order of things. Something very important is amiss."

Agravain sat silently on his horse for a time. He again surveyed the damage to the village, paying particular attention to the graves. "Let me be certain I understand, Mordred. You are saying Arthur is at least partially at fault for this storm and its destruction. And so, are you also saying it follows that he should leave the throne? Or do you think it is possible he could in some way atone for his offense?"

"Someone more knowledgeable than me must answer your question. However, I do know this: We must be prepared for any and all possibilities."

Agravain's horse became restless. He leaned forward and patted its head. "Whether what you say is true or not – and I'm not saying it's untrue – one should be cautious in expressing such sentiments about the king, especially considering your position."

"I'm not alone in expressing them. Vortigern has said the same."

"Ha, Vortigern. His comments about Arthur are to be expected. I merely disapprove of Arthur; Vortigern detests him."

"And Lancelot has said as much."

Agravain's horse started to move forward, and he pulled back on the reins. "Lancelot! Did you say Lancelot?"

"Yes, he became disenchanted with Arthur as he watched rain pour down through the missing roof of Camelot's tower."

Agravain sat quietly for a few moments mulling over this information. "Lancelot, too. This news puts the situation into a very different perspective."

CHAPTER 19: **A Different Sky**

Gawain lost count of the number of days the Norse ship had been at sea, but he was certain they had continued north-northwest farther than he thought possible. Where they were going or what they hoped to find, he had no idea. Clad in animal skins, his hair grown long, he could almost pass for a Norse. One Eye paid him little attention other than an occasional unpleasant stare, and most of the others onboard seemed to be accepting him. He was even learning some of their language, the bare necessities such as the words for food, water, boat, sea and danger.

The helmsman turned the ship more westerly. The ship was getting more assistance from the wind, and the crew was given a rest period. Gawain sat stretching his back and rubbing the calluses on his hands, and he wondered where in the world they were. Wherever it was, it was cold and the nights were longer and the days shorter than at home in Britain.

Just before sunset, land came into view. If it was an island, it was a large one. Gawain could see distant mountains, their snow-capped peaks glistening in the last rays of the sun. In need of stretching his back and legs, and sleeping somewhere more comfortable and warmer than the Norse boat, Gawain was delighted when the ship made straight for the land. As they approached the shore, the fading light made it difficult to see the features of the island in much detail, but there appeared to be no towns or villages, no castles or fortresses, and no people. However, there was a makeshift dock with wooden posts driven vertically into the shore where vessels could tie up.

Gawain was among the last to leave the ship. His legs were unsteady on land, and his balance shaky. He accidentally brushed against One Eye – of all people – as he came ashore, and his apology was met with a grunt. The Norsemen were going to camp here for the night. He assisted them in gathering firewood and unloading what they needed from the ship, including some large sacks of grain, far more than they would need in a few weeks' stay here. He hoped they weren't remaining that long.

Dinner was especially good because their food could be heated and because they ate it by the warmth of fires. And with fires to warm him and room to stretch out his legs, Gawain had the most restful night's sleep he had since they put out to sea.

Gawain awoke with the sun the next day, and in the morning light saw the island was unlike any land he had seen before and beautiful in its own strange way. It was more open and more barren of vegetation than Britain. There were long vistas ending in snow-covered mountains and what appeared to be large fields of ice. And except for the dock, there was no indication that any man had ever set foot here before. He was eager to see more of the island.

Immediately after breakfast, the Norsemen, carrying the large sacks of grain, began to hike inland. Where they were going they did not tell Gawain, and he did not ask. The terrain they trekked through had more ice and snow than Britain this time of year, and the island had more mountains and lakes or perhaps it seemed that way because the mountains and lakes were more visible in the distance. While the Norsemen trudged steadily forward, Gawain turned from side to side to take in the scenery, and occasionally he fell behind to study some particularly beautiful or unusual aspect of the landscape.

Always, he knew where One Eye was.

The Norsemen hiked with speed. They covered a great distance, and before midday a large camp came into view. It had a dozen or more huts, and Norsemen were building a large wooden structure Gawain thought too big to be one family's house. As they came closer, he saw there were also women and a few children among them. He also saw a herd of large sheep. Whether they were island sheep or sheep the Norse brought from home, he could not tell.

The most unusual feature of the camp was the small body of water it had been built near. In places a mist was rising a foot to a foot-and-a-half above the surface of the pool, and a distance out there was a large plume of what appeared to be smoke or fog. And yet, the weather and sky were perfectly clear with no sign of rain, snow or clouds.

Greetings were exchanged between the two groups of Norsemen, and the sacks of grain traded for fresh meat, dried fish and unusual white fox pelts. Gawain, who tried to be as inconspicuous as possible, later learned the foxes, unlike the sheep, were native to this island.

His attention was drawn to a handful of men from the boat who walked to the edge of the pool and were pulling off their clothes. As Gawain stood staring at them, Raevil came up beside him. "What are they doing, Raevil?"

"They will bathe in the water. You should try it, Gawain."

Gawain waved his hand at the snow-capped mountains. "It must be almost cold enough to turn water to ice. Certainly the water can in no way be comfortable."

"No, it's warm." Raevil took Gawain by the arm and led him to the pool. "I'll go in too."

While Raevil took off his clothes, Gawain bent down and put his hand into the water. "It's not just warm; it's actually hot."

"I told you, Gawain."

Gawain again looked at his surroundings and held up his wet hand to test the temperature. The air was cold. "I'm not dreaming that it's frigid here. I don't understand how such a pool of water is possible."

"Nor do I." Raevil, who was naked, walked slowly into lake, emitting small grunts and sighs of pleasure.

Gawain dropped his animal skins to the ground and pulled off his tunic. The cold air on his shoulders and arms made him shiver. He stripped off his leggings and walked into the pool. It was hot, almost too hot. "I don't understand how this is possible."

"Just enjoy it, Gawain." Raevil was in water up to his neck.

Gawain walked in slowly, and when the hot water reached his chest and upper arms, he emitted the same kind of sighs Raevil had. He went in up to his neck, leaned back and floated while moving his arms in small circles. "This is wonderful – amazing. I never knew water could feel this good. Usually lakes, rivers and streams are too cold, and I prefer to avoid them, but I could bathe in this pool every day."

Gawain was the last person to leave the water that afternoon, and the cold air against his warm body almost undid the benefit and pleasure of soaking in the hot water. Supper was served, and the sun began to set early. Gawain was not tired enough to sleep, and he sat outside watching the daylight disappear behind the mountains.

Lights flashed in the sky, somewhat like distant lightning. The lights grew brighter, and their flashing became more frequent. The entire northern sky suddenly turned bright green, and the lights flashed as though there were a great fire in the sky. This was not lightning nor was it some strange vestige of the sun in the wrong part of the sky. He could not help but wonder whether a natural disaster was about to befall them or if this might even be the end of the world. He thought he should warn the others but noticed several Norsemen nearby, two watching the lights in the sky, a third paying no attention to them. They had not panicked; therefore, he should remain calm and conceal his fears.

The lights continued to flash across large sections of the sky, and the dominant color remained green. If the heavens were on fire, they burned with different colors than wood and oil. Finally he sought out Raevil and asked him about the lights in the sky.

Raevil looked up at the lights and shrugged his shoulders. "I understand these lights even less than the hot water, Gawain, but there is nothing to fear. I saw them on my other journey here, and those who live in this place say they happen often."

Later that night, Gawain tried to sleep but kept opening his eyes to watch the lights. When the sky finally turned back to its normal color, he was able to fall asleep.

The next morning Gawain could not resist venturing into the water again. While he was enjoying its warmth, Raevil called to him from the shore. "Gawain, there is something I want to show you before we return to our ship."

Gawain continued to float in the pool. "Is it as pleasurable as this hot water?"

"No but as interesting, perhaps even more interesting."

Reluctantly, Gawain left the water, exposing his body to the cold air, and dried himself off. As soon as he was dressed, Gawain followed Raevil on a hike through a pass between the nearest mountains. They spoke hardly a word until they reached the other side of the pass when Raevil pointed ahead. "There."

Gawain looked in the distance and saw smoke coming from the top of a mountain. "The mountain is on fire? That is not as unusual as a pond or a lake that almost boils amid an ice field."

"Look closer, Gawain. Do you see the red mud running down its side?"

Gawain strained for a look and saw a thin line of glowing red mud flowing down the mountain like a stream.

"Sometimes the mud flames," said Raevil. "If you were to step in it, Gawain, it would burn your foot off. They say it destroys everything it touches."

"But how?" He strained his eyes for a better look. "How does mud burn?"

"They say the fire burning at the top of the mountain ignites the mud. It must be special fire or special mud. The only *mud* I've ever been able to burn is dung."

Gawain and Raevil watched the burning mud a while longer and returned to the camp, where their party remained one final night.

The following morning Gawain observed an animated conversation between Alrood and Hauk, the leader of the Norse settlement. When their conversation ended, everyone assembled at the edge of the steaming pool of water. Raevil explained it was a prayer ceremony to the Norse god Odin officiated over by Hauk. Hauk, the palms of his hands turned skyward, chanted while all the others remained silent. The ritual did not last long, and it culminated with Hauk walking a few feet into the water and throwing a battleax far into the pool.

With the ceremony concluded, Alrood led his men on the hike back to their ship, and during most of the journey, Gawain was lost in thought. To survive, a man had to understand nature, how to plant, tend and harvest crops, the habits of the prey they hunted, how to deal with rough seas, floods and droughts, how to recognize poisonous plants and to avoid bogs that could swallow a person whole. Gawain prided himself about such knowledge, but this strange island with its steaming pool of water, mud that burned and sunless sky that glowed bright green had turned his understanding of the natural world upside down.

Gawain would rather have been home in Britain, but if he had to take a long voyage to an unknown place, he thought the visit to this island was well worth the journey. He had not only seen some interesting new things, but he had learned the world was not always as he expected it to be, not always as it was in Britain and the parts of Gaul and Germania he had seen.

But he changed his mind about the positive aspects of the journey when they boarded their ship and pulled away from the dock. They were not heading home. The ship turned southwest, not southeast. Surely they had already gone as far as they dared, as far as they could. The edge of the world could not be too much farther. He had no doubt the world had an edge to it just as the top of a table had. He pictured in his mind the sea dropping off the edge of the world and their ship going down with it. But into what? Nothing? How could there be nothing below if it was being deluged with water? Could it be dropping into the Underworld, if there was an Underworld? No one had ever described the Underworld as having perpetual rain. What would it feel like going over the edge? How long and how far would they drop? Would they die before hitting bottom or fall endlessly?

Gawain had worked himself into a cold sweat. He looked at the other men in the boat; they seemed no different from how they looked any other day. He had to trust that they would stop the vessel short of disaster, that they would turn back before the edge was reached.

CHAPTER 20: **Warnings for Arthur**

Morgan le Fay stood with Lancelot in the vestibule of his castle's main tower and pulled herself away from his embrace. His hair was mussed from their lovemaking, and not bothering to fully dress, he was wearing only leggings and an undergarment over his upper body.

"Why must you leave now?" he asked. "Can't you stay at least a few more days?"

"We have discussed this. I respect your beliefs. You must respect mine whether or not you accept that I have the powers of an enchantress. I need to leave now for reasons you would not understand or if you understood, would not accept."

He seemed to have learned he would not change her mind once she made a decision. "Then, when will you be back? Soon? A few days?"

"I told you I don't know. I'm not an ordinary woman, and you should not treat me as such."

"I know. And I don't. I've never treated you as ordinary. Never." He reached out for her, and she backed away.

"And you will miss me, I know. But I will tell you something about yourself, Lancelot, that you may not yet know, but that I do. I am much older than you, and someday you will not find me so attractive." Before he could deny it, she held up her hand to silence him. "It's true. I will age and wrinkle and turn gray. There will be other women, younger women. There will have to be. It's the way of the world. Men are like bulls and roosters, in need of constant conquests in bed as well as on the battlefield."

His feelings were hurt. "Now you are treating me like an ordinary man."

"You may be extraordinary, Lancelot, but you are still a man."

He was becoming more possessive and trying to become more controlling. Morgan had to say goodbye several more times before Lancelot finally let her go. Fortunately, her time with him was nearing an end. Part of her plan was to stoke his passion as much as she could – and she had succeeded well – then to disappear, leaving him in need of an equal or greater female conquest. In her mind, if not his, such a conquest could only be Guinevere.

Lancelot's castle had not felt the brunt of the storm as Camelot had. There had been a downpour here and strong winds, but no flooding, no roofs or shacks blown away, no livestock drowned or pummeled by the wind. More good fortune for Morgan. It helped *prove* Lancelot was favored by his god.

She rode out of the castle, but instead of heading north in the direction of the decaying castle where she and Mordred lived – the place she told Lancelot she was going – she turned southwest and rode to Camelot. It was not a long ride. Her approach was noticed by a sentry, who hailed her, and when she entered into the courtyard, Arthur was there to greet her.

Arthur took the reins of her horse, helped her down and before he could welcome her, she spoke with some urgency in her voice. "This is not a casual visit, Arthur. I have much to discuss with you." He appeared more confused than worried, probably wondering what she could have to say that was so important.

"We'd best go inside," he said. He instructed a servant to tend to her horse and led her to a small tower room he used for royal audiences. Arthur ignored the throne to lead her to adjoining seats and waited patiently for her to speak.

"I want us to begin anew and forget the distant past, Arthur, if you are agreeable. Some of what I have to discuss is difficult for me to say and will be difficult for you to hear." Arthur enjoyed talking about times past, the battles he had won, his early days as king, the training and tutoring he had received from Merlin, but the *incident* with his half-sister was a part of his history he never discussed, and Morgan was going to enjoy his discomfort. "I know you blame yourself for what happened between us years ago, but I am equally to blame and no longer hold it against you." His cheeks turned red, and he seemed unnerved by the mention of their sexual encounter of many years before. "And I will confess I have not always support-ed you."

Arthur hung his head, his eyes staring blankly at the ground. "I know you haven't and I understand why."

She placed a hand on his arm. "It was inexcusable, and I am sorry."

He looked up at Morgan and covered her hand with his own. "We can forgive each other and put behind us all the animosity that should never have occurred between brother and sister."

She took a deep breath for effect. "Arthur, I come to you now for an important reason and not a moment too soon. I come to you with news and with a warning. Actually with several warnings." She paused to pique his interest. "All this talk about the Grail. . ."

He grew annoyed, not at her, but rather at the topic. "I'm being blamed for its loss, and its loss is said to be the cause of the terrible storm."

"Those comments are exactly what I have heard as well. I just learned Mordred was in the forest a few days ago and heard a strange chanting. He followed the sound and found hundreds of peasants in some dark ceremony, a primitive ceremony during which there were human sacrifices."

Arthur seemed stunned by this news. Before he could speak, she went on. "There is more. They were sacrificing to their gods – or perhaps to their demons – for relief from the harm of the storm, and their anger – I am told reliably by Mordred, who was lucky to leave the forest with his life – their anger was directed at you."

He sat back in his chair, mulling over this information. She knew Arthur wanted to believe life in Camelot was as close to perfect as possible, and this news was difficult for him to accept.

"There is still more," said Morgan, "and perhaps this information will be useful to you. You have doubtlessly heard I was there at the siege of Horsa's castle. Can I continue to speak without giving the details of exactly how I came to be there?"

"Of course, you can. Have we not just both agreed the past will stay in the past?"

"Lancelot was in Gawain's tent after the battle was won. Lancelot told me this last night: The Grail had been kept in Gawain's tent but was stolen from Gawain before he left Germania. Do you understand what that means? The Grail was not on Gawain's ship. If his ship sank to the bottom of the sea, it did not take the Grail with it. Someone else, one of your own knights most likely, took the Grail for his own purpose, and it is here in Britain."

Arthur appeared both concerned and confused. "If this is true, why didn't Lancelot say this before I sent ships to search for it? In fact, Lancelot was the one most eager for the search, he and Percival. Why would he do such a thing?"

"Whatever Lancelot's reason, the presumed loss of the Grail has created problems for you among the peasantry." She stared at him and folded her arms across her chest, knowing he was not eager to challenge her after they had just put many years of distrust and animosity behind them. "I can't answer for Lancelot's actions except to say that having spent as much time with Lancelot as I have, his actions no longer surprise me. In fact, I would not be surprised by anything he might do."

"I don't understand what his motivation would be for being deceitful about the Grail and for prompting a sea search for it?"

"I can't explain," said Morgan. "It's bizarre that he told me about his deception. and it was disloyal to you to let you organize a futile search of the sea when he knew better."

Arthur shook his head. "It's difficult to believe, but I suppose one can never be certain what to expect from people – although knowing Lancelot, he might have been trying to teach me some lesson. He has a tendency toward being sanctimonious, but he is the one person whose loyalty I considered beyond question."

Morgan wasn't certain whether Arthur had fully accepted her comments or was just avoiding a disagreement. But she knew she was making some headway. "Perhaps Lancelot is what you have always believed he is, but what is it Merlin always told you? Expect the unexpected and doubt has always held him in good stead."

Arthur seemed to be weighing her comment. "Do you think, Lancelot, himself, has the Grail?" he said finally. "Concealing his own guilt is a reasonable explanation for why he might have argued for a useless search of the sea."

Morgan smiled at Arthur's comment. "I haven't seen the Grail. But whoever has it, Lancelot or another of your knights, you must find it and stop people from believing its loss is the cause of all the harm that has befallen them."

Arthur was uncharacteristically unnerved by this conversation. "Let's think this out to its conclusion. What if Lancelot or another of my knights does have the Grail? I can't confront any of them directly, especially Lancelot." She could see frustration welling up in him. "A chalice could be hidden anywhere. How could I hope to find it and do it in such a way as to not alienate my best knights?"

She leaned closer to him and spoke softly. "You are neglecting the fact that, for whatever reason, one of your knights, possibly Lancelot, is already alienated. If it is Lancelot, it may be because he sees himself more righteous than you." She raised her voice again. "As for the Grail, it has special powers, does it not? Maybe it can reveal itself to you. Maybe a worthy person will be able to sense its presence."

"I don't know what to believe." He sat quietly for a few moments, apparently still doubting the accusations she made against Lancelot.

"You, yourself, have had the experience of encountering an enchanted sword in the forest, and Merlin's sight has aided you your entire life. Stranger things have happened than you finding the Grail. Don't you think it's worth making another effort?"

"Of course, you're right. I can have my best knights search for the Grail as soon as I can organize them."

"Haven't you been listening to me?" Morgan's tone was emphatic, almost angry. "Organize a search to divert suspicion, but also have your best knights searched as well, or at least their castles and manor houses. My guess is one of them took it or at least, knows who did and where it is."

"This information is most useful, Morgan. I am most grateful." He moved to the edge of his chair about to stand up, as if he was preparing to assemble his knights that very instant.

"One last thing, Arthur. Something else that will be both hard for you to hear and difficult for you to believe. I have seen a side to Lancelot hidden from you."

He sat back in his chair. "Morgan, you have known Lancelot well only for a short time. I have known him long, and truthfully, what you have told me already is difficult to believe – not that I'm saying I disbelieve you."

"As long as you have known him, would you ever have imagined he would take up with me?" Arthur couldn't counter that point. "Don't be naïve, Arthur. I share the man's bed. There are things he tells me he would not tell anyone else, least of all you." She paused to take a deep breath. "Lancelot is jealous of you."

Arthur shook his head and looked at her in disbelief. "Lancelot! I don't believe it."

"You, yourself, say he is the best knight in the world. And is it true, as you have often said, that his physical strength is based on his strength of character?"

"That's exactly my point. His strength of character."

"That is exactly *his* point as well," she said emphatically. "Lancelot believes his strength comes from his purity and also believes he is more worthy than anyone else including you. He now says the proof of his worthiness is that his castle was not damaged by the storm while Camelot was battered so badly the tower roof blew away. He is also angry that you have been credited with the victory over Horsa when you weren't even in Germania. He has not said this directly, but I believe he even doubts the validity of your kingship." Arthur's eyes opened wide at that comment. "I'm fairly certain he believes the Sword in the Stone was just a trick of Merlin's."

Arthur's face turned with anger, and he bit his lip, seemingly unwilling or unable to respond to her accusation. And she still had one last ploy to use.

"You may not have noticed," she said, "but your loyal and pure knight has developed a discriminating taste for women. Have you seen how he looks at Guinevere?"

Arthur's eyes flared, and he squeezed the arms of his chair. His regression from emotionally balanced king to hot-tempered young knight was complete. She was looking at the old Arthur, the one who was quick to anger and too quick to act.

"Perhaps I am seeing more in the situation than is really there," said Morgan. "Perhaps I'm just a jealous woman whose fear of losing her man causes her to imagine things," she said in a more relaxed tone. "But my advice to you is this: Keep an eye on Lancelot when he is near Guinevere and at all costs, don't allow Lancelot to be the finder of the lost Grail. It would do you no good and would only strengthen his standing among many others."

CHAPTER 21: **The Grail Knights**

Arthur, still agitated after his conversation with Morgan, left his bedchamber and started toward the meeting he had called of his Roundtable knights. From the corner of his eye, he saw someone in the hall approaching from the shadows. He was so upset this day he thought he might be in danger and prepared to defend himself, if necessary, with his bare hands.

"Good evening."

Arthur, who had been holding his breath, exhaled. "Merlin, must you always?"

The wizard stepped into the light. "Always what?"

"Never mind. I'm sure it is useless to complain. It has been useless up 'til now."

"I wanted to see you privately before your meeting of the Roundtable. Does that trouble you?"

"Of course, not. But you could have come to my chamber and knocked on the door instead of lurking here in the hall."

"I was not *lurking*."

"And you won't change my mind." Arthur waved his hand as if to dismiss Merlin. "You may not approve of me sending knights to find the Grail, but that is exactly what I intend to do."

Merlin lowered his disorderly white eyebrows into a scowl. "Change your mind! I'm not here to change your mind. I want to encourage you to find the Grail or at least make the effort."

"Then, you also believe it has special powers?"

"Of course not. It's just a cup. The real Grail is a stone. The Grail Stone has been known since the very beginning of time. Didn't I tell you about it before?"

Arthur placed his hands on his hips. "No, you most certainly did not."

"It must have slipped my mind. Be that as it may, I hear what is being said in the villages and towns and even among your own knights. You must make the attempt to recover this Grail. You need to do whatever you can to demonstrate you are making an effort and making some progress until all this concern about storms and grails dissipates and is replaced by some other irrational fear."

"Thank you, Merlin. Your advice is well taken, especially since searching for the Grail is exactly what I planned to do anyway. Now, it is best if we are not seen together. I've been accused of being unwilling to abandon the old ways."

Merlin became indignant. "And you believe it is wrong to honor the old ways?"
"Not necessarily. But some do believe the old ways should stay in the past, and this is a particularly delicate time."

The wizard would not drop the issue. "And what if the old ways, or at least some of them, are correct and powerful?"

"I have no time for a philosophical discussion with my mentor at the moment. The Roundtable is waiting. We can argue old versus new another time." Arthur left Merlin and continued along the corridor to the tower stairs.

Merlin shouted after him. "I would welcome such an argument."

Down in the great hall, fewer than a dozen of his knights were seated. There had been insufficient time to gather many of them, and Lancelot was not invited. Arthur sat in his usual chair and looked from one end of the Roundtable to the other, skipping over the empty chairs and looking at each of the knights who were present. "I have gathered you for a special purpose, and I apologize for the shortness of the notice."

"We know why we are here." There was some antagonism in Gareth's tone. "But I thought Gawain had the Grail and it was lost at sea."

"That may still be the case," said Arthur. "But I have new information that it may be here hidden somewhere in Britain."

"If that is so, how in the name of all that is holy are we expected to find a cup somewhere in Britain? If, in fact, it is in Britain at all."

Percival, who sat next to Gareth, put a hand on Gareth's arm. "It's not just a cup, Gareth. If it was just a cup, we wouldn't need to find it."

"Being more than a common cup still doesn't make it any easier to find."

Again Percival responded. "Lancelot said it might be seen floating in air surrounded by light."

"Lancelot may be correct," said Arthur. "Or what he and Percival have described might be just an image of it, a sign of where it actually is. If the Grail has the power that some say. . ." Arthur looked at his knights. "If it has the power that some of *you* in this very room believe it has, there may be ways of locating it beyond just the use of the sense of sight."

"We should pray for divine guidance in our quest," said Bedivere. "If God wants it found – and without daring to speak for the Almighty, I assume He does want it found – if God wants it found, we will find it."

Gareth turned his skepticism on Bedivere. "Do we just ride through the forest waiting for a sign from God?"

"As your king, Gareth, I tell you if that is the best you can do, then yes, just ride through the forest and wait for a sign. Some of you are more enthusiastic about the quest and will find better ways of searching for the Grail. I would not ask you to take on this task if it were not important. There seems to be mounting discontent everywhere, and finding the Grail will go a long way in quelling it. I understand this seems like a daunting task, but there are places where you should begin the search."

Arthur hesitated to look at the faces before him. "It is possible, it may even be likely, that one of our own number took the Grail – perhaps for a good reason – during the siege of Horsa's castle or shortly thereafter. That is where and when it disappeared. The starting places, then, are the castles of our own knights."

Gareth still appeared skeptical. "Do we just ride into a castle and say of its master, 'Have you stolen anything of value in recent times, such as the Holy Grail?'"

Arthur gave Gareth an angry enough look to cause him to squirm in his chair. "Even you, Gareth, are capable of more discretion but apparently not at the moment. In any case, all of you should use discretion. You are the flower of British knighthood. I'm asking you to find a cup, not to battle a Saxon army single-handed."

Gareth sat quietly.

Arthur looked over the group. "A final issue. We must also consider that someone in this hall took the Grail. For whatever reason, I do not care. I care only that it is returned." Arthur withdrew a dagger from his belt and placed it on the table, its point facing away from him. "Before I retire for the night, I will check the dagger. If it is facing the other way, I will know one of you has the Grail and will return it."

This last comment caused the assembled knights to look at one another, some with puzzled looks, others with suspicion.

That night Arthur checked the dagger. Its position was unchanged.

CHAPTER 22: **Bedivere's Quest**

Bedivere and his squire rode side by side to the home of Agravain. "You realize," said Bedivere, "of all the knights present at the Roundtable, I was given the most difficult assignment: Agravain, who has never been a supporter of Arthur's and may, in fact, detest the king."

"Is 'at why you sent word ahead you were goin' ta visit Agravain?"

"Yes, this is not a time for surprising people, especially powerful knights who may be hostile to our cause. There is discontent even among the Roundtable. Gareth was discourteous to Arthur to the point of being belligerent."

"But Sir Agravain weren't at the siege. So how could he be the one ta have the Grail?"

"No indeed, he was not at the siege because he is not a strong supporter of our king, and for that very reason he is under suspicion." Bedivere continued his explanation in a patronizing tone. "Agravain did not need to be there himself. Someone might have acquired it for him, or he might have obtained it later."

The squire considered those possibilities. "Sir Bedivere, if ya don't object to me askin' another question, what did ya tell him, Sir Agravain, that is – about why we're comin' to his castle?"
"I just said we were coming for a visit." Bedivere allowed himself a smile of satisfaction. "I believe the approach I plan to take is quite good. After we have engaged in conversation – about how bad the weather has been, how good the hunting is – I will describe the quest I have been given and ask his advice."

"Beggin' yer pardon, Sir Bedivere, but what does 'at accomplish?"

Bedivere stared at the squire from the corner of his eye. "You fail to see the subtlety of the plan. Failing to see subtleties is, in fact, a shortcoming of yours. If Agravain knows where the Grail is and wants to give it up without confessing to its theft, he can guide me to the right path in the guise of giving me advice."

"And if he don't want ta give it up?"

"Sometimes an untruth can be detected in the words a person uses and how the words are delivered. If I determine Agravain is being deceitful, I will leave it to the king to actually retrieve the Grail. But prying information from Agravain may not be necessary because some of the Roundtable knights, Percival chief among them, believe the Grail will make its presence known in some manner, some supernatural manner, like just appearing in the air right in front of you. Having it show itself certainly would make things easier." He pointed at the squire. "You, too, my lad, will also play a part in all this."

The squire put a hand to his chest. "Me?"

"You will have supper in Agravain's kitchen, no doubt. Learn what you can from the kitchen staff and any other household servants you may encounter. But use discretion."

"Discretion?" The squire pretended to be confused about the meaning of the word. "Ya mean subtlety?"

"You are not being so subtle now that I fail to see you are trying to dispute my earlier remark."

Their pace was leisurely, and it took longer to reach Agravain's manor house than it should have. Storm damage was still visible in the pile of debris off to one side of the house and the construction work being done on the stable roof. Two servants came out to meet them.

The first addressed himself to Bedivere. "Welcome, Sir Bedivere. Sir Agravain eagerly awaits your arrival in the great hall and has a meal prepared."

The second servant tended to the squire. "Follow me to the kitchen. You shall eat with us."

Before the squire left, Bedivere gave him a wink. The squire winked back.

The main hall of the manor was empty except for a small table and two chairs set before a fire in the hearth. Agravain rose from his seat to greet his guest and was so cordial Bedivere was immediately put at ease. They sat at the table, where Agravain had a tankard of mead waiting for Bedivere. Bedivere took a swallow and began to chat. He talked about the recent weather, which led to a conversation about the great storm.

Next, as food was served, Bedivere changed the subject to a more pleasant one and talked about hunting. The more he ate and drank, the more Bedivere talked. And the more he talked, the more he ate and especially the more he drank.

His lips wet, his words slightly slurred, Bedivere brought up the subject of discretion. "Have you ever noticed, Agravain, how some men can be discrete or subtle while others cannot?"

Agravain did not appear particularly interested in the topic but answered. "I believe there is a difference between discretion and subtlety." Bedivere paused with the tankard of mead part way to his mouth to listen to the explanation. "It is easier to be discreet. Even squires and servants are required to be discreet in keeping the confidences of their masters. Subtlety is much more difficult. A person must affirmatively undertake a task or a conversation without revealing his true intention."

Bedivere slammed his tankard down on the table. "You're right. I've never thought of it that way, but you are ab-so-lute-ly right."

"Now that we have distinguished discretion from subtlety, good Bedivere, what is the true purpose of your visit?"

Bedivere laughed. "I'm not nearly as subtle as I give myself credit for. I was just telling my squire. . ." He paused in mid-sentence. "What I told my squire, is, of course, of no consequence. But since you ask, good Agravain, I tell you in all candor I'm here about the Grail."

"The Grail?"

"You have not heard of it? Or that it is missing?"

"Of course, I have. But why do you come here?"

Bedivere noticed someone standing by his side and turned his head to see who it was. "Mordred, I didn't "

Mordred swung a mace up from his hip into Bedivere's face, smashing in parts of his cheek, forehead and skull, and sending him over backwards onto the floor, blood spurting in all directions.

"Damn you, Mordred," shouted Agravain. "You said you would strangle him. Look at the mess you created."

Mordred delivered another blow to the fallen Bedivere. "This is much faster." He reached for the tankard Bedivere had been drinking from and finished what was left.

"And the squire?"

Mordred placed the tankard back down on the table. "Also dead."

CHAPTER 23: **Percival's New Task**

Percival, who was in the stable saddling his horse, looked up to see Arthur approaching him. "I'm honored, my king, that you would come to see me off."

Arthur did not speak until he was standing directly before Percival. "I've come to give you a different task from the one I gave you in front of the other knights." Arthur looked about to be certain there were no stable boys in the barn. "It's a task of great delicacy, one I could only entrust to a knight I have complete faith in. Understand, Percival, I accuse no one of wrongdoing, but a man doesn't have to be disloyal to have his own view of things. Such a man might, perhaps unwittingly, not pursue the best interest of his king. I cannot take such chance with any knight, not with the current state of the kingdom."

Percival appeared both confused and troubled by this comment. "I realize you have some cause for concern among your knights, but I think it's more a matter of misunderstanding than disloyalty."

"Whether it is or not, there is also the matter of equal treatment and fairness, Percival. I have sent men to question and investigate some good and loyal knights as a precaution. I cannot remove a favorite knight from this kind of consideration, not even the great Lancelot. No one, not at this moment at least, should be above suspicion."

"Are you sending me to Lancelot's castle?"

"Yes."

Percival frowned. "I was with Lancelot on the boat when we were searching for the Grail at sea. When he thought he saw it, he became very excited, and his excitement was genuine. I can't believe he of all people would have the Grail."

"I don't doubt what you observed, and I'm not saying this about Lancelot specifically, but in general, such a reaction would be an ideal way to divert suspicion from one's self."

Now Percival was deeply worried. "So, am I to explain to Lancelot the reason for my visit and say he is under suspicion?"

"No, of course not. And you should not mention there was a meeting of the Roundtable yesterday."

"But I cannot lie to another knight. I could no more lie to Lancelot than lie to you."

Arthur sighed. "There is no need to lie. Just tell him you are questing after the Grail. That much is true. Say we are no longer certain it was lost with Gawain, which is also true. There is no need to say he or anyone else is under suspicion."

"But withholding all the truth is telling a half truth and a lie of sorts."

"Percival, Percival." Arthur was exasperated. "Priests and bishops could have a lengthy debate about whether not volunteering information is a lie or not. The future of the kingdom and perhaps all of Britain has been thrown off course by the storm and this issue with the Grail. You and I have no time for philosophical discussions."

"If you are ordering me to be less than forthcoming with Lancelot, I will do as you instruct me."

"I'm not ordering you. I'm asking you. No lies. Just don't say more than you have to. It serves no purpose to get Lancelot upset unnecessarily."

"I cannot refuse a request from my king." Percival resumed saddling his horse.

"Remember, Percival, what you yourself said. You may see a sign of some kind, in which case there would be no need to confront Lancelot in any way."

Percival, sadness in his eyes, looked at Arthur. "Let us both hope there is a sign and the sign is a testimony to Lancelot's innocence."

He left Arthur and rode toward the castle gate. Instead of leaving, however, Percival turned back to the chapel, tethered his horse, and went inside. It was empty. Only a few candles were still lit; the others had burned themselves down to cold stumps. Percival knelt at the altar, looked up at the cross and prayed aloud. His first request was that he be shown where the Grail was, not for personal glory but to prevent animosity from developing between Arthur and Lancelot, the two most important men in the kingdom. If he was not to be granted his first prayer, he asked he be given some sign here, or along the way, or at Lancelot's castle, that Lancelot was not the Grail thief. And if he was not to be granted either of these two prayers, he asked at the very least that Lancelot not ask him any questions that would force him to choose between lying and not carrying out his duty to Arthur.

Percival left the chapel some time later and rode toward Lancelot's castle, allowing his horse to stop whenever it pleased to nibble at grass or other vegetation. He occasionally mumbled prayers under his breath and was on constant lookout for a sign.

Morgan stood in the center of the great hall of Lancelot's castle calling his name. He finally appeared from the kitchen, a stained napkin tucked in at his neck to protect his white tunic. He pulled out the napkin, wiped his hands on it and handed it to the servant who followed him out of the kitchen.

"You're back! Wonderful. I'll finish eating later," he said to the servant, and he rushed to Morgan, taking her into his arms.

She gently pushed him away. "I am not back, not permanently. I made a special trip just to tell you something important."

Lancelot released her and backed off a step. "You've been distant lately. More than a little distant. I'm beginning to lose my patience."

"Forgive me. I'm not in the best mood, and you will understand why when you hear what I have to tell you. Arthur has organized a search for the Grail."

"What! At sea?"

"No, he believes it is here in Britain. He thinks it was taken by one of his own knights."

"This must be a story, only a rumor. The Grail was with Gawain. And why would this rumor put you in a foul humor?"

"It's more than a rumor. Arthur believes the Grail was not with Gawain, and I'm telling you that a search for it here has begun." She moved a step closer to Lancelot, who seemed somewhat dumbfounded by this information. "Have you been asked to seek the Grail? No, you haven't. Did you attend the meeting of the Roundtable today? Were you even invited? No."

Lancelot shook his head. "Now I am confused, thoroughly confused, or perhaps you are. There was no meeting of the Roundtable today."

"Indeed, there was. You just weren't told about it."

"I don't believe it!" He looked away from Morgan for a moment, apparently composing his thoughts. He looked back at her. He was angry. "You are certain about this? Positive?"

"Positive. I can even tell you which of the other knights were there."

He shook his head. "This makes no sense."

"It does if Arthur thinks you have the Grail. Or maybe *stole* it is a better word."

Lancelot went to one of the armchairs by the fireplace. He sat down, his face flushed with anger, nervously looking from side to side although there was nothing to see.

Morgan stood over him. "Are you confused about the meaning of what I just told you?"

"No," he answered without looking at her. "Just confused about the reason I would be suspected of stealing and lying and be left out of this quest. Have I committed some offense? If so, what?"

"Your offense is obvious or don't you see it? You are better than Arthur, and your reputation reflects it. He is jealous of you. After all, he is supposed to be the great king, the one chosen by destiny. But you are better than he is. You defeated Horsa and are getting the credit for it, not Arthur. And he thinks you are not all you purport to be." Lancelot's nostrils flared at that remark. "You claim purity, and yet, you have sexual commerce with me. Such a man in Arthur's view might easily find the Grail an irresistible trophy."

Lancelot stood up to face her. "Is that what Arthur said? Those very words? He is damning both of us and using our union to accuse me of being a thief?"

She shook her head. "He doesn't have to say it. I know he believes it."

"He has nerve. Do you know that before he was king, he was unfaithful with the betrothed of his brother? Many have forgotten that indiscretion over the years. And he seduced his. . ." Lancelot stopped in mid-sentence.

She finished the thought for him. "Seduced his own sister. I could hardly forget that."

Lancelot began to pace before the fire, speaking more to himself than to Morgan. "This is how he treats me! Me! What can the other knights think of this insult? He has damaged, if not ruined, my reputation by suspecting me of theft and excluding me from the Roundtable. And I am the one who has fought all his battles and has been his best knight."

"You have been too good. He resents you. The more you accomplish, the more resentful he becomes."

He turned toward her and pounded his chest. "If it were not for me, much of his army would still be bogged down in a hopeless siege of Horsa's castle."

"I know that as well as anyone, but Arthur still tries to claim the credit for that victory."

"No more." Lancelot swung his arm out from his chest as though angrily clearing a table. "The next time he needs help from me, he will have to apologize and beg for it although accusing a man of being a liar and a theft is a stain that cannot be removed. And even if he apologizes and begs, I may choose to keep to my own affairs or perhaps challenge him to one-on-one combat."

Percival rode the trail in the twilight nearing Lancelot's castle, his eyes continuing to search the woods in all directions in the impossible hope that the Grail would show itself in the forest. He heard a rustle of bushes on his left. He turned in time to see a pole being thrust at him and clutched his saddle to brace himself. Percival took a blow to his ribs that broke several of them but managed to hang on and stay mounted. He reached for his sword, but someone was on the other side of him restraining his arm. The pole crashed down on his head, and he almost fell. His horse began to rear and throw its head from side to side. More attackers surrounded his mount and tried to steady it. Again the pole crashed down on his head. He began to sway in the saddle. Several sets of hands grabbed at him. He was dragged off the horse and thrown to the ground. One attacker beat him with the pole while the others kicked him until he stopped moving.

They chased the horse off back in the direction from which it came, took the motionless Percival by the feet and dragged him deep into the woods.

Morgan stood at a tower window looking for the signal. She had managed to put Lancelot off this evening. For a change, it had been easy. He was too insulted and angry about the accusations against him to be interested in her.

There it was, a torch being waved on the forest trail. She grabbed a cloak, wrapped it around herself and hurried down the tower stairs. She crossed the courtyard, checking periodically to see she was not being observed, and exited a small wooden gate in the castle's south wall.

It was not long before a hooded figure approached her from the darkness. "Well?" she asked.

The man came closer and removed his hood before speaking. "Dead. Percival's dead."

"Good."

"And we've hidden his body where it will never be found."

"Fool!" He was stunned by her anger. "I want the body found, not hidden. Found! I told you that clearly. I want Percival to be found near Lancelot's castle. I don't want people thinking he may have ridden north or to Wales in search of this Grail."

The man held up his hands to calm her. "It isn't too late. We'll simply drag the body back from where we left it."

"Then, do it. Now! I will wait for you here."

She waited impatiently, and waited and waited. She had to put up with so many fools; sometimes she wondered if all this effort was worth it if she couldn't count on anyone but herself. When the hooded figure finally returned, he was winded and reluctant to speak. "Well?" she asked.

"He's not where we left him."

"What! He's dead, isn't he?"

"Yes."

"Then, he could hardly have walked away, could he? You and the other fools looked in the wrong place."

"It's dark."

"I can see it's dark!" She pointed in the general direction of the forest road. "Go back and find the body if you have to look until sunrise tomorrow."

CHAPTER 24: **Beyond the Edge of the World**

Gawain felt himself falling. He was dropping straight down as though he had fallen into a great hole in the earth. Not a hole, he realized, it was the edge. They had finally gone over the edge of the world. He threw his hands out in both directions reaching for something to grasp onto. His right hand touched wood. It was the side of the ship. He grabbed on.

The sensation of falling stopped. He opened his eyes to see he was aboard the Norse vessel and it was still sailing level in the night sea.

Gawain sat up. His face and neck were covered with sweat although the night air was cold. He wiped himself as dry as he could with the sleeves of his tunic and looked straight ahead. It was too dark to see anything, but somewhere out in the night there was an edge to the world, and they would eventually sail over it, perhaps at any moment. They had to sail over it because there had to be an edge. It made no sense that the world would be otherwise.

Gawain wondered if it was his destiny to die in water. He had almost drowned when he was washed overboard during the storm that left him stranded, and now he knew he might have been intentionally drowned during their last stay on land. After they had sailed away from the land of bright green night skies and burning mud, Raevil explained to him the strange ceremony they witnessed just before they left and the argument that took place between Alrood and Hauk. Hauk had been troubled by nightly visits from ghosts, and he decided to make a sacrifice to the god Odin to keep the ghosts away. Odin preferred human sacrifices, and Gawain, as the outsider, was selected by Hauk to be the victim. However, Alrood protested and persuaded Hauk to use his prized battleax as an offering instead, saying it was worth far more than the life of a Briton. The ax, rather than Gawain's half dead body, had been thrown into the steaming pool.

Twice Alrood had saved him.

Gawain again strained his eyes to see what might be ahead of them, and he decided to stay awake the rest of the night looking for the edge of the world, hoping that if he saw it, he could warn the Norsemen in time to turn the ship around.

When the sun rose the next morning, there was still plenty of sea before them. They sailed for days longer, and one afternoon to the crew's delight – no one was happier than Gawain – land came into view. There was a landmass, a large one, where the world should have ended. But what they saw now was only the beginning of a vast expanse of land. They turned south and sailed on, day after day, passing more and more coastline. Gawain had sailed the length of Britain from its southern tip to the land of the Picts. This was much bigger. And he had sailed portions of the coasts of Gaul and Germania. This was bigger still.

Was it possible, he wondered, that there was more land here, where there was supposed to be nothing, than there was land in the world he knew?

As they continued south, the weather became milder, and Gawain was beginning to enjoy the sunshine and relative warmth and the sight of a lush shore. Even being aboard a ship no longer bothered him.

One of the men in the bow of the ship called out. In the distance there were several narrow streams of smoke rising into the air as if from campfires. Gawain thought they might be approaching another Norse settlement, but when the source of the smoke came into view, he saw a village unlike any other – British, Saxon or Norse – he had ever seen. The tents were small, round at the base and narrow at the top, and the boats were also small, only large enough to carry a handful of men, and they were not of Norse design.

Villagers came to the shore to greet them, and they were even more unusual in appearance than their oddly shaped tents and small boats. The villagers were dark-skinned and had black hair. The women wore their hair braided as did some of the men. Other men, all of whom were clean-shaven, had long hair draped over the front of their shoulders and down their chests. Some wore cloths tied across their foreheads; many wore feathers, and men and women alike decorated themselves with colorful jewelry. Unlike Britons and Saxons, who wore woven cloth, or Norsemen, who preferred animal fur, these men and women dressed in smooth deerskin.

The crew took to their oars and rowed to the shore. "These people, Gawain, they are much like us, like Norsemen," said Raevil. "They are fierce warriors, but also they know the value of trade."

Gawain never took his eyes off the people on the shore. "And what is traded?"

"They have no metal; so, knives and daggers and especially axes are much prized by them and metal cups and plates, and also mirrors."

"And in return?"

"We receive hides mostly. The hides here are of high quality, and some are of animals unlike any of our own. We also take plants for spices and medicines. These are of little value to us but can be traded to the Saxons for cloth and grain."

Some of the dark-colored men came to the water's edge and helped them beach their vessel. The women kept a distance from the visitors, but curious children gathered around them. Gawain had not seen children in a long time and seeing these made him smile; he especially enjoyed their curiosity about the visitors and the fact that they, unlike the adults, made no attempt to conceal it. Gawain, Raevil and several other Norsemen, with children standing just behind them, began unloading the boat of the sacks of goods they brought to trade while Alrood went to greet the leader of the village, who stood a few dozen feet away observing the landing. The leader was dressed like the other men although he wore more feathers and more jewelry.

It was the man just behind the village leader who attracted Gawain's attention. This man, older than most of the others, was clad in a furry animal skin. The lower jaw of the animal's mouth had been removed and the rest of the head was still attached to the skin and worn like a hood over the man's own head. The skin was unusually furry, as was the animal's face, which was topped by horns that curved inwards. The animal was somewhat bull-like and somewhat ox-like in facial appearance but clearly was neither and was unlike any beast Gawain had ever seen. Indeed, the animal's face was somewhat demonic looking.

Raevil nudged Gawain, who had paused with a sack of grain over his shoulder staring at the man. "I see, Gawain, you are curious about him."

"Yes, and I wonder what kind of animal the skin he is wearing came from."

"The man in the animal skin would be called by a Celt a magician or an enchanter and by a Christian a priest. And the animal is one that lives only here. I've never seen one alive but have eaten its meat. We might receive some of those hides in trade but without the head. Only he wears the head."

After the ship was unloaded and their trade items were laid out on blankets, Gawain and Raevil were instructed to help make camp while the senior members of their party began trade negotiations. Sunset was nearing. As soon as the camp was set up, the Norse party ate their supper. They would continue trading the following morning and do some hunting with the permission of the villagers. The Norse needed meat for the return voyage and did not want to have to trade for it.

While most of the others decided to go to sleep, Gawain remained by the campfire long after the sun had gone down. He felt happier and more relaxed than he had in months. One at a time he threw some sticks onto the fire and watched them ignite, letting his mind go blank as his eyes focused on the flames. When he ran out of sticks, he decided to walk along the beach. The water was calm, and he found the gentle roll of the waves a pleasant sound. Occasionally he looked out over the vast sea to the east.

There was something on the sand ahead of him. He did not recognize its shape in the dark, but since it was not moving, he went closer. Gawain was almost on top of the figure before he realized it was a man sitting in the sand and not moving. Even without the animal robe Gawain recognized him as the man Raevil called the village enchanter or priest, and for some reason Gawain could not articulate, he thought the man might be trying to experience nature – the beach, the sea, the sky – more intimately. Or perhaps he wanted to actually blend in with nature somehow.

Gawain was intruding on the priest/magician and was about to turn around to leave when the man looked up at him and motioned for him to sit down. He sat, and the priest turned away to resume his concentration. Gawain glanced over at the man and tried to emulate first his posture and then the depth of his concentration. He had to adjust himself several times to find a comfortable enough position so the aches in his legs and hips from being many days aboard ship did not disturb him. He tried looking out at the sea without focusing his eyes. Next he tried closing his eyes and listening to the sound of the sea while attempting to release the tension in his mind.

His mind went blank for a few moments and quickly filled again with thoughts. He tried over and over. Sometimes he did better; sometimes not. Always thoughts streamed through his mind about anything and everything, and he got no closer to nature. But he kept trying. Finally his mind went blank for a longer length of time, and he found it relaxing to not be concerned about himself, not to be worried about where he was and how he would get home, or about all the things he regretted and all those things he wanted to accomplish and had yet to achieve.

He looked at the priest/magician. He seemingly had not moved in the slightest the whole time Gawain sat next to him.

This became Gawain's pattern night after night. When the others went to sleep, he came out to the beach and sat near the priest/magician, the two sitting silently, never attempting to communicate. Gawain found this motionless sitting relaxing, and he was improving at clearing his mind, but not once did he experience anything close to what he assumed the priest/magician was experiencing.

It was nearing the end of their stay here. The sun had set; most of the others were sleeping. Gawain, as usual, went to the beach and spent a good portion of the night there sitting still. On this night he was able to clear his mind more thoroughly than he ever had before.

Gawain glanced up at the heavens. His eyes had been closed just a few moments, but the crescent moon, which had been just above the horizon, was now high in the sky. More time had passed than he realized. He should return to camp to go to sleep, and he started back toward his tent.

There was something odd about all this.

He reached camp and saw the tents of the Norsemen and the few of their number who had chosen to sleep outside by a fire. He examined each tent and each man. By the fire he noticed mice picking clean some of the bones the Norsemen had discarded after dinner.

Something was very odd. But he could not say exactly what was wrong.

He moved about the entire camp effortlessly and silently. But he was not walking. He was floating, not flying like a bird but rather being carried along several feet above the ground without moving his limbs. He could not say how he was able to move is this manner or how he was able to change direction, but it was effortless. He raised himself higher into the air to look down at the entire Norse camp from above. He circled the camp by just wanting to do so, then glided to the village over the smoke rising from the tents and above a pen that held sheep.

Now he was over the beach. Below was a solitary figure sitting in the sand. He moved in for a closer look. What he saw should have shocked and amazed him, but he was unmoved by what he saw as though it was the most ordinary of sights.

He was looking down at himself.

The cold seawater rolled over his feet jolting him. He was sitting on the beach again. He looked for the village priest. He was gone. Gawain stood up, and with his wet feet caking with sand as he walked, he went back to their camp and to his tent. As he neared the campfire, mice scurried away into the darkness.

CHAPTER 25: **Failing Sight**

The peasant pushed a two-wheeled cart of hay along the forest path with great difficulty. The road was strewn with rocks, and there were many depressions in the mud, causing the cart to bump and dip as its wheels squeaked. He hit a smooth patch, picked up a little speed and rounded a bend in the road. He had not gotten far when the left wheel dropped into a hole and tipped the cart to one side. He pulled the cart back as far as it would go and gave it a shove. The cart shot ahead, spilling some of its load onto the ground. Cursing under his breath, the peasant bent over and began to recover the fallen hay.

He noticed a body lying off to the side in the bushes. Most of the man was hidden under the brush, but his arm was protruding onto the edge of the path. The peasant quickly gathered the rest of his fallen hay, grabbed the handles of the cart and pushed it ahead a few feet before looking back at the fallen man. He stared at the body for a few moments, rested the cart handles on the ground and cautiously approached the corpse. He bent over and pulled back the top of a bush to see more of the man. From his dress, the man was clearly of the nobility and apparently a knight.

The man moaned.

The peasant turned the knight onto his back and saw a face swollen and discolored. The knight moaned again. The peasant gently shook his arm, but the man did not awaken or open his eyes, one of which was black and puffed out to twice the size of the other. "What ta do? What ta do?" the peasant said to himself, as he looked from the knight to the cart. "Oh well. Nothin' else ta do about it." He wedged his arms under the knight's armpits, lifted his upper body off the ground and dragged him toward the cart. The knight moaned louder. "Sorry, sorry, sorry. A few more steps and I'll have ya in the cart." He managed to get the knight's upper body onto the bed of the cart, then swung his legs up and in, bending the knight in an odd manner and causing him to cry in pain. "Sorry, sorry, sorry. All done."

The peasant grabbed the handles of the cart, now with a much heavier load, and began to roll it forward.

A panicked servant rushed into the great hall to summon Arthur, who was in conversation with Kaye. "Sire, there is an injured man outside." The servant pointed back to the courtyard. "In a cart on a load of hay. It's a knight. I can't be sure, but I think it's Sir Percival."

Arthur, followed by Kaye and the servant, hurried out to see the injured man. The peasant who brought the cart to the castle stepped aside so the king could have a better look. "It is Percival," said Arthur, "although it is a wonder anyone could recognize him in this condition." Percival was not moving. Arthur turned to the peasant. "Is he alive?"

"Yes, m'lord. Leastwise, he was."

Arthur touched Percival's wrist and felt a heartbeat. Percival began to moan. "Let's get him inside and into a bed." Arthur and Kaye each grabbed one side of Percival's back and shoulders; the servant and the peasant each lifted a leg; and the four of them carefully carried Percival inside and up the tower steps. Arthur looked down at the swollen, blackened eye and the long cut on Percival's forehead that was caked with dried blood. "Whoever did this will pay for it."

Once Percival was laid on a bed and covered with a blanket, Arthur ordered the servant to bring food and water in case Percival woke up. He instructed Kaye to find a priest and to look for Merlin, then he thanked the peasant for his effort and rewarded him with several coins.

The servant was the first to return and carried with him a tray of food and a goblet of water. The priest arrived next and gave Percival the holy rites. No sooner had he finished than Percival opened his eyes and began to mumble. Arthur tried unsuccessfully to get Percival to drink some water from the goblet. He took the bread from the food tray, tore off a piece, dunked it into the water and placed it into Percival's mouth. Percival sucked on the wet bread and tried to raise his head. "Don't try to get up. You need rest, Percival."

Arthur coaxed him into putting his head back down. Percival moaned. "It's Arthur, Percival. Do you understand? Arthur." He didn't seem to be attentive. "What happened to you?"

Percival rolled his head from side to side. "Where am I?"

"Camelot. Do you know who attacked you?"

"What happened?"

"You were attacked. Do you know who did it?"

"I don't know what happened." He shook his head again, and this time the motion appeared to hurt him.

Merlin arrived and stood in the doorway. "Better let him rest, Arthur. Maybe after a long sleep he may be able to tell you what happened. Maybe he will never remember."

Arthur left the bed and walked to Merlin. "Whatever happened to him occurred while he was riding to see Lancelot."

"Surely," said Kaye, looking at Percival's disfigured face, "you don't suspect Lancelot had any involvement with this."

Arthur maintained his stern look. "I'm not sure what to think. Nothing seems to be as it was or as it should be. Lancelot is arrogant and self-centered and always has been although I have chosen to overlook it. Now he has become somewhat antagonistic. This could be retaliation for an insult by me because I didn't invite him to the last meeting of the Roundtable."

"Yes, Lancelot is arrogant and self-centered," said Merlin, "but why would he do this? I see no reason he would have Percival pay for your insult – if he knew about the insult and was offended by it, both of which are uncertain. You've let your emotion get the best of you, Arthur, just as when you were a youth."

"Don't always be reminding me of my youth." Arthur turned from Merlin toward Percival. "Look at him. How could I not be angry? He was on a mission for me. Is it just coincidence that he was nearly beaten to death?"

"I don't question the suspect timing of this assault or the depth of your anger but only caution you to be careful where you direct your anger. A beating such as this does not smack of Lancelot. If Lancelot wanted to kill Percival, he would not now be in that bed moaning. How could you even think such a thing is a possibility, even an unlikely possibility? It's disturbing, very disturbing. I cannot believe the extent of this sudden break between you and Lancelot."

Arthur backed down. "Realize, Merlin, I didn't say Lancelot did it. I just don't dismiss the possibility either. Aren't you the one who told me the unexpected often happens and distrust has always held you in good stead?"

"Well, yes. Although I believe the word was *doubt* not distrust. Doubt always held me in good stead."

"You're right in one thing, Merlin. This doesn't appear to be Lancelot's work, but that doesn't mean others did not do it on his behalf."

Merlin shook his head in exaggerated fashion. "Getting others to do his fighting does not smack of Lancelot either. This appears to me to be the work of peasants, and it may well be only what it appears to be and nothing more. Taking it at face value is a good assumption until you have evidence to the contrary. You realize, Arthur, the recent storm and the missing Grail have the peasants agitated. Peasants can be irrational, especially when they are frightened, and peasant irrationality may be the cause of this beating."

"Then, take a closer look at him, Merlin. See if your *sight* can tell you anything about what happened."

"I thought you didn't believe I have the sight," he said, and then under his breath, he mumbled, "At times I'm not certain myself. Can't always count on the sight. Not these days."

"Of course, I believe you have the sight – just that it isn't always reliable." The wizard appeared reluctant. He walked slowly to the bed, looking back once at Arthur, and stood silently over Percival. "Well? What do you see?"

Merlin did not answer at first but rather merely remained standing over Percival. He shook his head. "Nothing. I can see nothing. I'm sorry, Arthur, but I can't help you."

CHAPTER 26: **The Gift**

Raevil, noticing Gawain was not at the morning meal, looked to see if he was still asleep in his tent. He was not there. It was the day the Norse party was sailing for home, and Raevil wanted to make certain Gawain had not wandered off and gotten lost. He checked the village – he had seen Gawain playing with the children there several times – but there was no sign of him. Next he went down to the water's edge. In the distance he saw what could have been a pile of rags on the beach. As he got closer, Gawain's shape became more distinct. He was curled up, asleep, his back turned to the wind and a small mound of sand piled up against his body.

Raevil bent over and shook his shoulder. "Gawain, you need to get up." Gawain, groggy, opened his eyes. "You need to get up, Gawain. You don't want us to leave without you."

Gawain sat up and brushed the sand away from his face and out of his hair. "I wouldn't mind staying longer. I like it here. But I haven't seen my home and family in a long time."

Gawain stood up and with Raevil alongside him, walked to the edge of the sea. He dipped his hands into the water, cleaned the sand off them and splashed his face.

"How did you end up sleeping out here on the beach?"

Gawain dried his face with the sleeve of his tunic. "If I told you, you'd call me mad."

Raevil put a hand to his chest. "I swear I won't."

"I was trying to *blend* in with everything else."

"What!" Raevil studied Gawain's face to see if he was joking; he was not. "You're mad, Gawain." Raevil waited for him to continue, and when he did not, Raevil asked, "Aren't you going to explain yourself?"

As they started walking back to camp, Gawain attempted to explain in a casual, matter-of-fact tone of voice. "Each man spends his life seeing himself as more important, more special, more entitled than everyone else, and as being separate from everything else. At least, knights and the nobility see themselves that way. I don't know about peasants and tradesmen. I've always viewed things in a similar manner, but I had this dream, a vision of myself as a single oak leaf that had forgotten it was part of the tree."

Raevil looked more closely at Gawain. "What were you trying to do, Gawain? Attach back onto the tree?"

Gawain nodded. "Reattaching is a good way to describe it. One night I saw the village priest/magician on the beach sitting like a stone. He appeared to be sensing the air and the water and the sky in a way I didn't understand. He didn't seem to feel the wind, or if he did, he wasn't chilled by it. And he was touching the wet sand but wasn't disturbed by its moisture or grittiness. Understand?"

"I don't, no," said Raevil. "But I assume you tried to do what the magician was doing."

Gawain stopped walking and turned toward Raevil. "I tried and failed the first few times, but I succeeded on the night before last. I found myself floating."

Raevil frowned. "You were floating on the water?"

"No, I was floating in the air over our camp. And here is the most unusual part. I saw myself on the ground below."

Raevil waved his hand dismissively at Gawain. "Often when a person dreams, he doesn't know he is dreaming."

"It was no dream. Is what I experienced any stranger than Hauk seeing ghosts?"

"Ghosts are real."

"Is what I told you any more unusual than Hauk throwing an ax into water to appease Odin and rid himself of his specters?"

Raevil looked up at the sky. "Be careful, Gawain, what you say about Odin." Raevil's attention was drawn to something ahead of them. "We'd better hurry back to camp, Gawain. It looks we're almost ready to leave."

The Norsemen were loading their ship with their tents, weapons and food, and the skins they received in trade. Gawain quickly packed his few possessions and stored them in the vessel near his rowing station. He joined his shipmates, who were taking their leave of the villagers. Many of the children, who had come to know Gawain during the few days they were here, came to say goodbye.

There was one child in particular that Gawain wanted to see a last time. He sought out the youngest member of the village, a baby girl only a few months old who was being held by her mother. He did not know if the baby would recognize him, but when he brought his face close to hers and made an animal sound, the baby broke into a broad toothless smile and waved her arms excitedly up and down. He enjoyed this reaction. If the priest/magician could become as indifferent to this life as a stone, this infant fully embraced the smallest life experience. Gawain had learned to enjoy the two opposites, ignoring the physical world completely and being able to enjoy every aspect of it.

Gawain turned from the infant and mother and found himself face-to-face with the priest/magician. They had never spoken a word – neither knew the other's language – but they had developed a rapport during the nights they sat quietly on the beach a few feet from each other. The priest held his animal skin robe across his two arms and extended it toward Gawain. Gawain looked down at it. The priest extended the robe farther, and Gawain took it from him. He started to put it on but waited for the priest to nod his approval before continuing. He wrapped the fur around his shoulders and pulled the animal's head up over his own.

Even had Gawain been able to speak the priest's language, he would not have known what to say. Tears welling in his eyes, he smiled at the priest, who smiled back.

CHAPTER 27: **The Saxon Warlord Hengst**

Vortigern sat in a chair nervously tapping his fingers on the armrest. Mordred, who was sitting at the edge of his seat, stood up and angrily paced before the fireplace.

"I didn't realize we were going to have to chase Hengst all the way back to Germania just to speak to him," said Vortigern. "It was such a long voyage and even more difficult than I expected. Now Hengst keeps us waiting, not that the wait in itself bothers me. Well, actually it does, but what the wait symbolizes troubles me more. Hengst might not be much interested in our plan."

"You worry too much." Mordred's tone was dismissive.

Vortigern pointed at him. "And look at you, Mordred, pacing like an animal in a pen. I wish Morgan could have come with us. If she had, I'd feel better about this."

"You know it wasn't possible for her to come. She had to deal with both Arthur and Lancelot. And Lancelot would have been ornery and suspicious had she been away too long."

The great hall of Hengst's castle was not like any either man had ever seen. Rather than being the ground floor of the main tower, the great hall was a separate building connected to the tower. The reason for the unusual arrangement was apparent. The great hall had its own roof rising four stories high, and near the top of each of the four walls were four windows that could be opened or shuttered by long ropes hanging down almost to the floor. One set of windows, those on the west, was open to catch the late afternoon sun, which streamed across the great hall. The sunlight augmented by the many lit torches and oil lamps made the room almost as bright as the outdoors. The nature of the illumination was one reason this great hall was so unusual. The other was there was not a sword, lance, battleax or shield decorating the walls – most unusual for a warlord. Instead the walls were decorated with tapestries, all of them colorful but all having white as the dominant color.

Vortigern looked at Mordred. "You should sit down."

"I don't wish to sit down."

"Please, Mordred. You are in the castle of a powerful Saxon warlord we have not yet met. We cannot afford a display of your temper."

Mordred relented, although he stared angrily at Vortigern, and sat down.

"We should have no difficulty winning over Hengst," said Vortigern. "I don't know why we should be concerned."

Mordred crossed his legs and grunted. "You are the concerned one, not me."

"We have a very persuasive story to tell, one that will certainly appeal to him."

"Then, why does he keep us waiting this long?"
A Saxon appeared at the entrance of the great hall. He was young and thin, and he squinted as he looked at the Britons who had been kept waiting for Hengst. "My apologies. I have only just learned you were here and awaiting Lord Hengst. I am Narl, his advisor."

Vortigern stood to greet him. Mordred would have remained seated had Vortigern not poked his arm. "My apologies," said Narl. "At the moment, life at this castle is not as it usually is. I'm afraid Lord Hengst has not recovered from the loss of his brother."

"He has kept us waiting an unreasonable length of time," said Mordred, and Vortigern gave Mordred a disapproving look.

Narl did not appear angry or offended. "I will see if Lord Hengst is ready to receive you." He started to leave them, then turned back. "Please, be prepared. He might appear somewhat unusual to you – unusual in the manner of his dress, that is. It is his custom from time to time."

Mordred followed Narl's exit with his eyes as the Saxon advisor walked to the far end of the great hall and opened the door to what appeared to be a small chapel. A short time later Narl emerged from the room, followed by an older man who was tall, gray haired and stern looking. He was dressed in the white robe of a monk. The robe was what Narl had referred to as unusual.

Hengst was cordial in the manner of a man who was fulfilling a duty. "Sorry for keeping you waiting. I was praying. And sometimes when I pray, I wear a monk's robe to remind myself of the importance and power of prayer." Hengst introduced himself to his two visitors and sat in a chair opposite them while Narl stood at his right shoulder.

As Morgan instructed them before they left Britain, Vortigern began to make the case for why Hengst should send an army to assist in deposing Arthur from the throne of Britain. "Permit me, Lord Hengst, to give you an assessment of the situation in Britain and why it is ripe for conquest. The Roundtable has been severely weakened. Lancelot, the best of all the British knights, will not fight by Arthur's side, thanks to the work of our enchantress, the exquisite and clever Morgan le Fay. Three more of Arthur's best knights, Gawain, Percival and Bedivere, are dead. Uriens is too old to fight. Ector and Kaye are of no consequence."

Mordred, because of his young age and temperament, was told he should engage in the conversation only if necessary, but he could not resist making a point. "Agravain, a powerful knight, will fight with us."

"That is correct." Vortigern nodded to Mordred. "And many other of Arthur's knights, the skilled warrior Balin included, are off on a quest. Who knows when they will return?"

Hengst did not respond.

"Understand also, Lord Hengst," said Mordred, "that my army and I will pretend to fight with Arthur on his flank. Arthur is sentimental enough to welcome the support of his only son without questioning it. At the proper time, we will turn on him and compromise his flank."

"Yes," said Vortigern, "and it is likely Mordred will be close enough to Arthur to strike him down with his own hand. There will be no better time to attack Arthur. He will never be as weakened as he is now."

Hengst sat quietly and allowed Narl to respond. "What you say may be true – and we in no way doubt it – but we, too, have suffered loses. We, as you surely know, lost Lord Horsa and most of his army. Any invasion force we could mount now would be less than it would have been had Lord Horsa not been defeated."

"Your loss of troops is an issue that can also be argued in support of our proposal," said Mordred. "Your weakened circumstances might entice Arthur to send an army to attack you here. And might not such a siege result in the same outcome as happened at Horsa's castle? Isn't it better, with our support, to make the place of the battle Arthur's castle, not yours, and the time of the battle of our choosing – before Arthur can reconstitute the Roundtable?"

Hengst still sat quietly. Again Narl answered. "Of course, an attack on us here is a possibility we must give serious consideration to, but to take the offensive is likely a much greater risk."

"And what about avenging your brother, Horsa?" said Mordred. Vortigern squeezed his arm, but he continued. "He was decapitated. Did you know that? He was taken alive and decapitated like a common criminal."

Hengst's eyes opened wide at that comment. Finally Hengst began to speak – softly and as though he was far off in a dream state. "I am aware of what happened to Horsa but am not prepared for another military adventure. The last one failed completely and cost my brother his life. And I feel partly responsible."

Hengst now appeared more present than he had been a few moments before. "We – my brother Horsa and I – were certain he could easily withstand a siege. Having a British army in Germania would weaken the defense of the British homeland, we thought, and free me to establish a foothold in Britain. Establishing a foothold, or even mere coastal raids, we were certain, would force Arthur to bring warriors back to defend the homeland and in doing so, it would weaken, if not end, the assault on Horsa's castle. We would divide Arthur's forces to his detriment; that was the idea. Now I know that I should have sent men to Horsa's defense and should have helped end the British siege when I had the opportunity."

The sorrow and regret in Hengst's tone were powerful enough to prompt Mordred to remain quiet.

Hengst continued his explanation. "Also understand why I fought in the first place. It was not for mere conquest. Kings are kings by the will of God. Arthur became king by supposedly pulling a magic sword from a stone, a pagan superstition and no way to enthrone a king. Britain is full of superstition, heresy and debauchery. We hear tell of human sacrifices – an abomination in the eyes of God. And Arthur claims to be Christian but still allies himself with the Wizard Merlin." Hengst looked to his guests for confirmation, and Vortigern gave it to him with a nod of his head.

"Better to not be Christian in any manner than to be a corrupt one." Hengst looked directly at Mordred. "Forgive me, young man, if I give offense because I know your mother is said to possess some of the same skills as Merlin, but I cannot help but speak the truth." Hengst turned to Vortigern. "Your land is full of paganism and barbarism. To end paganism and barbarism is a worthy goal. And a king who claims to be Christian but remains in part pagan is more of an offense to God than a pagan king who admits what he is. But as I have already said, our plan, Horsa's and mine, was folly. Now he is dead, and I am full of regret."

Hengst finished, and the room remained in silence. Mordred needed an opening of some kind to continue to make their case. Hengst gave it to him.

"We have even lost the Holy Grail," Hengst said as an afterthought.

"I know where the Grail is," said Mordred. "That is, my mother knows."

Hengst was intrigued by this comment. "And she can return it to us?"

Mordred, suppressing a smile, shook his head. "It is in a British castle, and it will take a sizeable force of men to take it back from those who stole it, more men than Vortigern and I have."

Narl began to speak, but Hengst interrupted him to question Mordred further. "Do you have any conception of the power of the Grail?"

"I do not. But I do know it's in the wrong hands and should be taken back."

"It's far more powerful than you could possibly imagine." Hengst raised a clenched fist. "If what you say is true, it changes everything."

The nature and the tone of the conversation improved from that point forward. Hengst agreed to join Vortigern and Mordred in an attack on Arthur, although Mordred would not say whether the Grail was in Camelot or another castle. They spent the remainder of the afternoon discussing the Saxon preparations for an invasion of Britain and planning the nature and timing of the attack on Camelot. When the subject of expenses arose, Hengst excused himself to return to the chapel, leaving Narl and Vortigern to negotiate the details of how the British would help fund the Saxon invasion.

Vortigern was smiling when they finally left the castle at dusk.

But Mordred appeared angry. "Vortigern, why did you say I would probably kill Arthur during the battle?"

"Isn't that what you have said? Certainly, your mother has said as much."

"I did not mean it as a guarantee; neither did she. And if I challenged Arthur among his own warriors during the battle, I'd have little chance to escape alive."

"I didn't mean you would take on Arthur and his entire army. Besides, what does it matter what I tell Hengst? Once Hengst's army is in Britain, it will be too late for him to change his mind. And you will do as you please anyway. But there is another matter I need to discuss. What about our arrangement? You haven't changed your mind, have you? "

Mordred pulled a vial from under his tunic and offered it to Vortigern. "This is my part of the agreement."

CHAPTER 28: **Into the Mist**

The sea was mildly unsettled. The Norse ship rode up and down the rolling waves in a fairly steady rhythm. On the journey out, it would have been enough to disturb Gawain but not now on the return voyage. He had learned to be calm and to ride with the waves rather than resist them. And this he attributed to his sitting as the priest/magician had, or *stone-sitting*, as he thought of it, which he did every evening when the crew pulled in their oars for the night. He thought he was getting quite good at it although his success varied from night to night.

He had figured out where the ship was heading even before Raevil told him, back to the land of ice and burning mud. He was looking forward to visiting that strange land again, although he hoped Hauk was no longer having visits from ghosts. But he was not unduly fearful of Hauk. Gawain thought he had earned new respect among the Norse crew, even from One Eye, when the priest/magician gave him his special robe. Although he had it neatly put away now, it was his intention to wear it when they hiked to the village by the steaming pool. He assumed it would impress Hauk as it had the others.

The sea gradually calmed, and by sunset they put away their oars and let the ship drift without the aid of any wind. Gawain decided to stone-sit for a short time before going to sleep. The nature of his dreaming had changed – this too he attributed to stone-sitting. There was nothing special about the content of most of his dreams, but they had become far more realistic. He saw colors, heard sounds, engaged in extended conversations and most unusual of all, felt things such as the texture of stone against his fingers and the wood of the ship's hull against his feet.

That night there was nothing special about his stone-sitting, and he did not dream at all. In the morning, after they ate a meal, the crew took to their oars until the vessel caught the wind. They sailed the rest of that day and for a half dozen more days before the land of snow and the steaming pool came into view. They made for shore, and when they landed, they followed the same procedure on this visit as they did on the last, unloading what they needed to camp as well as some of the deerskin hides they acquired in trade.

Gawain put on his special robe and pulled the animal head up over his own.

They began their hike to the Norse settlement. Again Gawain enjoyed looking at the distant mountain peaks covered with snow and the fields of ice as well as the openness of the landscape and the absence of the presence of man. The journey seemed shorter this time, and before he expected it, the settlement by the steaming pool was just ahead of them.

Many of the settlers walked out to meet them. All of them, it seemed, were a little awed or frightened by the demonic horned animal face Gawain wore over his head. Even Hauk, who may not have recognized Gawain, seemed wary. Hauk engaged Alrood in conversation, and as Hauk listened, he nodded several times while his eyes remained on the strange animal skin.

Gawain thought he had surmounted another hurdle in his effort to get home; in watching Hauk's reaction he knew he would survive his stay in the Norse settlement here. But soon he would have to ask Alrood to put him ashore somewhere, anywhere, in Britain so he could make his way back to his family. He was uncertain how the Norseman and his crew would react to his request to leave.

That night Gawain waited until after dinner and after everyone else was asleep to walk to the edge of the steaming pool and stone-sit. He found a comfortable place to sit down, closed his eyes and tried to quiet his mind and shut down his senses. He rearranged his position a few times and opened his eyes more than once. Often he caught himself in thought, either memories of home or this voyage or his plans for when he finally returned to Britain. Each time he failed to concentrate, he tried again.

He didn't know the exact point of transition, but he succeeded in becoming like a stone. He was aware of the wind and the cold but did not sense them in the usual way; it was as though he was observing them from outside. That sensation, in fact, was the explanation. He was no longer inside his body. He was not floating in the air as he had done once before. He just was not in his flesh. And while his mind was quiet and dull in one sense, in another his mind had never been sharper and more active.

He began to move, not to leave one place for another but rather to spread out like a fog and cover more space. He became aware of the steaming pool sensing its wetness and heat. He extended toward the camp seeing all who slept inside their tents and feeling their breathing as their lungs and chests expanded out and sank back in. He reached the mountaintops, delighting in how the moonlight glistened on the snow. And he approached the burning mud, glowing red and occasionally flaring tongues of fire. He sensed its heat and was captivated by its bright color.

As much as he enjoyed all this, it lasted all too brief a time, and he found himself centering, returning to his core being while also remaining in this extended, vapor-like body. A white fog began to form around him. The fog grew denser, and as it did, he could make out the vague shapes of humanlike faces but perhaps not humans at all. The face of a woman with golden hair became the most distinct although she was little more than a specter. No words were spoken, but somehow they conversed.

Gawain had achieved a special status, she communicated to him. And somehow he already knew as much. He could see things most people could not; he could understand things most would refuse to even consider. And he was developing the *sight* like Merlin, the ability to see things not physically present and to anticipate the future. This ability was coming just in time, he was told, because Merlin was losing his powers. Gawain would become the next Merlin, the new Merlin.

This was both an honor and burden, but he did not understand how he could *become* Merlin.

One of the other shapes in the fog was communicating with him now. "Merlin" was a title not a name, it said, although the distinction was usually lost on the people around the wizard over time. The old

Merlin would soon be forgotten, and eventually people would not remember Gawain had ever been called by his original name.

But Merlin led such a strange life, living alone in the forest, dressing in rags, and talking in riddles. This was not for him, whether he was called Merlin or Gawain.

Times change, the lady communicated to him. Such things are no longer necessary although symbolic dress such as the robe he now owned and speaking in riddles could be useful in certain situations and with many people who took a more simplistic view of world.

Gawain became aware of dozens and hundreds of shimmering shapes surrounding him in the mist. Almost as soon as they became more distinct in form, they began to fade like stars blinking out behind clouds.

Gawain came out of his trance with a jolt. He bent forward and gasped to catch his breath. The experience was at once wondrous and frightening, but how could he be certain it was real? He wanted to experience it again to be sure it was not a dream, but he would not try again tonight and perhaps not for days. It had taken too much out of him.

Gawain got up from where he sat by the pool and walked to his tent. It took some time for him to fall asleep, and in the middle of the night, he awoke with a sense of dread. Something terrible had happened or was about to happen at home. He did not know what it was or how he knew, but he was sure of it. This was the beginning of his new life. He had to return to Britain as soon as possible.

GODS IN THE MIST

CHAPTER 29: **The Morning After**

Morgan awoke with one of the worst headaches she ever had. And she was confused, not remembering what day it was or even where she was. She heard loud snoring. She glanced over to see Lancelot, his back to her, rolled under a blanket. But the shape did not look like Lancelot, and now that she listened closer, the snoring did not sound like him either. And she was naked. She never went to bed without a nightgown.

She slowly and cautiously slipped out of bed, hoping what she was beginning to fear had not actually happened. She went around to the other side of the bed and saw one of the last people she ever wanted to share a bed with – fat, ugly, slovenly Vortigern. She felt faint and though she might have to sit down to keep from falling down.

How could this have happened? She searched her memory and remembered she and Mordred had been in a small chamber in Vortigern's castle having dinner to celebrate their alliance with Hengst and his Saxons. She remembered the room being dark except for two candles on the table and a small fire in the hearth. "Cozy," she remembered was the word Vortigern used to described the room. Now she realized he meant it to be romantic. There was not much food, and she remembered complaining she was hungry, but there was plenty to drink.

Vortigern had woven a trap for her, one that seemed so obvious now, and she had fallen into it. She felt faint again.

Why hadn't she been more wary? Mordred had been with them, and the presence of her son was one reason she had not sensed danger. But Vortigern found a reason to send Mordred away, and the two of them were left alone. She remembered they sat next to each other on a bench by the fire. She thought she would vomit as she recalled caressing his fat cheek, calling him "dear boy," and complimenting him on his eyelashes. His eyelashes! How drunk could she have been? One instant she was asking where was Mordred and where were the servants with the rest of their supper; the next instant she was suggesting she and Vortigern go to his bedchamber.

Remembering her aggressiveness was the thought that sparked her understanding. She might have been so drunk as to accept his invitation, although that was doubtful. But for her to have suggested they bed together meant more than just drink was involved. Somehow Vortigern had used magic on her.

All her plotting and scheming, all her cleverness and persuasion, this is what it had brought her to, the bed of a swine. For a few moments she considered abandoning her clever plot against Arthur and going somewhere to recover and forget what had happened to her – if it was possible to lose this memory. But no. She had waited a long time to exact her revenge on Merlin and Arthur. She could wait a little longer. And she could add another victim, Vortigern, to her list.

Morgan crossed the bedroom floor, unsteady on her feet, and found her dress and undergarments on a chair. She lifted the dress, and there underneath was the dagger she kept always strapped to her leg. She pulled the dagger from its sheath, walked back to the bed and stood over the snoring Vortigern trying to decide whether to stab him in the back or cut his throat.

A voice in her head said, *Don't; you still need him.*

"Yes, I still need him," she whispered. She could wait a few days to avenge herself on this swine. It might even be better to wait. She could give him hope he would bed her again, and after they had defeated Arthur, she would lead him to a bedroom, let him think he was going to take her again and then stab him to death.

She put the dagger away, hurriedly dressed and slipped out of the bedchamber. Her mind was muddled, and as she descended the tower stairs, she tried to think what kind of magic Vortigern might have used. There were several love incantations, but none of them really worked. Neither did mandrake root, despite what common people believed. The only magic that truly worked was Merlin's potion.

Merlin!

The thought caused her to pause on the staircase. Could Merlin have been involved? It made little sense because the old wizard never allied himself with Vortigern. But then, she, herself, was dealing with the likes of Vortigern, Hengst and Lancelot to advance her plans. Why would Merlin be any more discriminate in his choice of co-conspirators than she had been? There was no one else it could have been. Perhaps Merlin had suspicions about her and Vortigern plotting against Arthur. Of course, what better way to put an end to their alliance than this? It was almost a perfect plan. She could have easily killed Vortigern just now and fulfilled the old wizard's hopes.

She owed the old fool Merlin a long-standing debt, and she did not need him alive as she did Vortigern. Indeed, he was just wily enough to escape the doom she had planned for Arthur.

In that moment she vowed to kill Merlin at the first opportunity.

CHAPTER 30: **Vow in a Crypt**

Forty-nine men knelt in seven columns of seven rows. Each man was clad in a black robe, a scarlet cross over the left breast, a black hood pulled down far enough to conceal his face. The large crypt was dimly lit by two torches. Standing before a sarcophagus was a tall man in a black robe with a golden cross on the left breast, his hood also concealing his face. He led the group in a prayer, calling upon God to bless their mission and make it successful. The prayer ended, and he led them in a slow chant, deep voices emanating from their chests, the sounds resonating through the crypt and echoing off its stone walls.

The chant sounded almost supernatural in nature.

The chanting stopped, and everyone remained silent and still until the last echo faded. Their leader took a torch from the wall and lit a tall brazier. As it flamed up, he pulled a dagger from under his robe and laid the lower portion of the blade into the fire. The leader pulled back the sleeve of his robe, extended his right arm and turned it palm up to expose his forearm. The man in the first row of the first column stood and came forward. Waiting until the tip of the dagger was red hot, he pulled it from the flame and stood by the leader's side.

The leader lifted his head and spoke. "I swear by Almighty God that I shall seek the Grail and either return with it or die in the effort." The attendant pressed the red-hot dagger blade into his flesh. The leader never flinched and made no sound. The dagger was returned to the flame. The leader lifted his arm to show in the dim light the three-inch-long burn.

The attendant who had burned the leader now lifted his own sleeve and exposed his forearm. The leader pulled the dagger from the flame and burned the man's arm. He, like the leader, did not flinch and made no sound. One by one, starting with the man in the second row of the first column, the others came forward, made the same vow and were burned by the leader with the dagger blade. A few sucked in air loud enough to be heard, but none cried out. Several more shuddered when burned, but none moved his arm.

Narl came to the door of Hengst's chamber, knocked and was told to come inside. Hengst was sitting in a chair seemingly lost in thought. "I know this will not please you, Lord Hengst, but the abbot is here to see you."

Hengst looked up at Narl. "Who?"

"The abbot."

"Brother Mark, the meddlesome monk! Can't you put him off?"

"I tried, Lord Hengst, and was fortunate enough to hold him at bay this long. He insists on seeing you on a matter of great urgency."

Hengst sighed. "Very well." He rose from his chair and walked with Narl down to the great hall, where the young abbot awaited him. Brother Mark was a sickly looking young man but had a well-deserved reputation for being intense and unyielding. The two men exchanged greetings, and the abbot moved his eyes from Hengst to Narl, signaling he wanted a private conversation with the warlord.

"Ah yes, you may leave us, Narl," said Hengst. "Thank you." As Narl took his leave, Hengst pointed to a chair. "Please sit down."

"Thank you, no. I'll be brief, but please do not be deceived by my brevity. The matter I wish to discuss is very serious." Hengst, who stood almost a head taller than the monk, opened his eyes wide in anticipation of what the abbot had to say. "I have heard talk of a secret group, a secret society. . ."

"That rumor?" Hengst dismissed the comment with a wave of the hand. "There is always such talk."

"And this secret society has been formed in the name of God or so I am told."

"You may have heard as much, Brother Mark, but have you actually witnessed this yourself? I need not tell you that all manner of rumor may be heard here as well as in any other castle."

"No, I have not witnessed it myself. But know, Lord Hengst, any secret society invoking the name of God must be contained within the auspices of the church. All things pertaining to the Almighty are the province of the church. We cannot let every man decide what God means us to do and what is right and what is wrong."

"I am not every man."

The abbot bowed. "Of course, not. You are my lord when it comes to all things temporal, but when it comes to the eternal, you are part of my flock. The whole reason God created his church was to serve as intermediary between himself and the faithful." The abbot hesitated and softened his tone. "I know I vex you, but I never trouble you about affairs of state. I only speak to you about those things that are part of my responsibility."

"I appreciate your discretion, Brother Mark, and we have no quarrel in that regard." Hengst motioned to a chair. "Are you certain you won't take a seat?"

"Thank you, but no."

"Why tell me all this now? Is this the matter of urgency you wanted to see me about, this rumored society?"

"Yes, but there is more. I have heard – I cannot say where – that there will be, or has been, a blood ceremony held with God being called upon to serve as witness. It is said warriors will be asked, or have already been asked, to swear to return from your expedition to Britain with the Grail or to forfeit their lives. Such an oath is neither pleasing to God nor sanctioned by the church."

Hengst broke into a broad smile. "You say I think you vex me. Actually I admire your courage to come here to speak to me as you have, Brother Mark. Few men would dare to." He rested a hand on the abbot's shoulder. "Such rumors would occur naturally because of my expedition to Britain, but I can assure you I know of no blood ceremony and will not permit any of my warriors to participate in one. Now, has your mind been put at ease?"

"Yes, it has. That assurance is what I came for. Thank you, Lord Hengst."

As Hengst withdrew his arm from the abbot's shoulder, the monk noticed the burn mark. "You were recently injured, Lord Hengst?"

"Yes, but it is nothing."

As the new day began, Hengst's army was assembled in the courtyard. Every other member of the castle – ladies and children, house servants and stable boys, the elderly and the infirm – lined the periphery of the courtyard or watched from atop the castle walls. Brother Mark, attended by two of his monks, stood before the assembled army. At his signal, first the warriors, including Hengst, followed by all the observers, knelt. The abbot performed a brief prayer ceremony asking God to bless Hengst and his men on their journey to Britain and to protect them from harm. As he prayed, Brother Mark spread out his arms and raised his eyes toward the heavens. When he finished, he hung his head and remained silent.

The two attending monks lit incense burners they held by thick chains. They positioned themselves on either side of the abbot. Brother Mark raised his head and slowly walked through the ranks of the kneeling soldiers, blessing them by tracing a cross in the air over their heads while his attendants waved the smoking incense at them. The ceremony did not end until the abbot had blessed every warrior.

Hengst stood up and called his men to order. He pulled on his helmet, and the others followed his lead. The warriors lined up in more than a dozen columns across the courtyard while the onlookers scurried to line the main gates and the road leading away from the castle.

With Hengst in the lead, his advisor Narl at his side, they marched out to the cheers of the onlookers. People waved at them, patted them on the arms and shoulders as they went by, and handed them flowers as they exited the castle and began their journey to Britain and their hoped-for conquest of Camelot.

CHAPTER 31: **Escape**

Gawain came up behind Raevil as he was carrying the last of his gear to their vessel. He tapped Raevil's shoulder. "I must speak to you."

Raevil turned toward him. "You look very serious, Gawain. Is there a problem?"

Momentarily forgetting Raevil was the only Norseman who understood his language, Gawain checked to see he could not be overheard. "I must get home. Twice Alrood has saved my life, and I don't know how much more I can ask of him." Raevil smiled, which Gawain interpreted as meaning that he was being foolish if he was considering asking Alrood to take his vessel off course and put Gawain ashore in Britain.

"I think I know what you are about to say, Gawain, and there is no reason to worry. Alrood is not satisfied with what we received in trade. The voyage has not been profitable enough considering its length." When Gawain did not immediately respond to this comment, Raevil playfully shoved his shoulder. "Don't you understand, Gawain? There is no need to ask Raevil for a favor. We are going to Britain."

Gawain smiled, then quickly frowned. "To raid?"

"Naturally. And I assume you plan to sneak away after we land?"

Gawain could not possibly be party to one of the Norse bloody raids. It was one more compelling reason to leave this company. "Yes, my plan now is to sneak away. No sense asking permission to leave if we are making a landfall in Britain. The answer might well be no."

The Norse ship with men at their oars put to sea in the morning. For the first time since he left Horsa's castle many days before, Gawain was moving in the direction of home. Knowing he was heading to Britain increased his energy and strength, and he rowed harder than he ever had. There was little wind that day, and he rowed long as well as hard. At night when it came time to sleep, he started to nod off as he was eating his supper. He decided to save what was left of his meal and carefully wrapped it away. He would need it later as he walked from whatever coastal landing the Norse made to the nearest British town or castle.

He soon fell asleep.

Some nights on this journey he had difficulty distinguishing strange experiences from dreams, but this time he knew he was dreaming. Even so, it was a special dream. He was observing a conversation in a castle. Several dark figures were sitting in a dimly lit hall by a fire. He could not make out any of their faces nor could he hear what they were saying, only an unintelligible murmuring. But somehow he knew they were conspirators. That was the reason their faces were not visible and their words not audible to him. And they were plotting something dire.

The dream disturbed Gawain. He did not fully awaken but turned over and repositioned himself on the ship's hard hull. Soon he was dreaming again. Now he was seeing a vessel. He could barely make out its shape in the fog. More of it became visible, and it was clearly a war ship. His vantage point had changed. He was much higher, and he could see the fog breaking up in various places, and everywhere the view was clear he saw another war ship. It was an invasion fleet.

Gawain awoke. He pulled himself up to a sitting position and looked about the vessel. Everyone else was asleep. The dream haunted him. He knew wizards and enchanters claimed they could see the future in dreams. He was neither a wizard nor an enchanter, at least not yet, but he had been told by the figures in the mist he had become a *seer*. This might be his first vision, his first test, his first important mission.

Gawain reached over the side of the ship, dipped his hand into the cold sea and wet his face as he began to consider the possible meaning of the dream. One part was easy. The invasion fleet had to be Saxon. It would not be the first group of Saxons to invade Britain; Arthur had beaten them back several times before. And it was not a stretch of logic to consider that Hengst was retaliating for the defeat and execution of his brother Horsa.

With this as the context, the unintelligible conversation among the dark figures was also easy to decipher. Hengst had one or more collaborators among the British. If his dream was prophetic, then Gawain was meant to get home in time to warn Arthur.

They spent several more days at sea. Gawain used the time visualizing how he would sneak away from the Norsemen and determining how much food he should try to carry with him. There was a slight chance the Norsemen might excuse his leaving, but there was no doubt they would object to the theft of their food. He also attempted to calculate how long it would take him to travel – on foot, by horseback, aboard ship – from the north of Britain, where they were likely to land, south to Camelot. Traveling on foot would take too long. He would need to acquire a horse or a ride aboard a ship even if it meant contact with the barbarous Picts.

They finally made landfall one night well after sunset. Gawain knew where they were, in the very north of Britain in the land of the Picts. The Norsemen pulled their vessel ashore and began to make camp. It was too late in the day to raid. They would spend the night here and raid the nearest village in the morning.

Gawain, concealing his cache of food in his blanket, bedded down by a fire on the edge of the encampment. Pretending to be asleep, his eyes scanned the camp checking to see if the others were asleep. They appeared to be. It was time to get moving.

He stood and casually walked across the camp to see if he would attract any attention. He did not. He went back to where he had been pretending to sleep, strapped on his sword, rolled up his bedding and slung his sack of food over his shoulder. "Oh no," he said to himself. He had left his animal robe in the ship, and one or more of the crew might be sleeping aboard the vessel. He briefly considered leaving it behind but decided he had to retrieve it. Resting his load on the ground, he walked to the ship and cautiously looked into its interior.

Of all people, it was One Eye who was asleep in the bow of the ship, and of all the incredibly bad luck, his head was resting on the sack containing Gawain's robe.

Gawain stood over the sleeping Norseman pondering the two most obvious options: leaving the robe or slitting One Eye's throat. Neither was acceptable. An idea entered his mind, perhaps one Merlin might have suggested because of its audacity. He climbed into the ship, grabbed a deerskin pelt and rolled it up. He knelt next to One Eye and gently shook his shoulder. The Norseman opened his good eye but was not fully awake. "You are resting on my sack, and I need it." Gawain pointed to the bag his head was resting on. Confused, One Eye lifted his head to see what Gawain was talking about. Gawain quickly substituted the pelt for the sack with the robe. "Never mind," he said with a wave of his hand. One Eye rested his back down, adjusted the deerskin and went back to sleep.

Gawain smiled. The maneuver had been almost too easy.

He hurried back to his sleeping spot and retrieved the rest of his load. It might be safer to walk a distance along the shore before turning inland, although he was certain that if he were caught sneaking off into the night, the direction of his travel would not spare him punishment or death. He walked along the beach, casting an occasional glance back at the camp. He thought he saw a figure moving in the darkness but decided it must be his imagination because a Norseman would either give an alarm or attack him, not follow him silently. Soon he was out of sight of the camp, but again he saw a figure in the darkness, and this time he was certain it was a man. He quickened his pace. So did the figure behind him.

"Gawain." It was Raevil. His one friend among the Norsemen had caught up with him. "I wanted to say goodbye."

"Thank you Raevil, but you take a risk leaving the camp like this."

Even in the dark Gawain could see the pained expression on his face. "I considered going with you."

"Then, come with me. You were born a Briton, and I cannot imagine you are at heart a Norse raider."

"No, I'm not, Gawain. Not me. They kill every living thing. Sometimes I worry they'll see I don't fully engage in their blood lust and I will pay the price for it. But, Gawain, I cannot go with you. My life all these years has been with them. I even have a Norse wife and young child. But I wish you well."

"I understand, Raevil." Gawain grabbed the young man by the arm and squeezed it. "I thank you for your friendship and wish you good fortune. Now please return to the camp before you are caught with me."

It was too much to ask a man to give up his whole life, especially when it involved a woman and a child, even if he found parts of that life unpleasant or dangerous. He left Raevil, knowing he would never see him again.

Gawain continued his journey south, moving inland in search of a path or road. Travelling on foot was far too slow. He had to find a horse or a boat. If it had been bad luck that the Norsemen landed far north in Pictland, he might have had a change of fortune in the nature of a light he now saw in the forest. He followed the light through the woods toward its source. As he walked closer, he saw there were actually several campfires. He laid down his load and carefully moved through the trees and underbrush for a better look. Even before he could see the encampment, he heard the whinny of a horse.

It was a Pict encampment and a fairly large one. Most Britons never said the word "Pict" without prefacing it with "barbarous." But they were not as murderous as the Norsemen he had just left. They, like he, were Celt, even though they were of a different tribe, and he needed their help.

Gawain unrolled his animal skin robe, put it on, lifted the animal head over his own and walked toward the Pict encampment.

CHAPTER 32: **Wizard's Sleep**

The cawing of a crow perched high on a tower windowsill was the only sound in the courtyard of Vortigern's castle. A servant held the reins of two horses, their breath streaming out white in the cold morning air. Mordred exited the tower and quickly mounted his horse. Morgan followed him. Vortigern, with the little hair he had left on the top of his head plastered down with oil, was a step behind her.

"Must you leave so soon?" said Vortigern. "I feel we are just beginning to know each other."

She turned back to face him and whispered so Mordred could not overhear. "I think we have gotten to know each other a little too well and much too fast." She smiled at him and playfully pinched his cheek. "Just because we had one adventure, dear boy, doesn't mean we will have another anytime soon. But keep trying. It's the only way to succeed."

He appeared love sick. She knew the look. He followed her lead and spoke in a low voice. "It wasn't just an adventure for me."

She grabbed hold of his cheek and gave it a good squeeze. "I really must be going, or do you want to call off our plan and end our alliance with Hengst? There are things I must attend to, or you will never see the inside of Camelot."

"I'll help you up onto your horse."

"I can mount him myself." He assisted her up anyway.

Morgan and Mordred turned their horses around and rode out the castle gate and toward Camelot. Mordred, a sly smile on his face, looked over at his mother. "What was that whispered exchange with Vortigern about?"

"Nothing." Her tone was dismissive. "I get weary of men fawning over me, which is why you are going to see Lancelot."

"Me! Why me? You have a much better *relationship* with him."

Morgan showed a flash of anger. "I don't like the way you said 'relationship.' And I don't think I like the look on your face either. Whatever has transpired between Lancelot and me benefits you. Or have you forgotten? But I am almost as tired of Lancelot as I am of Vortigern, although my tolerance for Vortigern is completely exhausted. As soon as we no longer have need of him. . ."

"You will kill him, I know. Just be certain to wait until he is of no further use."

"Let me be concerned about Vortigern. Your immediate task concerns Lancelot. This is what you need to tell him."

"Mother, I know what to tell him. I've heard all this before."

"You must work it into casual conversation. Don't make Arthur the purpose of your visit. Say you were looking for me, but as you converse with Lancelot, be certain to mention Arthur is jealous of him."

"Yes, of course."

"Even more important, you must say Arthur doesn't believe Lancelot is all he pretends to be. The more you stress that Arthur believes Lancelot hides behind a false face the better."

"Don't worry. I am my mother's son and will get Lancelot worked into a state of great agitation."

Late in the morning Camelot became visible in the distance. Mordred continued south while Morgan turned east and rode to Camelot. She smiled when she saw the peasants who had taken up residence in hovels outside the castle walls. These farmers, she knew, were among those whose homes and crops were wiped out in the great storm and had come here in desperation. If not much of a threat to Arthur, they were at least a reminder he was being held responsible for their plight. As Morgan rode among them, their Druid leader stood watching her. He nodded subtly to her, and she nodded back just as subtly.

Morgan entered through the castle gate, gave her horse to a servant to stable and feed, and paused before entering the tower to dab a little powder around her eyes. Once she began to tear, she entered the great hall walking slowly, her head hung low.

Arthur hurried to greet her, his smile turning to a frown when he noticed her eyes. "You've been crying." He took her by the shoulders. "Are you well?"

She wiped moisture from her eyes. "I'm just upset."

"Come sit by the fire and tell me about it." He put his arm around her and walked her to the hearth.

She sat head down, eyes lowered. "There is no use in speaking about it."

"It always helps to talk about the things upsetting us, and there is certainly no harm in doing so. We've had intimate talks before."

"It's Lancelot, his temper. It's terrible."

She could see the simmering anger in Arthur's eyes. "And are you the brunt of it?"

"No, not me, not so much. Usually it's the servants but sometimes also his warriors and even closest advisors. It's very unpleasant to observe and creates constant tension in the castle."

Arthur looked away as though searching for an answer. "I'm both shocked and disappointed by this news. Lancelot continues to surprise and disappoint me. But I must say I have never seen his temper except in battle."

"Of course not." Morgan caught herself. She was becoming too animated for the mood she wanted to project. "No, you would not have seen it," she said in a softer voice. "He only displays it before those he is superior to." She wiped away a tear. "And the things he says about you. I couldn't stand it any longer. I said, 'Lancelot, if you don't respect Arthur, your king, at least respect me, your lover. I'm Arthur's sister and should not be obliged to hear these things.'" Arthur turned red with anger. "I haven't slept well or eaten well in days."

Arthur stood up, walked closer to the fireplace and stared at the flame. "Things are as bad with Lancelot as I thought." He looked back at her. "Your association with him is over, then?" She nodded and wiped away more tears. Arthur took a deep breath as he composed himself. "Let's get you something to eat."

"I'm not hungry, Arthur."

"Exactly why you should eat. You'll feel stronger, and it will help you put all this behind you, although I really don't know what to do about Lancelot except never to count on him again."

Arthur went to the kitchen and instructed the cook to prepare a meal for two. Soon he and Morgan were eating by the fire. She kept a close eye on his expression. Although his conversation was light, he still appeared troubled.

There was a figure in the shadows at the far end of the hall.

"Merlin," Arthur called to him. "Here you are appearing unexpectedly as usual and as often happens when there is food to be eaten. Come sit down."

The arrival of Merlin immediately improved Arthur's mood. Morgan could see that her half brother was still reliant on the old wizard, and she worried Merlin might undo some of what she had managed to accomplish recently with Arthur. One more reason to hate the old fool.

Arthur told a servant to bring more food and another plate. Merlin uncharacteristically sat down without saying a word. He did not speak until after he was served and had eaten several mouthfuls of food. And then he spoke as though far away. "I have a feeling, Arthur, a foreboding."

"About what?"

"I'm certain about the feeling but not its cause. Of course, it takes no special sight or wisdom to see signs of trouble here. Too many of your best knights are spread all over Britain in search of that damnable Grail, and angry peasants now live just outside your walls. I feel the kingdom is vulnerable."

Arthur showed a flash of anger. "You, yourself, said I had to make the effort to find the Grail."

"Perhaps I was wrong," said Merlin. "The solution to an immediate problem may have created a problem of longer duration."

Arthur slammed his goblet down on the table. "That is just what I needed to hear from my advisor."

"Don't be annoyed with me, Arthur." Merlin was not his normal combative self. "I have grown very old and don't see things as clearly or with as much confidence as I once did."

Morgan decided to enter the conversation. "There is a simple solution to this problem, Merlin. Arthur should just send other men to retrieve the knights on the Grail quest."

"On the other hand," said Merlin, "finding the Grail – if it can be found and I doubt that it can be – is also important."

"Make up your mind, Merlin." Morgan turned toward Arthur. "Does he always speak in such contradictions? What good is his advice if. . ." The sight of Percival entering the great hall caused her to pause in mid-sentence.

Most of the swelling was gone from Percival's eye although it remained discolored. There were cuts and bruises on his cheeks and forehead, and he walked with a slight limp and with a hand to his chest where several ribs had been broken. He teetered for a moment before regaining his balance. Arthur and Merlin rushed to help him.

Morgan was shaken by the sight of a knight she thought dead, but she quickly recovered. This was her best chance to deal with Merlin because he and Arthur had their backs to her and Merlin's drink sat unguarded on the table. She fumbled to open a small metal box she had hidden in her sleeve. She dug a nail under the latch and pulled hard. The box snapped open too easily. Yellow powder spilled onto the table, and Morgan cursed to herself. She quickly dumped some of the remaining yellow powder into Merlin's goblet. She began to brush the spilled powder on the tabletop into her hand intending to put it too into Merlin's goblet, but she noticed Arthur, who was assisting Percival to a chair, was turning toward her. She swept the powder to the floor and again cursed to herself.

Percival took a seat at the table, and Arthur called for more food.

"What happened to you, Percival?" Morgan asked.

Arthur answered for him. "Percival was brought to us in a hay cart badly beaten and barely conscious." He looked to Percival. "Do you still not remember what happened to you?"

"No, I think I dreamed about it last night, but I don't remember the dream."

"Well, Percival, you look much better today," said Arthur. "I'm sure it will come back to you soon, and then, we can deal with whoever attacked you."

Merlin took a swallow from his goblet. At first, he paid attention to the conversation between Arthur and Percival. Morgan was careful to note, however, that Merlin did not join in. Soon he lost interest in what they were saying, and she saw him yawn. A few moments later his eyes fluttered and closed momentarily. It was not long before the old wizard could not keep his eyes open. Morgan said nothing, but Merlin drew attention to himself when he began to snore. A small portion of the powder had worked too quickly. He needed to have taken more of it for a fatal dose.

Arthur laughed and grabbed the wizard by the arm. "Wake up, Merlin. You are not so old and worn that you should be excused for falling asleep at the supper table." But Merlin did not awaken. Arthur shook his arm with more force, and he still did not stir. Arthur dipped his fingers into his water goblet and gently wet Merlin's face. No reaction. "I have never seen him like this."

"He is old, very old," said Morgan. "Old men fall asleep at supper and at the most inopportune times."

"I don't think this is a natural sleep."

"Perhaps he is ill as well as old."

Arthur called for help from the servants in the kitchen. He asked one to stay with Percival, who insisted he needed no assistance, and with the help of a second carried Merlin to a bedchamber. They placed him onto the bed, and Arthur gently covered him with a blanket.

"Stay with him," Arthur said to the servant. "Let me know if he awakens or has any distress or difficulty breathing."

"Arthur." Morgan was in the doorway behind him. "You are being overly concerned."

"You, yourself, said he is very old and possibly ill. This seems to be a time of caution for many reasons."

He started to leave the bedchamber.

"Where are you going?" she asked.

"To recall the Grail knights. I hope I can get them back before Merlin's bad feeling, whatever its cause, comes to fruition."

CHAPTER 33: **The Picts**

Gawain, dressed in his animal skin robe, stood at the edge of the Pict camp. All the Picts appeared to be asleep, and there was so little moonlight he might have been able to sneak in without being seen. However, if he tried to steal a horse and any of the horses tethered at the edge of the camp gave a sound, he would likely be caught. So, he made the first of several difficult decisions he would have to make this night and walked boldly into their camp. He slowly went to the center of scores of sleeping warriors and stood by the most central of their campfires.

"I bring you a warning," he said in a voice loud enough to awaken most of the camp.

Groggy Picts opened their eyes and looked at the strange sight of what appeared to be a half-man/half animal. The combination of his strange appearance and the boldness of his sudden arrival among them may have caused the majority of Picts to wonder if he might be a supernatural being. In any case, they hardly moved.

One man, who had propped himself up on an elbow, slowly reached for his sword. Gawain, noticing him from the corner of his eye, pointed a finger at him. "Leave your sword sheathed." And the man did as he was told. Gawain looked around the group. "Who is your leader?"

A battle-worn man with long white hair stood up. "I'm Caelleigh." The other Picts also stood up. Gawain was surrounded by them.

"I am Merlin," said Gawain. This was the second decision he had made. He was certain these men knew of the wizard but doubted any of them knew what Merlin looked like. If incorrect in that belief, it would be a fatal mistake. He took the risk because a warning from Merlin would be taken far more seriously than a warning from Gawain. He again looked around the Pict warriors. So far, his bluff was succeeding. "I bring you a warning, and I ask a favor in return." He looked at Caelleigh, who nodded for him to continue.

Gawain had come to his third and final decision, the one causing him the most consternation. Raevil was his friend; Alrood twice saved his life. But the Norsemen were ruthless raiders who killed every man, woman and child they encountered on their raids. As savage as most Britons considered the Picts, they were less barbarous than Norsemen. "There is a Norse raiding party not far from here," said Gawain.

There are few things he could have said that would have drawn a stronger reaction from the Picts, who began to talk excitedly among themselves. Caelleigh held up his hand. "Quiet." And when they grew silent, he continued. "How many Norsemin and where are they?"

"One ship. About two dozen men. But first the favor. Although Britons and Picts are often enemies, we are all Celts, and we now face a common enemy."

"The Norsemin," said Caelleigh.

"Worse than the Norsemen. Saxons. Worse, because the Saxons are coming to conquer not just to raid. Their target is not here. It is Britain. But if Britain falls, you will have a hostile neighbor to the south, one that might well plan the conquest of you next." He paused to allow them to weigh his words. "I ask only for a horse so I can warn the Britons as I have warned you this night and give them the opportunity, as I have given you, to defend themselves."

Gawain could not determine if the Pict leader was confused, doubtful or fearful. "You're sayin' there is both Norsemin nearby and Saxons on the way?"

"Yes, Norsemen nearby," said Gawain. "And a fleet of Saxon warships under sail." Caelleigh looked at his men as though not certain what to make of these claims. "I will tell you where the Norse are, and after you have dealt with them, you will lend me a horse. Agreed?"

Caelleigh again looked to his men and said finally, "Agreed – if all is as you say."

Raevil had to relieve himself. He got up from his blanket, left the warmth of the fire and walked to the edge of the small Norse camp. He was about to urinate on a tree when he heard the snap of a twig and looked in the direction of a sound. He heard a grunt and was about to call out when a thrown ax sliced into the middle of his chest and split open his rib cage. He fell to the ground making a gurgling sound as Picts, shouting battle cries, ran out of the woods and attacked the Norse camp.

Caelleigh led the assault and with his sword hacked down a Norseman who was just getting to his feet. The Picts struck down two more Norsemen before the raiders could defend themselves. As the Picts swarmed into the camp, the Norsemen grabbed their weapons and met the challenge. The Norsemen, wielding their axes, were more than a match for the Picts individually, but they were outnumbered. Alrood was holding off two attackers by swinging his ax in a double circle from left to right and back again. The Norseman next to him was engaged with one attacker but was struck down from behind by a second. Another Norseman was felled nearby.

Alrood managed to cut one of his attackers across the belly, but the man was able to stay on his feet. Alrood used a forward swing of his ax to hold off the second attacker on his left and a backhand to finish the wounded man on his right. With only one Pict to deal with, Alrood was able to steal looks around the battle. "We are greatly outnumbered," he shouted. "To the boat."

Shouting to one another the Norsemen backed toward their vessel, coming closer together to form a defensive line. A few of them at the rear pushed their ship into the water, but it appeared the Picts would not be content to simply drive them off and continued to fight them as they approached the edge of the sea.

One Eye gave an animal-like shout and tore into the Picts, swinging his ax wildly with two hands. The Picts backed off. More of the Norsemen reached their ship. One Eye again charged the Picts, challenging at least a half dozen of them. The Picts responded by encircling him. One Eye took a cut to his leg and a blow to his left arm. A Pict charged in and stabbed the wild Norseman in the side.

In retaliation One Eye took off his head with a swing of his ax. A Pict charged from the other side and delivered another thrust to the Norseman's side. One Eye lowered his weapon and staggered. He was knocked to the ground, and as he lay prone, the Picts continued to chop and stab at him with their swords.

The remaining Norsemen reached their ship and quickly put to sea, leaving behind more than a half-dozen dead.

At the Pict camp, Gawain sat motionless by the fire. His two guards rested nearby. Gawain kept as still he could and fixed his eyes in a stare, thinking the more bizarre his behavior, the more wizard-like he would appear. One of the guards soon tired of watching the motionless man wearing the strange animal skin with the dead creature's head worn like a helmet, and he nodded off to sleep. His companion woke him. But the next time the first guard fell asleep the second did as well.

Seeing the two guards sleeping, Gawain laughed to himself, a rare bit of relief in a tense night, and he waited patiently for Caelleigh and the others to return.

Gawain heard the sounds of horses in the night forest and thought the Picts were returning too soon to have fought a battle. What if they had not found the Norse raiders? They would consider him a fraud and likely not give him another chance. His guards heard the approaching horses as well and got to their feet. The returning Picts rode into camp, and Gawain noticed there were several corpses strapped over their horses.

Caelleigh rode up to Gawain and dismounted. "Thank you, Merlin. We found the Norsemin and drove 'em off. We lost some men but inflicted more casualties than we received."

Gawain took a moment to compose himself. He had almost forgotten he had used the wizard's name. "And the horse for me?"

Caelleigh motioned behind him. "There's four men, as you see, who no longer have need of a horse. Choose among their mounts."

Gawain gave the Pict leader a slight bow in appreciation for the gift. He selected a horse, and although Caelleigh invited him to spend the night in the Pict camp, Gawain rode off immediately. In Britain, Merlin had a reputation for wandering the woods at night and foraging in the forest for his food. Whether the Picts knew about that reputation or not, it was safer to act as the real Merlin would have.

Gawain traveled a short distance from the Pict camp and waited to make certain he was not being followed. He then retrieved the rest of his belongings and his store of food, which were hidden in the hollow of a tree, and continued his journey south.

He rode during most of the night and reached the coast as a great orange sun was rising over the sea. Gawain paused to watch the bright beams of sunlight shoot skyward through a low bank of clouds. It was a marvelous sight. But it was another impressive sight that stole his attention. A distance out to sea, appearing as small as sea birds, a large fleet of ships was anchored.

CHAPTER 34: **Saxon Arrival**

Vortigern, his chief advisor Kierwyn by his side, stood atop the wall of his castle watching the Saxon army approaching in the distance. "Can you estimate their number, Kierwyn?"

The advisor held up a hand to shade his eyes from the sun and squinted. "Not yet. There could be many more of them beyond the hill."

The two men were silent for a time as the figures in the lead of the Saxon force became larger and more distinct and more Saxons came up over the distant hill. Vortigern, without taking his eyes off the approaching army, said to Kierwyn, "I hope there are enough of them to defeat Arthur. It will require a sizeable force."

"One thing is for certain. There are more than enough of them to take this castle if they turn out to be treacherous."

Vortigern looked at his advisor with an expression exhibiting both anger and worry. "Why do you say that? I know you don't approve of my bargain with the Saxons, but why would you make such a comment?

"Just estimating their number is all," said Kierwyn apologetically.

"Find a better way to estimate their number, then." Vortigern turned back to look at the Saxons. "I wish Morgan were here."

"Why isn't she?"

"You know full well. She and Mordred are to pretend to be allies of Arthur."

Kierwyn emitted a low grunt. "I don't trust either one of them, especially Mordred."

"Well there, Kierwyn, is where you are wrong. I made a private arrangement with Mordred, and he did exactly as he said he would." Vortigern held a finger in Kierwyn's face. "But you are to tell no one of my arrangement, no one."

He grunted again. "I still don't trust them."

The Saxons were close enough for Vortigern to recognize tall Hengst in the lead. "I must prepare to meet them. I don't want Hengst to find me here watching his approach like a peasant. Bring him to the great hall, Kierwyn. I'll receive him there."

Vortigern hurried down from the castle wall and up to his bedchamber, where he changed into his favorite tunic and smoothed down his sparse hair with oil. He went down to the great hall, positioned several chairs by the fireplace, and picked one to sit in. And there he sat with stiffened back awaiting the Saxon warlord.

He heard the sound of footsteps entering the vestibule. Kierwyn appeared first in the great hall. Behind him came Hengst, the same tall, severe-looking man he had met in Germania but more impressive looking wearing armor rather than a monk's robe. Hengst carried his helmet in the crook of his right arm, and with a warrior on either side of him and his advisor Narl in the rear, he approached Vortigern, who stood to greet him.

"Welcome, Lord Hengst." Hengst did not smile or soften his stern expression and merely nodded a greeting to Vortigern. "Please sit down."

Hengst took a seat. Narl stood by his right shoulder; the two Saxon warrior escorts remained a few steps back. Hengst began the conversation with a complaint. "I thought, Vortigern, you would have assembled more of an army than the number of men I saw in your courtyard. Are you relying primarily on me to defeat Arthur?"

"Agravain has not yet joined us, and remember Mordred and his men will pretend to protect Arthur's flank. We have far more men than you've seen here, but, yes, you and your men are an important part of this effort."

"We've no time to wait for Agravain. He should be here already. One cannot land an army as large as the one I brought here and have it stay a secret for long. We must assume Arthur will be warned and will use the time to gather troops and prepare his defense. We can't give him more time than we are forced to. My men will camp outside your walls tonight, and tomorrow we will march on Camelot."

"And Agravain? Should we not wait for him?"

"He has until morning to join us." Hengst leaned forward toward Vortigern. "Mordred promised me the Grail. Is it here?"

This question made Vortigern uncomfortable. "Only Mordred's mother Morgan knows where it is, although it may well be in Camelot."

"I am a man who keeps his word, and I will hold you and Mordred to yours."

At first light the next day, the two armies ate their morning meal and assembled for the march south, Vortigern's men gathering in the courtyard, Hengst's Saxons just outside the castle walls. Vortigern rode ahead of his men to be in the lead of the joint forces with Hengst. He could not help but notice dozens of Hengst knights were clad in identical black tunics with a scarlet cross over the left breast and Hengst was similarly dressed except his cross was gold. He asked Hengst if there was some special meaning to their attire. Hengst did not answer.

CHAPTER 35: **A Lone Rider**

After making sure Arthur was nowhere in the vicinity, Morgan crept up the tower stairs to the bedchamber where Merlin had been sleeping. She pushed open the door to the room, and the female servant sitting by the bed stood to greet her. "How is he?" Morgan thought she delivered her question with more concern than was believable, but it was nothing the servant would dare mention to anyone, even if she noticed the insincerity.

"He's not awakened." The servant looked back at Merlin. "He continues to mumble, and finally I can understand a few words, but if there's some meaning in them, it escapes me."

Morgan took the woman by the arm and pulled her to the door. "You must need a rest. Let me stay with him a short time, and you can tend to –
tend to whatever needs tending to." She ushered the servant out into the hall and closed the door. Morgan walked to the bed and looked down at the sleeping Merlin. She put her right hand up her left sleeve and withdrew a small vial. Merlin had not finished the drink she had poisoned, and so, she mixed her remaining poison powder with water. She leaned over the old wizard fearing if she put the vial to his mouth, he might twitch and spill what little of the precious poison remained or if he drank it, spit it out. So, she sat on the edge of the bed, opened the vial and wet the tip of her index finger with the liquid. She rubbed her moist finger across his mouth.

Merlin licked his lips. She smiled. "There, isn't that good? Your mouth must be so dry." She wet his mouth again. He licked his lips, then made a face at the odd taste of the concoction and turned his head away. "Just a little more." She put her finger to his lips, and despite being asleep, he shook his head with enough speed to avoid the contact of her finger.

The door burst open. Morgan pulled the vial close to her chest to conceal it. It was the servant. "I thought you would want to know, mistress, that your son, Mordred, has just arrived."

Morgan looked down at Merlin. She sighed, put the top back on the vial and hid it in her sleeve. "I'm coming." This method of killing him was too slow and had become less than certain. When Arthur and his warriors left to face the Saxons, she might suffocate or strangle him or just take a knife to him.

She went down to the courtyard, where a large number of people were gathered, Arthur, Ector and Kaye among them, all standing before Mordred and his men. Morgan stifled a smile as she picked up pieces of conversation. The Saxons were coming, Mordred warned them. Vortigern and his warriors were with the Saxons, it was said. Lancelot refused to help. Mordred, himself, had begged him without success. Some of the assembled knights were arguing to march out to meet the Saxons on a battlefield away from the castle. Others, Kaye chief among them, recommended that because of the small number of warriors assembled here, they should take a defensive position and prepare for a siege.

Arthur held up his hands to quiet the group. "There is no time to lay in provisions for a siege of any length. And have you forgotten all the people now living outside our walls? They have to be fed as well, and as the Saxons approach, more villagers will surely join the peasants already here. We have no choice but to ride out to meet the enemy. I know Balin is on his way here, and it's my hope he will arrive in time to hold one flank. Maybe some of the Grail knights will return as well."

Mordred stepped forward. "And I will man the other flank."

Morgan saw the look of pride in Arthur's face and thought he might have a tear or two in his eyes.

The group again broke into dozens of separate conversations as Mordred's men unloaded their gear, and Arthur stood speaking with his closest advisors – Ector, Kaye, and for the first time, his son, Mordred. A female servant threaded her way through the crowd until she was almost inside the circle of advisors. "Beggin' your pardon,

Sire. Beg pardon, King Arthur," she said in a louder voice. "Merlin is awake and callin' for you."

"I'd best go to him alone," said Arthur. "A group of people may be too much for him in his present state."

Arthur followed the servant up to Merlin's bedchamber. She opened the door for him and remained in the hall while he entered. He walked to the bed. The old wizard appeared to be asleep. Arthur gently shook his shoulder. "Merlin."

Merlin's eyes opened. He stared blankly at the ceiling for a few moments and looked at Arthur. "Arthur." His mouth and throat were parched, and the words barely came out. Arthur took a goblet from the table near the bed, lifted Merlin's head and gave him a drink. The wizard took a long swallow, water spilling down his chin. He coughed a few times and caught his breath. He seemed to have gained a little more energy and to have become a little more alert.

Merlin looked up at Arthur. "How are things?" Arthur would not answer at first. "Bad? You can tell me. You cannot hide things from me."

"Yes, bad, very bad."

"Details?"

"The Saxons have landed an army and are coming this way. Vortigern is said to have joined with them."

He motioned for more water. "The Grail knights?"

"All sent for." Arthur helped him take another drink. "None are yet here. But Mordred is here. . ."

"Mordred!" The mention of his name caused Merlin to cough again. "Better Lancelot than Mordred."

"Lancelot will not come."

Merlin paused to take a deep breath. "You tell me of too many coincidences. Grail knights gone. Mordred here but not Lancelot. What did I always tell you about coincidence?"

Arthur would have preferred not to answer, but he was happy just to see his old mentor awake and challenging him again. "To be suspicious of them. But these may be just coincidences."

"Be suspicious." He held up a finger and wagged it at Arthur. "There is more to all this than you see and more than I can see as well," he said, his voice growing weak as he finished his warning.

"Do you know that for certain?"

"I'm just certain that I am weak and tired, very tired." The wizard closed his eyes.

"What can you tell me about all this?" He did not answer. "Merlin?"

The old wizard seemed to have exhausted himself and was asleep again.

Arthur left the room. The servant was waiting in the hall. "Don't leave him for a moment." She bowed in acknowledgement of the instruction. "And take careful notice of anything he says – particularly if he says he is using his *sight*."

"His what?"

"Sight. Just remember anything and everything he says."

Arthur went down to the great hall, where he assumed his advisors would be meeting to discuss battle strategy, but they were still in the courtyard discussing – and at times, arguing about – what they should do. Kaye was still advocating defending the castle and preparing for a siege although few appeared to be supporting his position. Mordred, exuding great confidence, argued to take the offensive. The situation was chaotic, too many opinions, too many voices trying to be heard at the same time. Arthur began tapping his favorite advisors on the shoulder and telling them to meet him in the great hall.

A sentry from atop the castle wall called out. "A rider approaches."

In times of peace such announcements were not made, but now the kingdom was at war.

"Perhaps, it is one of the Grail knights returning," said Kaye.

"Let's find out." Arthur and Kaye, followed by a handful of the other curious knights, went to the castle gate. The rider approached slowly. He was not clad in armor as a Grail knight would have been. "I cannot make him out."

Kaye shook his head. "I don't recognize him either. I wonder if he has come to join us or if he brings a message from the enemy."

CHAPTER 36: **Surrender of a Castle**

Agravain's army had Bedivere's castle surrounded, but the dead knight's warriors, who lined the top of the castle walls, remained defiant. Agravain cupped his hands around his mouth as he shouted up at them. "Your lord is dead. There is no purpose to your resistance."

The man who seemed to be their leader shouted back at him. "You've shown us no proof Sir Bedivere is dead."

Agravain turned to his second in command. "Had I known I would have to show them the body, I would have brought it with us. Not that it would have done much good. That damnable Mordred bashed Bedivere's face so badly they wouldn't recognize him anyway." He looked up at the men on the wall and again cupped his hands around his mouth. "I give you my word as a knight Bedivere is dead."

"Your word! Ha! If you were an honest knight, you would not now be trying to take Bedivere's castle." The man next to the leader tapped his arm and pointed in the distance. There was a dust cloud on the horizon that could only mean a large army was approaching. "Now we shall see what we shall see," he shouted down to Agravain. "Our king is riding to our rescue. You'd best leave before he arrives."

Agravain turned but could not see what they were referring to. "Take command," he said to his aide. "I will see to this myself."

Agravain rode in the direction Bedivere's man indicated and had to mount a hill before he saw the cloud of dust that had excited the man. He traveled down the hill and up another and broke into a broad smile when he saw who was approaching: Vortigern and a large army, including Saxons.

Vortigern and Hengst, leaving their warriors behind, rode ahead to meet him. Agravain greeted them with a wave of his hand.

"Where have you been, and where is your army? Why did you not join us earlier?" asked Vortigern.

"I decided to take what I have earned in our bargain, Bedivere's castle."

"Aren't you acting prematurely?" said Hengst angrily.

Vortigern quickly interceded. "This is Lord Hengst."

"Since the castle is now mine," said Agravain, "I decided to take it. Now is as good a time as any. And there are dozens of good fighting men in Bedivere's castle who should join us." He stood up in his saddle to see their joint army stretching down the road behind Vortigern and Hengst. "It appears you already have more than enough men to defeat Arthur and storm Camelot if necessary."

"Yes, more than enough." Hengst gave Agravain a hard stare. "Let's put a quick end to what you started here. Lead on."

With Agravain at its head, the combined British-Saxon force approached Bedivere's castle and spread out in a wide formation, creating a semicircle around the front part of the castle. More of Bedivere's men appeared on the walls and looked down at the large army and at Hengst as he rode slowly toward them. Hengst stopped his horse, which whinnied and tossed its head to the side. He shouted up at Bedivere's men. "I will say this but once. You have only moments to surrender the castle and join with us or we will take the castle by force. If using force is what we must do, those of you who survive our assault will wish you had not."

Hengst turned his horse and slowly rode back to his army. Behind him the castle gates opened, and Bedivere's men surrendered.

CHAPTER 37: **A Knight No Longer**

Gawain, his hair grown long and unkempt, his clothes worn and dusty from his long journey, rode into Camelot, where there was a crowd of knights in the courtyard. He could see Arthur did not recognize him. Neither did Kaye or Ector or any of the others. Gawain slid down off his horse and stood face to face with Arthur. "It's me, Gawain, returned from a journey through many worlds."

Arthur's eyes opened wide in disbelief. He studied the shabby-looking creature before him and smiled when he saw it was actually Gawain. Arthur threw his arms around Gawain and hugged him. "You can't imagine how happy I am to see you." Arthur stepped back for a better look him. "Yes, under all this hair and dust, it is Gawain."

Kaye stepped forward and hugged Gawain, who was quickly surrounded by old friends wanting to greet and speak to him. And they barraged him with questions and comments. Where had he been? They thought he had drowned. How did he manage to get home? Some thought he was attacked at sea; others that his vessel sank in a storm. Was he in Germania all this time? In Gaul? In Britain? Lost at sea?

Eager to speak with Arthur privately, Gawain gave all their questions short answers and told them he would explain more later. "Thank you for your welcome, and I am happy to see you all, but I have a matter of some urgency to discuss with Arthur. King's ears only." Gawain took Arthur by the arm and led him toward the far end of the courtyard. "Perhaps, if we keep walking, we can speak in private."

Arthur looked at Gawain in anticipation of what he had to say. "You said it was a matter of some urgency."
"Yes. The Saxons have assembled a large invasion fleet and are likely headed this way."

"I know. We were just now discussing whether to march out and face them or take a siege."

"You knew! I'm not certain whether to laugh or shout or curse." He turned and pointed back to where he left his horse. "Do you know where I got that animal? From a party of Picts. I walked right into their camp and bargained for him so I could get to you with the news of the Saxon arrival."

"I'm sorry, Gawain, that you took such a risk unnecessarily. Of course, I had no idea —"

"Oh, I've taken many risks. I've visited Picts and journeyed with Norsemen. I've been to places in this world and other worlds you cannot imagine." He noticed Arthur's expression of disbelief. "Don't look at me as though I'm mad. I was able to see the Saxon ships in a dream long before I saw the actual fleet anchored off the coast."

"You sound like Merlin, the old Merlin. He hasn't been able to see much lately."

"But, Arthur, if you knew about the invasion, you must have assembled the Roundtable. Yet, I didn't see Lancelot or Balin, Percival or Bedivere or many of the others when I arrived. Are they here? Or on the way?"

Arthur did not appear eager to answer. "Balin is on his way from the far north but may not arrive in time. Bedivere is missing; Percival seriously injured; Lancelot uncooperative; and many of the others off on a quest for the Grail."

"The Grail! I have a suspicion about it as well, and my suspicion involves Lancelot."

Arthur shook his head. "He is not the old Lancelot, I'm afraid. I still have difficulty believing it, but he has become an adversary."

Gawain looked about the courtyard. "Things here, if you'll forgive me for saying so, seem to have fallen apart."

"I know," said Arthur, nodding his head. "And Merlin says to be wary of the several coincidences that have put me in this position. Even he has been ill and sleeping for days. He has brief periods of consciousness, but mostly he sleeps."

"Of course, Merlin is right." Gawain became more animated. "There are too many coincidences to be just bad luck. In my dream, when I saw the Saxon fleet, I also saw traitors but couldn't make out their faces."

The remark interested but did not surprise Arthur. "Vortigern is the most likely traitor."

Gawain let the name run through his mind. "Vortigern, yes, but more than Vortigern."

"Lancelot?"

It was the arrogant and self-righteous Lancelot who Gawain was fairly certain took the Grail from his tent. "The mention of his name gives me unease but not in the same way as Vortigern. I still remember the old Lancelot, not the one you describe as adversarial to you. But my mind is muddled. All this is new to me. Take me to see Merlin. Later I want to discuss the Grail with you and what might have happened to it, but first I must see Merlin."

Arthur took Gawain to Merlin's room and left him to convene a war council. The servant attending to Merlin took her leave and said she would wait in the hall. Gawain leaned over Merlin calling his name several times without a response. Gawain's instincts told him Merlin's condition was more than the consequence of illness and old age. He gently shook the wizard's shoulder and again called his name, but he could not bring Merlin to full consciousness. Merlin did open his eyes more than once, and he mumbled several times, mostly things Gawain could not make out or make sense of. But two words, or rather two names, he said clearly – Lancelot and Morgan.

Gawain could not get any more from the old wizard, at least not now. He left Merlin and found Arthur in the great hall about to convene his war council, such as the Roundtable was with so many important knights missing. Gawain motioned to Arthur, and the king delayed the start of his meeting to confer with Gawain in the vestibule.

Arthur smiled at him. "It is good to have one more Knight of the Roundtable here."

"Something is wrong here," said Gawain. "I sensed it as soon as I realized Lancelot, Bedivere and the others were not here. Merlin could tell me nothing except he said the names of Lancelot and Morgan. Is there any significance to his mumbling or was he just rambling in his sleep?"

"No, it's understandable he would mention them. To the surprise of almost everyone, they have been or perhaps were a couple, albeit an unlikely couple. I told you he is not the old Lancelot."

Gawain thought back to his time with Morgan, how she watched Lancelot as he led a prayer service after their victory over Horsa and how she said she would find a way home to Britain. "All here is not as it appears, Arthur. Perhaps with the situation with Lancelot as well."

Arthur studied Gawain's expression. "Do you know this? Or just sense it?"

Gawain hesitated before answering. "Sometimes sensing is knowing. Do you have any idea of where the Grail is?"

"No. There was a great storm. Many people, peasants mostly, blamed it on the loss of the Grail. At first we thought it sank with you. Then, we learned it had been stolen from your tent."

"And you sent your best knights in search of it, and that's why so many are missing at a time you sorely need them?"

"Your tone admonishes me the way Merlin did when I was a boy. It was not a bad decision except for the timing."

"The timing is suspect." Gawain did not know how, but he was becoming *aware* of information about what had been happening here at Camelot. "And as for Merlin, I can tell you that he has been poisoned."

"Poisoned! By whom?"

"You must keep a guard on him. And I need a horse. The one I rode here is need of a rest."

"Of course, I'll get you a horse and armor to replace what you lost and you'll take your normal place at the Roundtable. But first, tell me who poisoned Merlin if you know."

"I won't say because all this is too new to me, and I could be wrong, but I can tell you this much with certainty. I can be of more use to you than just another sword." The remark seemed to further confuse Arthur. "I understand that with so many of your best knights missing, you are eager to have even one more join you in battle, but I must see Lancelot."

"Lancelot is a lost cause. Better you stay here."

"No, I must see him. For some reason, I feel he may be a key to unlocking the puzzle of all the *coincidences* you have been suffering."

CHAPTER 38: **Battle Lines**

Arthur and Percival, who claimed to be almost completely recovered from his injuries, sat side by side atop their horses outside the gates of Camelot, watching the procession of warriors riding out to meet the Saxon invaders. They were surrounded by the peasants who were now living just beyond the castle walls. The peasants watched the march with interest, and Percival, who kept looking from side to side, watched them with even greater interest.

Percival's eyes locked into a stare, and his expression went blank. "I remember now. It was peasants – peasants who attacked me."

Arthur put a hand on the handle of Excalibur. "These peasants?"

"No. I mean, I don't know if it was these in particular or not, but they were peasants – I'm pretty certain."

Arthur looked at the peasants and at the procession of warriors moving out of the castle. The contingent of knights had all ridden by. Now the spearmen were marching out on foot to be followed by the archers. "Come with me," said Arthur, and he and Percival rode back into the castle courtyard. There were several hundred spearmen in four columns walking toward the gates. Arthur cut off the last fifty with his horse. "You are to stay here and defend the castle." The fifty quickly moved out of the formation allowing the archers to move up.

Arthur rode back over to Percival and leaned across his saddle to speak to him. "Percival, I have an important task for you. Stay here with those fifty men, keep the castle gates closed and defend Camelot. I don't trust the peasants who are camped outside our walls."

"But you'll need me against the Saxons. And I feel perfectly fine."

"You obviously can ride. I'm not as sure you can fight just yet. Stay here. Don't weary yourself on a journey. Defend the castle against those peasants. Who knows what they are planning or what assistance they might receive if they try to storm the walls? There is no one other than you I can trust with that task."

Percival agreed although it was obvious he did not like the order.

The archers were now marching out. After them came Mordred and his men, forty mounted warriors and another forty on foot. When they were out of the courtyard and on the road north, Arthur ordered the castle gates closed and galloped to the head of his army.

They marched north throughout the day and did not rest until they were on the edge of the forest facing open farm fields that had been left barren by the great storm. Arthur, Ector, Kaye and Mordred gathered close together. "This may be the place we make our battle line," said Arthur. He pointed to the forest behind them. "We can position our men in the woods and force the enemy to cross the open field. Recall we did something similar at the Battle of the River Glein."

Mordred studied the open field and the woods on the far side. "Do we know how close the Saxons are?"

"The scout hasn't returned. Let's rest here and wait for him."

They were eating their midday meal when the scout finally returned. From the speed with which he rode toward them, it was evident he had spotted the enemy. The scout rode up to Arthur, who was drinking water from an animal skin container. "The Saxons are making camp in the woods on the other side of those fields."

Arthur wiped his face with his sleeve. "Do they know we are here?"

"Yes, I was spotted and narrowly ducked an arrow for my trouble."

"And their number?"

"I couldn't tell. It was too wooded. And they spotted me almost as soon as I spotted them."

Arthur tossed the scout the water container. "Here, drink, and get yourself some food."

Arthur spent the remaining daylight positioning his men in the forest and having a trench dug in front of their battle line and firewood gathered. He wanted as many campfires as possible to conceal their small number. By sunset they had done most of what they needed to do although men continued to work on the trench in shifts. With their own fires lit, Arthur stood at the edge of the camp watching the Saxon campfires blink into life.

Mordred came up behind him. "There appear to be many in the Saxon camp."

"Yes, unless they are using the same trick as we are." He had a distant look in his eyes. "It wasn't that long ago, Mordred, although it seems like a lifetime ago now, that I looked at an encampment such as theirs only the enemy was the Picts, and it was raining then, almost as hard as during the recent storm. It may not sound believable, but I was young and foolish enough to ride right into their camp alone and kill the Pict leader."

Mordred listened with great interest. "I have heard that story but always thought it was just a story, one of the many legends that have grown around the great Arthur and the Wizard Merlin."

"No, Mordred, it's true – not that I know what exaggerated version of the story you might have heard. The story was exaggerated the first time it was told, and I'm sure every time since."

Mordred studied the firmness in Arthur's expression. "You're not thinking of doing it again, are you? You couldn't possibly be considering taking such a risk."

"No, of course, not. I was lucky to survive such foolishness once. I wouldn't tempt fate again. Besides taking such a risk is not an adventure appropriate for a king. I was merely a warrior back then, a knight in desperate need of restoring his reputation. Kings must be far more cautious."

"But I could do it." Arthur laughed dismissively, and Mordred became angry. "You think I can't?"

"I shouldn't have laughed. It's not your courage I doubt. It's the situation. This is entirely different from what I faced."

"How so – other than they were Picts back then instead of Saxons?"

"One difference is it was raining so heavily that night I couldn't see more than a foot or two ahead, which concealed me even better than the darkness. Also, I was wearing Pict armor and riding a Pict horse.

Those things combined to allow me to move through the Pict camp without raising any suspicion let alone an alarm. And, Mordred, we had Pict hostages who told us what we needed to know and where the Pict leader was likely to be sleeping." Arthur gestured toward the Saxon camp. "Hengst is surely better guarded than the Pict leader I killed. And do you even know what Hengst looks like or where his tent is likely to be?"

"No, of course not. But I don't mean to kill him, but rather just to get the information your scout failed to get."

"Oh! Well, that's a different proposition." There was still uncertainty in Arthur's voice. "But still a very dangerous one."

"I have lived my entire life in your shadow and wish to establish my own reputation. Isn't concern for your reputation what caused you to enter the Pict camp? Give me this chance to show I am a man cut from the same cloth as my father. Is my request so unreasonable?"

Arthur appeared conflicted. "I worry about your safety, Mordred, but I am proud of your courage. I remember what it was like to be your age and would have likely made a similar request. But understand you would have to be more careful than you have ever been in your life. And you must promise me you'll turn back at the moment the situation appears too dangerous."

Mordred smiled confidently. "Don't be concerned about me. I can manage things better than you might imagine."

When it was determined the enemy camp had probably bedded down for the night, Mordred began his mission assisted by the other man who could claim to have spent his entire life in Arthur's shadow, his brother Kaye. The pair rode as close to the enemy line as they dared, and Mordred dismounted to walk ahead on foot while Kaye remained behind with the horses. Mordred crossed the rest of the open field undetected and moved into the forest on the far side. He withdrew his dagger and went in search of a sentry.

Mordred carefully walked the edge of the forest straining to see in the dark and listening for any sound that might be made by a warrior on night watch. He laughed to himself. He could hear whistling, not a signal, not an attempt to sound like a bird, but rather the idling whistling of a bored man. He focused on the sound and moved around to approach the man from the back. The whistling stopped. So did Mordred. The whistling resumed, and now he could see the silhouette of the man as well as hear him.

Mordred came up quickly from behind, put an arm around the sentry's neck, positioned the side of his leg against the back of the sentry's and flipped him to the ground. The man landed face down. Mordred was on him immediately. He turned the sentry over and put his blade against the man's throat. Mordred laughed. "Lucky for you I'm here to see Hengst." The man was breathing too heavily to speak. "I am Mordred. Take me to Hengst. And if you are a cooperative lad, I won't tell your lord what a terrible sentry you are."

The sentry got up, dusted himself off and led Mordred through the woods to the rear of the Saxon camp where Hengst's tent stood. A lamp burned inside. The sentry called from outside the tent, begged Hengst's forgiveness for disturbing him, and told the warlord he had an important visitor. Mordred, leaving the sentry outside, entered the tent, and Hengst stood to greet him.

"Mordred! What are you doing here?"

"Spying on you. The sentry who brought me here, I'd replace him if I were you. I snuck up on him and could easily have slit his throat."

"I will deal with the sentry later. Sit down." Hengst motioned to a stool across from his own. "Tell me what you can about Arthur's army."

"He has fewer than six hundred men. He had to leave fifty behind to defend Camelot against the peasant rabble my mother and I placed outside the gate."

"Then, we outnumber him more than four to one."

"When I return I'll estimate half that number to Arthur."

"What else can you tell me?"

"Lancelot remains at his own castle. Balin is on the way but certainly cannot arrive before sunrise. There will never be a better time for you to attack than morning."

Hengst suddenly had a far-off look in his eyes as though visualizing something in the future. "We'll attack at first light."

CHAPTER 39: **Too Convenient**

The man standing in the doorway looked like a woodsman, but Lancelot's servant said the visitor was an emissary of the king, which did not please Lancelot. "Tell Arthur," he said to the shabby-looking man, "the next time he sends someone to speak to me, to choose a knight, not a woodsman or a farmer."

"I am a knight; at least, I was a knight." The man with the long hair stepped into the room. "And Arthur didn't send me. I came of my own accord."

Lancelot squinted at him. "You look familiar."

"Perhaps you mean I sound familiar. It's me, Gawain, looking somewhat different from when last you saw me."

Lancelot looked disbelieving at first, then broke into a smile. "By all that's holy, it is you. It is. We thought you were lost at sea."

"I was."

"Here, sit by the fire and warm yourself." Lancelot motioned toward the hearth, and they sat down. "Would you like some food or drink? I must admit I'm stunned to see you. Stunned."

Lancelot was far more cordial to him than he had been in Germania, and Gawain now accepted some of the responsibility for the friction that occurred between them during the siege of Horsa's castle.

"We had given up on you, Gawain. Where have you been? Lost at sea?"

"I've been places unlike any you have ever seen, unlike any that any Briton has ever seen. But I'll tell you about my travels another time. My concern now is that I didn't return to the same place I left. Much here has changed." Lancelot frowned in anticipation of what Gawain was about to say. "Lancelot, Saxons are on the march, and Arthur needs you."

Lancelot was not touched by these words. "I didn't know about the Saxons, but I'm certain Arthur can manage without me. He needs – and values – me so little that I was not invited to the last meeting of the Roundtable. I was left out completely. He has also accused me of being a liar and a thief, unforgivable accusations. I can see from your face, Gawain, you were unaware of these insults. And it is likely you came here thinking I was the cause of the split between us. I'm always said to be at fault when it comes to an issue with Arthur. But I'm not at fault. Not this time. Whatever battles Arthur needs fought now, he has chosen to fight without me. He has the rest of the Roundtable to do it for him."

"You are correct, Lancelot, in that I didn't know what you just told me. You heard these insults directly from Arthur?"

"No, they were told to me, but I have no doubt about them."

"Who told you all this?"

"That's not important."

"It may be all important. Understand, Lancelot, the situation goes well beyond what has transpired between you and Arthur. Your differences can be mended later." Lancelot appeared skeptical. "But what is about to happen now could harm everyone in Britain, or at least, every loyal Briton. You said Arthur has his Roundtable Knights to fight for him. That's untrue. Bedivere is missing; Percival has been injured, and others are dispersed searching for the Grail."

"The Grail! But you have it, or at least, you did have it. We even organized a search of the sea to find it and you. Five ships searched the water until we encountered a storm."

"I had it until you took it." Gawain suddenly was no longer certain Lancelot had taken the Grail but made the remark to test his reaction. Looking at Lancelot now, he knew Lancelot did not have the Grail. "No, I'm wrong. I apologize. You didn't take the Grail."

Lancelot was insulted. "No, of course not. I never had it. And I don't steal. First, Arthur accuses me, then you."

Gawain was ignoring Lancelot for the moment and talking aloud to himself. "It disappeared from my tent before I left Germania. You showed so much interest in it, I thought it had to be you." His eyes opened wide. "It must have been Morgan."

Lancelot appeared as stunned by the mention of Morgan's name as he was to see Gawain back from the dead. "What has she to do with it?"

"She spent a night in my tent. She had access to it, and if she took the Grail, she took it for a reason. Everything she does is for a reason. Was it Morgan who drove the wedge between you and Arthur? Is she the one who told you Arthur called you a thief?" Lancelot didn't answer. It was one of the few times Gawain had seen Lancelot less than supremely confident. "When I sneaked into Horsa's castle disguised as a beggar, I saw Morgan there and assumed she was involved in some act of treachery."

"You can't know she was for certain," said Lancelot, who, nonetheless, appeared very concerned.

"And what was she doing in Germania at our camp? Have you given any thought to her strange presence there?"

"No, not much. She's an enchantress or thinks she is."

"But you don't believe she is an enchantress, so enchantment can't be a reason you should accept. And when I was there at Horsa's castle I had a feeling that to advance some plot of hers she had bedded Horsa and perhaps, Willayne as well."

Gawain had struck Lancelot's tender spot. "You can't possibly know that either. People change. She has. And much of her reputation is unwarranted. Completely undeserved."

Lancelot was on the verge of an eruption of anger; Gawain softened his tone. "This I do know. After we defeated Horsa, she spent the night in my tent in my bed – naked." He didn't need to tell Lancelot that nothing happened between them. "Morgan uses men as you and I use a sword or lance, as a weapon. She is alluring and clever and overpowering at times. For whatever reason, she first grabbed onto me to be a tool in her plans. Then, she saw you leading the men in prayer —"

Lancelot shook his head. "No, I don't believe this. It is too convenient for you to come here to tell me this now. Far too convenient."

"Listen, Lancelot, both to me and to your feelings. When Morgan needed a Saxon, I found her in Horsa's castle. When she needed a Briton, she spent the night in my tent and now she is with you. Morgan took the Grail and for what purpose I can't be completely certain, but I am sure now that she has it. And you mention things being too convenient. How too convenient is all this? Arthur's knights are dispersed seeking the Grail, which neither you nor I have but Morgan does. Angry peasants are menacing outside Camelot's gate. The Saxons, who Morgan has bargained with, have invaded Britain. This is all too *convenient*, to use your word, to be coincidence; it's part of a plan."

Lancelot turned red and could no longer look at Gawain. He was breathing hard as though the pressure inside him would be released in an eruption.

"And this, Lancelot, I offer you this as final evidence, the question I asked you earlier and you didn't answer. A wedge has been driven between Arthur and you, between the king and his best and most important knight. And just prior to a Saxon invasion." It never hurt to flatter Lancelot. "Was it Morgan who drove that wedge? And where is she now? Why isn't she here with you?"

Lancelot slammed his fist down on the table to the right of his chair and swiped his arm at it turning the table over and sending its contents scattering across the floor. He didn't speak. Gawain doubted he would. Gawain had done all he could except to make one final argument. "There is little time, Lancelot, for you to make a decision. If you join Arthur on the battlefield, and you are correct that he doesn't need you or that he has been disloyal to you, you can leave him after the battle. Leave him that day or the next day or the day after. What is one more battle to a knight of your skill and history? You will not have lost much. But if I am right, if Arthur needs your help, and you don't come to his aid because the two of you have been tricked by an enchantress, it will destroy him, and knowing the kind of man you are, it will destroy you as well."

There was nothing else for Gawain to say. And there was no time to say more. Someone was trying to kill Merlin, and now that Gawain was convinced Morgan was involved in a plot, he worried she was within striking distance of the old wizard. He left Lancelot sitting in his chair in a state of high agitation as a servant entered the room and looked at the overturned table and the small mementos of past battles strewn across the floor.

CHAPTER 40: **Surrounded**

The Saxons finally showed themselves. Approximately seventy foot soldiers marched out of the woods on the far side of the open field and approached the British position. Arthur, with Kaye on one side and Ector on the other, watched their advance.

Kaye wore a puzzled look. "There aren't many of them."

"They're testing us," said Ector.

"And we'll show them nothing." Arthur turned and shouted to his foot soldiers. "I want seventy men."

At least a hundred stepped forward. Arthur quickly chose an appropriate number of them and directed them to go out to meet the Saxon attack. Those selected walked out onto the barren field moving confidently but not in any particular formation. The two sets of warriors approached each other, and when they were a few dozen feet apart, both sides tightened into battle lines and crouched behind raised shields.

The air filled with the sound of metal striking metal. Both sides fought defensively, men slashing and pounding at one another's shields and taking few risks. Arthur leaned toward Kaye. "They are looking to see what we have hidden in the woods and looking to see if we will bring archers in support or send knights into the battle. They want to gauge our tactics as well as our number."

As Arthur watched the center of his battle formation, a British warrior took a misstep, teetered and was knocked off balance by a series of powerful Saxon sword strikes to his shield. Before he could regain his balance, he was stabbed in the left side. The warrior doubled over, lowering both his sword and shield. He took another sword thrust, this one to the chest, and fell to the ground.

"He should have been more careful," Arthur said to Ector. "We have too few men to lose even one to carelessness."

The battle between the two armies lasted a time longer with neither side trying to gain any significant advantage. As suddenly as the Saxons had appeared, for no apparent reason they began a fast retreat. Arthur shouted for his men to withdraw, and they did so, walking backwards a few paces until the Saxons were a safe distance away. The Britons turned and walked back to the cover of the forest.

The British remained on high alert, but the Saxons did not show themselves again for some time. When they finally reappeared, there were far more of them, several hundred at least. The Saxon foot soldiers took the center of the field; mounted warriors flanked them and remained a few dozen feet behind. The spearmen started to advance on the British, the mounted Saxons holding their position. Arthur put an equal number of foot soldiers into the field but kept his archers and knights in reserve.

The Saxons reached the middle of the open ground between the two forces. One of them gave a war cry that was echoed by all the others. They charged the British line, and the British ran out to meet them. The two sides collided man against man and shield against shield. With sword, spear, ax and mace, they attacked one another, slashing, hacking and stabbing, striking mostly shields, armor and helmets.

On the left side of the British formation, one Briton took a spear thrust to the neck and fell over backwards; a second was clubbed to his knees by a Saxon mace. The Saxons pushed back the remaining Britons several feet and threatened to break through the line.

Kaye, who observed this, turned toward Arthur. "Now?"

"Not yet."

Arthur kept his eyes on the Saxon knights, who remained a distance away. They began to advance, slowly at first; then, they broke into a gallop. Arthur ordered his archers out of the woods and shouted for them to target the approaching Saxon horsemen. He turned to his father and brother. "Let's seal that breach in our line."

The three of them rode to the left flank and waded in among the combatants. Arthur, wielding Excalibur, drove a handful of Saxon foot soldiers backwards. As they retreated, he glanced to his right where he heard a loud grunting. Kaye, trying to fend off a Saxon foot soldier on either side of his horse, was in trouble. Arthur moved in and took down the Saxon on Kaye's left with one swing of Excalibur. Kaye concentrated on the man to his right and delivered several good blows. In desperation the Saxon struck Kaye's horse in the ribs with the butt of his spear. The horse reared up, and Kaye barely managed to hold on. Arthur turned his mount and rode down the Saxon, nearly trampling him under his horse's hooves. The Saxon dove to the ground and rolled out of danger, giving Kaye an opportunity to calm his horse and recover.

The British archers unleashed a barrage of arrows on the Saxon horsemen, who were still a distance off, but did little damage. Rather than enter the battle, the riders pulled up in the face of another volley of arrows and called for a retreat. The Saxon foot soldiers also began to retreat, the British following them.

"Hold your positions," Arthur shouted. He kicked his horse into a fast trot and rode across the rear of the British battle line. "Hold. Don't chase them. Don't be pulled into a trap."

The vast majority of the British soldiers held their ground, but a handful pursued the retreating Saxons. As soon as they were safely out of arrow range, the Saxons turned, surrounded the few Britons who had followed them and quickly took them all down. Arthur could only watch and shake his head.

The British regrouped in the forest. Arthur dismounted and shouted for his men to prepare for another assault, while those who needed bandaging were assisted and those with damaged shields or armor tended to their equipment.

Word quickly spread through the ranks that British riders were approaching. Kaye passed the news to Arthur, who, more mumbling to himself than speaking to his brother, said, "This must be Balin and his hundred men. And just in time."

But it was not Balin who was leading the riders coming from the south, but rather it was Lancelot. And the number of soldiers with him was not as many as a hundred but closer to four dozen. Nonetheless Arthur smiled at the sight of his champion. During battle, past slights and disputes between men, even large ones, can easily be forgotten. Lancelot rode up to Arthur and dismounted. The two men grasped each other's forearms in a display of friendship.

"Whatever differences we have had, Lancelot –"

"Let's not talk about them now. We have a battle to fight." Lancelot looked around the camp paying special attention to the warriors who were treating wounds. "The situation looks bad."

"Bad, yes, but I'm not yet sure how bad. Mordred says we are out-numbered two-to-one. It's at least that bad. We have fended off two attacks but have yet to see the true size of the Saxon force."

"I hate to raise your spirits with my arrival only to tell you more bad news. As we approached, we saw in the distance a group of warri-ors, perhaps three hundred of them, at least three hundred. They appeared to be British, not Saxon, and at first I thought they would turn this way, but they continued south."

"It must be Vortigern. We have yet to see his men here. They must be planning to surround us."

Lancelot looked over Arthur's shoulder and pointed in the distance. "Look there. The Saxons are attacking in force."

More than a thousand Saxons had appeared out of the woods and spread out in a wide battle formation with two rows of spearmen in front and two rows of archers behind. As the British shouted for their men to line up in formation, the Saxon foot soldiers began their advance. Behind them came several hundred of their mounted warriors.

Arthur positioned all his spearmen in a defensive line a hundred feet from the edge of their protected position in the forest. Behind them he placed three groups of knights: Arthur commanding the center, Lancelot the left flank, and Mordred the right. The British archers remained hidden in the woods.

The Saxons moved steadily toward them. They reached the center of the open field and continued to within four hundred feet of the British front line. Arthur gave the command, and the archers unleashed a volley of arrows. The Saxon spearmen dropped to their knees and raised their shields high. The archers behind them fell to the ground as close to the protection of the spearmen's shields as they could manage. The arrows reached the highest point of their arc and dropped down on the Saxons. Arrows came down in groups of two, three and more sticking in shields and glancing off helmets and shoulder armor or harmlessly penetrating the dirt. But a few tore into the Saxon soldiers who lay on the ground.

The Saxon archers quickly stood up and fired a round back at the British. Only a few found their mark, taking down a handful of spearmen and a rider who sat on his horse less that fifty feet from Arthur.

The British archers let loose a second volley. Again the only damage the barrage accomplished was to strike a handful of the enemy.

The Saxon spearmen jumped to their feet and charged the British line while behind them their archers formed two lines and covered the advance of their foot soldiers by alternating volleys of arrows.

The two front lines met in a loud clash. The British held their own until the second line of Saxon foot soldiers waded in. Using their shields, the Saxons, who far outnumbered the British, began to push Arthur's troops back into one another and back toward the forest line. The Saxon archers moved forward, and although some of them were felled by British arrows, they continued to shoot at the British knights.

An arrow glanced off the left side of Lancelot's helmet, but he hardly flinched. One stuck in the right side of Arthur's saddle. He pulled it out and threw to the ground, and as he did so, he noticed something amiss on the right flank. Mordred's men had turned and were attacking Arthur's own men. And Mordred was leading the attack.

In a furor Arthur kicked his horse into a gallop and rode head-on for Mordred. Mordred saw him coming and cocked a lance in his arm. Arthur raised his elbow to wield Excalibur. Mordred threw. The edge of the lance sliced across Arthur's upper right arm just below the shoulder. He pulled down his arm and winced, somehow managing to hold onto his sword. The cut was deep and bled profusely, but the blade had not touched the bone. Mordred sat frozen on his horse as Arthur continued to bear down on him. Despite the pain and the bleeding, Arthur raised Excalibur and swung at Mordred, who lifted his shield just in time to catch the blow. Its force toppled him off the back of his horse.

Arthur wielded his horse around. He sheathed Excalibur and pulled a lance from the leather pouch hanging from his saddle. He cocked his arm and looked down at his son, who lay helpless on his back. Mordred stared up at his father in anticipation of the strike, but the strike did not come.

Mordred's men rushed to his aid. Pushing himself backwards with his feet and elbows, Mordred retreated between horse legs, then turned onto his stomach and crawled to safety.

Kaye and Ector came to support Arthur. With Mordred in retreat, his men followed him.

Ector saw the blood stains on Arthur's tunic, the large cut in at the top of his arm, and the fresh blood running out between the seams in his armor. "You need to be bandaged at once."

Arthur returned his lance to its holder. "When this assault is beaten back."

"No, Arthur, now. I've seen a few wounds in my time, and you will surely bleed to death if you are not tended to." Arthur hesitated. "Think of your men. You are only one sword in a battle line, but you lead them with your presence. Get yourself sewn and bandaged and forget about fighting until you are healed."

Reluctantly Arthur went to the rear of their line.

The British fought well, especially Lancelot and his men, and they held the left flank. But Arthur's army was in trouble. The center of their formation was pushed back, and the right flank was vulnerable now that Mordred and his men deserted to the enemy. Arthur had no choice but to order his men to retreat back into the forest. They would need the cover of trees to withstand another Saxon assault.

The Saxons watched their retreat but did not follow them. They were not yet ready to charge into the dense forest, where their superior numbers would not give them much of an advantage. Instead, they withdrew a few hundred feet and regrouped.

Kaye and Ector, joined by Lancelot, sat with Arthur as he tried to take off his tunic and armor. He could hardly move his arm. Ector cut away his tunic, and Kaye unstrapped his armor. The cut in his arm was four inches long, deep and still bleeding.

Arthur tried to stem the bleeding with his left hand but the blood ran out from under his fingers. "I'll have the wound sewn."

"Yes, have it sewn," said Lancelot, "but if you try to use that arm, you will reopen the cut. You will not fight again in this battle."

"I can't worry about anything beyond today, beyond this moment. There might not be another battle after this one, not for most of us here."

While Arthur had his arm stitched, they discussed their next move, and it did not take much debate to determine they had to leave this forest before Vortigern boxed them in from the south if, indeed, they were not already boxed in. They would leave a rear guard to make it appear they were still defending the forest and evacuate to a place on the coast where they could make a final stand.

Arthur's arm was bound to his side by a bandage to keep him from moving it. Kaye helped him on with a tunic and up onto his horse. Taking the reins in his left hand, he led the retreat out of the woods. They turned east toward the coast and continued south along the shore until they reached a sea cliff. There was an open stretch of flat ground between three and four hundred feet wide. This, Arthur decided, was where the last battle would be fought. On the seaward side they were protected by a sheer forty-foot drop to a sandy beach. And the Saxons could not easily attack from the inland side because it was covered with hills, boulders, and bushes, terrain not easily traversed in battle by horses. Arthur said they would defend this flank with archers and hope to funnel the main Saxon force between the rugged terrain and the sea cliff, squeezing the enemy into a narrow space to limit the impact of their numbers.

With that decided, they quickly made camp and began digging defensive trenches to augment their defenses. The men took turns eating while they waited for the Saxons to arrive, but they did not come, not until shortly before sunset.

Arthur and Lancelot stood at the front of the British position watching the enemy set up camp. "It is too late for them to attack now," said Lancelot. "It's too dangerous in the fading light with that cliff on one side."

"Same as this morning, we can expect an attack at first light tomorrow. Let's hope all the gods are with us."

CHAPTER 41: **Betrayal**

Gawain had not imagined he would ever see such a sight: peasants standing before the gates of Camelot shouting angrily at the few warriors who stood atop the castle wall above them. Percival, who was positioned between two stone pickets, his upper body bent down toward the crowd, appeared to be trying to reason with them, but every time he spoke, the peasants shouted him down. One man picked up a stone and threw it at Percival. He never saw it coming, but it hit harmlessly against one of the pickets.

On his journey here, Gawain constantly berated himself for taking too long to realize it was probably Morgan who was poisoning Merlin. He worried he would not arrive in time, and now he faced a new problem in the mob of peasants who blocked his entrance to Camelot. He had already bluffed his way into a Saxon castle as a beggar and into a Pict camp as a wizard. He had no better idea now than to try a similar approach and decided to call as much attention to himself as he could as though he were in total command of the circumstances here.

"Pardon me," he shouted at the peasants who stood immediately before him. "Make way, please." Several peasants stepped aside; a woman pulled her child out of his path. "Thank you. Make way. Coming through. Pardon me." More of the group turned toward him, and they moved aside, clearing a path to the castle gate. "Thank you. Thank you." He bowed from side to side. "Much obliged." He waved to Percival. "Open the gate please."

Gawain dismounted, hoping Percival would have the small gate in the large castle door open as quickly as possible. The door was not high enough to allow his horse through, and for an instant Gawain considered just leaving the animal to roam free outside. Instead he targeted a severe-looking man in a hooded cloak, who might well be the leader of the group of peasants. "Would you mind holding my horse, please? Just for a very short time." Gawain extended the reins toward him. The man hesitated but took control of the horse.

Behind Gawain, the small castle door opened. He bowed to the peasants again, turned toward the door and entered. Once he was inside Camelot, he hurried to the tower and climbed the stairs to the room where he had last seen Merlin. The same servant girl he had seen tending to Merlin before was in the hall. He was probably still alive. Gawain threw open the door. Morgan was leaning over the bed and came quickly to attention when she heard him entering the room.

He looked at her, thinking, as he had in Horsa's castle, that she was both very beautiful and very dangerous. "Morgan, he is an old man. Do you need to kill him when he is so old and feeble and so near to death anyway?" It was the only time he had ever seen her flustered. She threw back her shoulders, straightened the waist of her dress and took a deep breath. "How long can you sustain your vengeance, Morgan? Has it been thirty years?"

"Longer." She was unapologetic.

Gawain looked at Merlin, who was stirring in the bed. "Didn't you commit the same offense against Arthur as Merlin committed against Igraine using the potion? Didn't you even the accounts? And this vendetta, this consuming hatred of yours, how has it worn on you all these years?"

The intensity for which Morgan was known returned to her eyes. "Yes, I owe him an old debt, a very old debt, and it is still unpaid. But even you will see justification in my actions when I tell you he recently, as recently as a few days ago, committed the same offense against me."

The old wizard was mumbling and lifting his head up. He was finally awaking.

Morgan walked toward Gawain and stood toe to toe with him. "I woke up one morning in bed with the vilest of all men, Vortigern." She was screaming and on the verge of hysteria. "Vortigern! The last man in Britain I would want to touch me. Of course, I had no memory of how I came to be there. You understand what that means? Trickery! Magic!"

Merlin sat up in bed. He rubbed his eyes and the back of his neck. His eyes blinking, he looked around the room. "What is all the shouting about? And why have I been sleeping so long?"

Morgan looked back at the wizard and pointed a slender finger at him. "You helped Vortigern seduce me. It could have been no one else but you."

"Vortigern!" The old wizard was not troubled by the accusation if, in fact, he even understood it. "No, I don't think so, not Vortigern, no." He yawned. "Not that I remember."

"How was Merlin supposed to have accomplished this?" asked Gawain.

"The potion. How else? The same he used on Igraine."

"Potions?" Merlin didn't look as though he was following the conversation, but he was. "I know many potions."

"The love potion – improperly named. You should call it the lust potion, the deception potion, the hate potion. And you are the only one who knows how to mix it."

"No, not true," said Merlin nonchalantly as he stretched his arms and rubbed his neck again. Finally appearing fully awake, he focused his eyes on Morgan. "You know how to make it as well, Morgan. You used it on Arthur, remember?"

She put her hands on her hips and shouted at him. "Are you claiming I may have used the potion on myself?"

Gawain interceded. "Morgan, Merlin has never been an ally of Vortigern. It wasn't him. Think. Who are Vortigern's allies and who might also have access to Merlin's potion or to yours? It must have been someone who is both close to you and to Vortigern."

"There is no one . . ." She stopped in mid-sentence, the color draining from her face. Morgan teetered as though her legs might collapse beneath her. She staggered toward a chair, Gawain holding her arm to assist her. She sat down, a blank stare on her face. "Mordred is Vortigern's ally, and he was there the night it happened," she whispered. "My own Mordred." She looked up at Gawain. "Do you know what Mordred said to me? He said, 'I am my mother's son.' Now I know what he meant. He is capable of anything." She swallowed hard and closed her eyes. "What an evil being I have created that he could do this to his own mother. Why, I cannot fathom, but he did it to gain some advantage or perhaps out of spite. He has often accused me of having too much control over him." Gawain wanted to console her but doubted there was anything he could say. "My son betrayed me. Look at where my life has brought me?" She pointed at Merlin, who was now fully alert. "He still lives. After more than thirty years, he still lives, and I am betrayed. For all my trouble, instead of getting vengeance for what happened to my mother, I end up suffering the same crime as she – the victim of my own son."

Gawain gently touched her shoulder. "It's not too late for you to make some act of redemption."

She laughed bitterly. "Oh, it is much, much too late, Gawain. Arthur will almost certainly die at the hands of Hengst and his warriors. And if by some unforeseen miracle he lives, he will surely execute me. And with Vortigern and my own son conspiring against me, I no longer much care who wins the battle."

"The Grail," said Gawain. The mention of it caught her attention. "You have it, don't you?" She gave no answer and did not reveal anything in her expression. "There is a chance, albeit a small one, that returning the Grail to the Saxons might convince them to turn back."

The color returned to Morgan's face, and she became infused with energy. "No, you're wrong, Gawain. It's much more than a small chance. We had to promise Hengst the return of the Grail to coax him to come here. There is every chance you can strike a bargain with him. But first you will have to bargain with me. If I give you the Grail, you must allow me to escape, not chase after me when I leave the castle and not have me followed. Agreed?"

Gawain looked at Merlin, who was listening carefully. "You have my word, Morgan, and I will keep it as I kept your confidence in Germania."

"Then, we have a bargain, and this old fool is the witness." She hurried toward the door. "I'll return with the Grail."

As soon as she left the room, Gawain looked at Merlin. "That was the right decision to make, wasn't it?"

Merlin was now sitting with his legs over the edge of the bed, rubbing his legs to improve the circulation. "Absolving Morgan of her guilt in return for Arthur's life and having the Saxons stand down – if that's how it turns out? I would have done the same in an instant." Merlin sounded like himself although he looked frail. The old wizard studied Gawain's appearance. "You have become a seer."

Gawain was not certain if Merlin had asked him a question or had made a statement. "I'm not sure. Sometimes I think I see things in the future and in far-off places. But everyone dreams."

"Yes, how does one ever know? It's not easy being a seer, an enchanter, an influencer of the affairs of men – if they can be influenced."

After many days of being on his own, Gawain finally had someone to talk to, someone who understood what was happening to him better than he understood himself. "But I have recently done things I'm not proud of, things I have never before done or at least have rarely done." His guilt and uncertainty caused Gawain to avoid looking the wise and insightful Merlin in the eye. He pointed to the door to indicate Morgan. "I just now lied to her. I didn't keep her confidence from Germania, not fully."

"But you broke it for a good cause."

"Yes, to bring Lancelot into Arthur's fold again. And I also lied to a band of Picts. I told them I was you."

Merlin laughed so hard he began to cough. Gawain hurried to the bed and patted his back. "Told them you were me," Merlin said between coughs. "No one else in the history of the world has pretended to be me or wanted to." He laughed again, and the laugh was followed by another cough. "Surely, being me must be the worst thing you have done."

"No, I wish it was. I gave away the position of a group of Norsemen, including one who saved my life, to an army of Picts."

"Norsemen to Picts. I'm not sure I follow." Merlin waved his hand in the air. "No details, please. You'll only confuse me. Just tell me the rationale for your decision."

"To keep the Norse raiders from slaughtering the Picts and to get a horse so I could ride to warn Arthur of the coming Saxons."

"You've just answered your own doubt." Merlin slid to the edge of the bed. "Help me up. I've been in this bed too long, and I'm not certain I can walk on my own." Gawain assisted him to his feet and holding his arm, helped him to walk back and forth along the bed.

The old wizard was unsteady on his feet. "And once you get the Grail, Gawain, how do you plan to return it to the Saxons?"

"I haven't decided yet. I might just walk up to Hengst and hand it to him. That's the way I seem to be handling difficult tasks in recent times."

Merlin stopped walking long enough to frown at him. "And do you know where Hengst is?"

"No."

"Or Arthur?"

"Not precisely, no."

"Hmm! I suppose we can figure out where they are."

Gawain looked at the door. "Morgan has been gone awhile. Perhaps, I should have gone with her."

"She'll be back," Merlin said with confidence. "I sense a change in her, a small one but a change nonetheless, but nothing so great as to make her any less interested in her self-preservation. No one could offer her a better bargain than you did – the Grail for her life."

Nonetheless, Gawain wanted to check on her. He left Merlin sitting in a chair and started to search the tower for Morgan. Not knowing which bedchamber was hers, he flung open the door to several of them and finally decided to search the great hall and then check with the guards at the castle gate to see if she had escaped. She was not in the great hall, and as he started to leave, a kitchen servant called to him.

"Sir Gawain, beg pardon," said the woman. "You are Sir Gawain?"

"Yes, I'm Gawain."

"Mistress Morgan told me to tell you that what you seek is in a drawer in her bedchamber."

"And do you know which bedchamber is hers?"

"Yes, I can show you."

No doubt Morgan had already left the castle. He briefly considered chasing after her, but decided to go to her bedchamber for the Grail instead.

CHAPTER 42: **The Fog**

Gawain and Merlin, who was a little unsteady in the saddle, rode out of Camelot right through the angry mob of villagers, galloped north and soon encountered Balin and his warriors arriving to join Arthur's army. None of them knew exactly where Arthur and his army were, whether Arthur had encountered the enemy, and if he had, how the encounter had gone. Merlin had a dim vision of a forest, Gawain a strong vision of fog.

"My vision being weak," said Merlin, "let's follow Gawain's. Fog is most likely to occur near the sea, correct? Let's follow the coast north." And they did.

They had not ridden long when Merlin had to stop to rest. Balin, believing Arthur might need immediate help, continued on with his soldiers. Not long after, Gawain and Merlin resumed their journey, but several more times the old wizard needed to stop to rest. They made slow progress.

As they rode along the coast, they saw a mist out to sea, prompting Merlin to predict they would be enveloped in fog after nightfall, fulfilling Gawain's vision. Rarely had one of the wizard's predictions been so accurate or Gawain's vision been so clear. The mist eventually turned into a dense fog and came ashore after sundown making their travel even slower than it had been already. Nonetheless they continued their journey and passed most of the night on horseback.

Daybreak was not far off. Merlin was breathing hard and needed another rest, saying he was not sure he could go farther. The pair dismounted and sat on rocks by the edge of the sea. "Listen," said the old wizard. "I hear voices."

Gawain strained to hear them. "I don't hear anything."

"I think Arthur's camp is just ahead." Merlin motioned with his head in the direction of the voices. "Go on without me."

"I'll wait 'til I'm certain you'll be all right."

"I'll be fine. Even Morgan had trouble getting rid of me, and she apparently tried very hard." Merlin abruptly changed topics. "Tell me, Gawain, have you been to other worlds?"

He hesitated before answering. "It depends on what you mean by other worlds. Dreams are other worlds. But they aren't real."

"True, but neither is this one."

Gawain wanted to ask him what he meant, but the wizard had already changed the subject again. "You will find eventually, Gawain, that you are no longer *in* events but rather *outside* them. And you will attempt to influence important people and the course of important events; so, be prepared for disappointment and failure."

"Why failure and disappointment?"

"Because *they* are not ready. Men kill each other for glory and gain, out of anger and jealousy, for sport and differences in philosophies. Men will not change in your lifetime or even in many lifetimes. But this is one time, this very moment, when you can change the course of events. Go and don't be concerned about me."

Gawain knew the old wizard was correct. He had to keep riding. He patted Merlin on the shoulder, mounted his horse and continued forward, riding cautiously because he could barely see in the fog where his horse was treading.

Now he could hear the voices. Although it was still dark, Gawain found Arthur's army arrayed in battle formation facing north in the direction of an enemy hidden in fog. Gawain rode to the front of the formation where the leaders – Arthur, Lancelot, Kaye, Ector and Balin – sat silently on their horses. There were several reasons why Gawain did not want to explain what he intended to do to any of them, especially to Lancelot, who was wearing his most stern battle face.

Lancelot called to him. "You are not in armor, Gawain, and appear to be weaponless."

"No, Lancelot, no weapons for this battle," said Gawain. He turned toward Arthur. "With the king's permission, I wish to negotiate with Hengst."

"Negotiate! There can be no negotiation with the Saxons." Lancelot appeared to have recovered his force of character after his disappointment with Morgan.

"Lancelot, hear him out," said Arthur.

"But negotiation is pointless."

"Then there can be no harm in trying," said Gawain. "I have discussed it with Merlin, and we have a strategy that has a chance of success. But time is running out. I assume they will attack at first light, at which time it will be too late for talking. My understanding is we are outnumbered, and it would be in our interest to avoid a battle."

"Your understanding is correct, Gawain," said Arthur. "I don't know what you have in mind, but if Merlin agrees with it, it's worth an effort. You have my permission to negotiate and my hope you are successful."

Gawain dismounted, handed the reins of his horse to Kaye and walked into the fog separating the two armies. He could see only a few feet ahead and walked cautiously. When he estimated he was within easy shouting distance of the Saxons, he called out and was answered by a sentry, who asked who he was.

"I am Gawain, come on behalf of King Arthur to negotiate with Lord Hengst."

"Then, come forward."

"No, I have come nearly all the way to your camp. Hengst can meet me part way. Tell him I can give him what he has come here for."

Gawain had a wait before he heard a voice he assumed to be Hengst's calling to him. "Gawain, is it? Come on behalf of Arthur? Step forward."

"You must meet me part way. I am alone and weaponless. Come to me and come alone."

"If you were Christian, I would ask you to swear on the cross that you are telling the truth."

"I am not Christian, but I am telling you the truth and can give you what you came for."

"How do you know what I came for?"

"Because I have spoken with Morgan le Fay."

A long silence followed. Gawain heard approaching footsteps. The fog was beginning to dissipate. Although still hidden, the sun was starting to light the morning sky. Gawain could make out the faintest outline of a man in the fog. "I am just ahead of you," said Gawain. "Alone and unarmed."

The figure moved forward. A tall man with white hair wearing a black tunic and holding a dagger became visible. The man appeared startled by the sight of Gawain. Given his ragged appearance and shrouded as he was in fog, Gawain was not surprised.

"I am Hengst."

"And I am Gawain. You can sheath your dagger." Hengst continued to hold it pointed toward Gawain. "You want the Grail?"

"I have sworn an oath to return with it or die in the attempt."

"And if to have the Grail returned to you, the condition was you would have to break off this engagement and return to Germania, would you agree to the condition and swear an oath to fulfill the bargain?"

"I might."

"*Might* is insufficient. You have to agree. Understand what I am offering you. You can have the Grail or not have it. And to use your own words, you can die in a failed attempt to retrieve it."

"Very well, I would agree to such a bargain, to break off this engagement and return home. But I cannot say what these British traitors, Mordred and Vortigern, would do."

"Don't concern yourself about them."

"I must see the Grail to conclude this bargain, and I don't believe you have it."

"Tell me first that you would swear an oath to abide by the bargain?"

Hengst nodded. "Yes."

"You would swear on the cross, by your god?"
"I would, yes."

Gawain was stalling. Several shafts of sunlight had penetrated the fog to reach the ground behind Hengst. He waited for one to be closer to his own position. "Then, do we have a bargain? Remember if I fail to produce the Grail, there is no agreement."

"I swear on the cross that if you can produce the Grail for me, I will leave the battle that is about to begin here and return to Germania."

A sunbeam struck the ground a third of the distance to Hengst and off to the right. Gawain walked forward drifting slowly to the right as Hengst watched him with suspicion and tightened his grip on his dagger. Gawain was close enough. He reached under his tunic, withdrew the silver, ruby-studded chalice and held it up in the beam of sunlight. Sunrays caught the upper right corner of the Grail and seemed to set it afire. Whether this was a natural phenomenon or the Grail had some supernatural property, the impact on Hengst was overpowering, and he dropped to his knees.

Kaye pointed into the fog. "I see someone approaching."

Gawain walked slowly toward them, took the reins of his horse from Kaye, and mounted up.

"Well?" asked Lancelot.

"Well, I'm very tired. I feel like I have been travelling for a lifetime."

"How did it go with Hengst?" asked Arthur.

"At this moment he is breaking down his camp and preparing to go home."

Lancelot was skeptical. "And how did you accomplishment his withdrawal?"

"I gave him the Grail."

"But I thought you didn't have the Grail," said Lancelot. "And who said it was yours to give to Hengst?"

"I didn't have the Grail until this morning. Actually, I suppose it was yesterday that I found it. I've lost track of the days. And giving it to Hengst was the only way to persuade him to withdraw from the battle. He probably would have gotten it anyway at the cost of many dead Britons."

"To be clear," said Arthur. "You gave Hengst the Grail, and in return, he agreed to return home?"

"Yes, but Mordred, Vortigern and Agravain will stay and fight."

"They told you this?"

"No, but I foresee it, and with Hengst gone, you will defeat those who remain."

They could hear the sound of orders being shouted in the fog and braced themselves for an immediate attack.

"Those are the sounds of the Saxons breaking camp to return home," said Gawain.

Arthur looked in the direction of the sounds. More orders were being shouted, but no warriors advanced. The king turned to Gawain. "Is there more I should know?"

"I don't know if Agravain will survive the coming battle, but Mordred and Vortigern will. Keep a wary eye on them because they will likely try again. And, of course, remain wary of Morgan, who may or may not have had a change of heart."

"And other threats?"

"None that I can see now, Arthur. But remember this threat was mounted by your half-sister and your son. If there is a lesson in it, the lesson is, at the risk of sounding like Merlin, to expect the unexpected." Gawain turned his horse around. "Speaking of Merlin, I must return to him. I left him on the side of the road, and he didn't look well. And I'm not needed here any further."

Without taking leave of the others, Gawain rode back the way he had come. The fog had become a light mist, and he expected to see the old wizard from a distance off. But Merlin was nowhere in sight. Gawain thought he might be looking in the wrong place. It had been night and the fog had been thick when he left Merlin. It was difficult to determine where exactly he had left the old wizard. Nonetheless, he came across several large rocks that very well could have been the ones he and Merlin had sat on. He dismounted and inspected the ground surrounding the rocks. There were the footprints of two men and the hoof tracks of two horses. One set of tracks appeared to have been made by Merlin's horse returning in the direction of Camelot. He decided he would follow them.

Before he remounted, Gawain walked over to a small pool of water by the sea's edge and splashed his face. He was dirty, and he was tired. And he had not seen his family in a very long time. Returning to them was his next task. What was it Merlin had said? In the future he would not be in events but outside them. Maybe so. But he was not finished with being inside events either.

Gawain climbed atop his horse and followed the hoof prints south. They disappeared at times, but he was always able to pick up the trail again. They led away from the coast and into the forest. Ahead he saw Merlin's horse, untethered, feeding on some grass by the side of the road. He called for Merlin, but there was no answer. He looked for him, but found nothing. The old wizard could be anywhere between here and the shore where Gawain first started to follow the tracks. His instinct told him he could look all morning without success. The old wizard was gone.